Reckless

SIMON AND SCHUSTER

New York·London·Toronto·Sydney·Tokyo

Abandon

A Novel of Mystery and Romance

Sharon Singer Salinger

Simon and Schuster
Simon & Schuster Building
Rockefeller Center
1230 Avenue of the Americas
New York, New York 10020

Copyright © 1989 by Sharon Singer Salinger

SIMON AND SCHUSTER and colophon are registered trademarks
of Simon & Schuster Inc.

Designed by Elizabeth Woll
Manufactured in the United States of America

1   3   5   7   9   10   8   6   4   2

Library of Congress Cataloging in Publication Data
Salinger, Sharon Singer.
Reckless abandon: a novel of mystery and romance/Sharon Singer Salinger.
p. cm.
I. Title
PS3569.A459525R4   1989
813'.54—dc20   89-36776
CIP
ISBN 0-671-68344-6

For my mother and father, with love.

ACKNOWLEDGMENTS

I am fortunate in having many wise and loving friends.

Special gratitude to Herb Katz for his wisdom, warmth, and savvy.

Joe Singer and June Flaum Singer inspired me and taught me the ropes.

Robert Greenberg, thanks for the push.

Carol and Sam Whitehorn, Ian Singer, Darcy Salinger, Melissa Danckert, Nancy Powell and Eric Neudel, Jay Cradle, and Ann Kostant generously provided real assistance. Thanks folks.

Brett Singer, Valerie Singer, and Gary Flaum shared most valuable suggestions, tips, and encouragement.

Leslie Beale, Ellie Donner, Jeffrey Fine, Bob Ivanno, Maris Salinsky, Ruben Stern, Tony Temple, Joe Vitagliano, Katrin Winterer, and especially Zach Klein kept my feet on the ground and my head somewhere interesting.

Gratitude for skillful editing to Carole Lalli; thanks Carole and Kerri Conan for being so nice to work with.

Robin Beck, I would love to hear from you.

My admiration to the brave Greenpeace activists who are heroic in the face of cynicism, greed, and apathy.

Above all, boundless love to Seth, Natasha, Gabrielle, and Astro. Thanks for the hugs, kisses, and comic relief.

Reckless
Abandon

one

"MINE IS GOLDEN brown with green eyes," Lily says, her eyes closed. "He's slim but muscular. I love it when you can see the stomach muscles ripple."

"Who doesn't?" Kit agrees lazily.

It's nice to see my two best friends in agreement for a change.

"He's wearing a faded blue shirt and jeans," Lily continues. "And his eyes are lined from working in the sun. He's maybe a carpenter or something like that. He works with his hands, but he's smart. I like an intelligent man. He could be sarcastic too, a bit cynical."

Her own face takes on a tough little smirk.

"Like you," I say.

She grins at me, her blue eyes humorous, fine lines at the corners.

"And does he have a promising bulge in those faded jeans?" Kit teases.

"Does he not!" Lily affirms. "In bed he is wild, like a bee after honey."

Kit squeals and we all laugh, taking sips from our tall ice-filled glasses. It is a hot day, but we've found refuge on my deep and shady front porch. Kit's nine-year-old daughter, Ananda, lies reading in the hammock on the front lawn. Josh, Lily's four-year-old, splashes trucks into a wading pool. We are whiling away the golden summer hours, spinning delicious fantasies of dream lovers who float languorously above us in the still air.

Lily is not finished with her turn but Kit can't hold herself back any longer.

"Mine is tall and gentle, with a deep voice," she says, a coy smile on her lips. "And it doesn't matter how old he is in years, because in wisdom he's an ancient soul."

Lily grins wickedly at me, but I am determined that we will respect each other's fantasies, so I shake my head sternly at her. Kit breezes on, oblivious.

"He's very relaxed, he meditates, and drives something like an old BMW. He has a big sunny house in a meadow, all bleached wood and lofts."

That figures. Lily's man is working class, while Kit's, though spiritual, owns property.

"The minute I see him, I'll know him. I'll be somewhere like A New Basket, just picking out some vegetables." Kit acts out the selection of something plump and ripe. "I look up and across the artichokes I see him. Our eyes lock and though we haven't met before, we recognize each other. Soulmates coming together after many lifetimes apart."

She sighs. I picture Kit in her white dress waltzing with Mr. Goodvibes through the aisles of the gourmet natural foods market.

"Speaking of coming together, how is he on the old futon?" Lily asks.

"He's got a slow hand, he takes his time," Kit answers, changing direction without missing a beat.

Lily and I sit forward a bit.

"Yes, yes?" Lily says.

"Like this: First he would just lightly brush his closed lips over mine. He'd brush my eyebrows, along my jaw, my neck. Then with his teeth he'd pull the strap of my dress off my shoulder and nuzzle softly from my ear down my arm to here." She fingers the crease inside her elbow. She's got our undivided attention.

"And . . . ," Lily prods.

"And that's what he's like—fill in from there," Kit says primly. "Now it's Nell's turn."

Suddenly I feel shy. Dare I say what I really want? My friends look at me expectantly.

"Mine is a hero," I say in a soft voice. They look at me quizzically. "Like King Arthur. I fell in love with him when I was seventeen. Sweet, noble, willing to fight for what he believes is right. Sincere and compassionate and brave, and at the same time humble."

"I don't think there is anybody like that," Lily says. "And what about sexy?"

"To me that *is* sexy. I need someone I can respect. And he would have a sense of humor too, and sensual lips."

"Do those things go together?" Kit asks. "Truth, justice, and hot lips?"

"Why not? Do you think I have to choose between a good but dull man and a demon lover?"

"OK, OK," Lily laughs. "Wanted: Hot-blooded King Arthur type."

"And Jesus the carpenter," Kit adds teasingly.

"And Buddha," I say, "levitating in his BMW."

Lily laughs.

"It's just like an ad in the personals," she says. *"We R 3 lovely, loony ladies. U R Jesus, Buddha, K. Arthur. U soothe our souls, we'll ring your chimes. Let's rendezvous for . . . ,"* she searches for words.

"For sweet romance," I supply.

We all sigh.

"Hey, look," Ananda calls from her hammock. "Someone's moving in across the street."

A blue truck is pulled up across the wide tree-lined street, in front of an old yellow Victorian where I'd noticed a SOLD sign the other day.

"What a day for moving," Kit says, fanning herself. I loll more luxuriously in my chaise. A tannish dog jumps down from the truck and stretches deeply, front paws and head low, rump to the wind. He is a nice, funny-looking dog. Some guys begin unloading the truck. We look around for the new owners, but they're not in sight, so we check out their furniture instead.

Stripped to the waist, their backs glistening, the movers carry in a brass bed I could kill for. They unload a Chinese lacquered screen, followed by an enormous, old-fashioned bathtub, painted parrot green with gilded lion's claw feet. We watch totally fascinated as, cursing softly, they carefully balance an ornate, ceiling-high wall mirror.

"Someone's setting up a brothel in there," I hazard.

"For giants," Lily says.

An overstuffed red velvet couch curvy as Mae West is placed incongruously on the front porch. A white piano is followed through the wide double doors by a massive round oak table.

"Hey Guinevere," Lily says, pointing, "there's the Round Table."

One of the movers rolls a stone birdbath into a spot on the front lawn, or rather into the tangled weeds, grasses, vines, and flowers gone wild that flourish in front of the house. The man walks out to the street and cocks his head, studying the placement of the birdbath. His manner is very proprietary—maybe he is not a mover. We all take notice.

He is a man of medium height, muscular, with a mostly bald head, a short curling red beard, and a very shapely back. He whistles to the dog, who lopes over and jumps up, licking the man's laughing face.

"Aha!" Lily exclaims. "The Man With The Yella Dog." Lily grew up in the South and has a way with words. The Man With The Yella Dog we call him then and in the days to follow, during which we speculate about him. It is Kit who begins it.

"I don't see any signs of a Mrs. Yella Dog," she muses.

"Maybe she's coming later. Can't you just see her—big pink Cadillac, lots of makeup, latex pants, ample bosom?" Lily is off and running.

"A small pearl-handled revolver in her brassiere," I add.

"Why not a wooden leg and a parrot on her shoulder?" Kit complains.

"You're right," I sigh. "They're probably both dentists. Only able to walk on the wild side in the furniture department."

"Actually," Lily says, tapping a shapely fingernail on the rim of her gin and tonic, "I believe this is a single gentleman."

The object of our speculation returns to moving his belongings. We return to watching him. Eventually the larger items give way to the inevitable cartons, then the cartons give out, the truck is empty, the movers drink a beer with The Man With The Yella Dog and take off in the truck. The Man settles himself on the red couch on the porch with a guitar and a beer. He balances the beer on the porch railing and stretches out with the guitar. The yella dog flops in the shade under the couch.

"He's attractive," Kit says casually.

"He's not as handsome as Spence!" Ananda injects hotly. Spence is Kit's longtime fiancé, to whom Ananda is fiercely attached.

"Well, he looks kind of lazy and no-account to me," Lily sniffs. Her ex-husband played the guitar. He enjoyed himself hugely but worked seldom.

As though he's heard her, The Man jumps from the couch and begins unwrapping a large canvas-covered object. It looks like some kind of statue. Curious, I trot inside for my binoculars.

Looking—discreetly, I hope—from behind a pillar on the

porch, I examine the object. It is carved of wood, a large grey dolphin arching its back as though leaping through the air above the water. As he starts to mount it above his front door, I realize that it is a figurehead. Its weathered condition says it has seen long service at the prow of a boat. Carved on a wooden banner under the dolphin's flanks is the name *Reckless Abandon*. It is beautiful. With this detail, the wooden house now lends its own rather rakish and exotic nuance to the faded charms of Beau Cherry Lane.

A little guiltily, I turn the binoculars on the man himself. His bald head, tanned and well shaped, noble like a Greek head of Zeus, is surrounded by a vigorous cluster of dark red curls that grow into a fiery gold beard. His strong neck sits on a powerful torso. His broad shoulders and chest taper to a supple waist. Golden fuzz glints on his muscled forearms and the backs of his shapely hands. He is built like the sculptors I knew in art school. A warm and vigorous life force radiates from him, like heat from a wood stove. His white pants are spattered with paint drips of various clear colors. He is a spangled flame of a man. I feel as though I've been kicked in the stomach.

"Let me see," Kit demands.

Reluctantly I hand over the binoculars. Instead of hiding behind the pillar as I have done, she sits in the lotus position, square in her chaise, and trains the glasses right at him.

"Ooh, can I see? I want to see!" Ananda clamors. Josh too is tugging at Kit's sleeve and whining.

"Stop it," Kit hisses. Lily scuffles with Josh.

"Selfish! I always have to share. It's not fair," Ananda accuses her mother. In her world this is the ultimate crime. "Nell, can I use them, MAY I use them, PLEEZ!"

"Shush!" Kit waves her arm and knocks over a glass. Josh lunges for the binoculars. The Man With The Yella Dog looks up and stares. I slink down out of my chaise onto the floor, trying to hide behind the railings. Kit whips down the binoculars. The Man With The Yella Dog bows deeply to us. Lily and the children laugh in delight. Then he crouches down and waves a special little hello just to me. Weakly, I wave back.

People are never satisfied, I muse later in my bath. Here we are, Lily, Kit, and I. In the past two years each one of us has come back here to Merrivale to start over. In this odd tucked-away pocket paradise each of us has fared rather well. I'd been dissatisfied with my life in Manhattan; I dreamed of living in a small seaside town. When I found the courage to move here to Merrivale, it seemed as if I'd made my dreams come true. This village was just as I'd fantasized it, like a seacoast village in England. The streets and lanes curving up the hills and along the sea. The crooked wooden houses with their foolish windows wearing an air of amiable looniness. The walls and fences covered in rambling roses, the cries of the gulls and the clanging of lines against masts as boats rocked in the harbor.

I found the perfect house my first morning out. It had every feature I'd recited over and over to myself like a promise in my tiny New York bedroom: a small garden with a huge old tree, a fireplace in the living room, a big upstairs kitchen with a pantry. Best of all, there was a large light studio for me to paint in, with windows on every side and, if you stood on tiptoes, a view of the sea.

I found a lover here too. Paul lives in the city but he is close enough to drive here in less than an hour. He is a charming, complex, witty man, and very good to me. And I have my friends.

I met Kit my first week living here. She too was a new-comer, a recent divorcée with a daughter, and she too had come to Merrivale following a dream. Kit, though ethereal in appearance and spiritual in philosophy, is really a practical person. She didn't leave Charles, her wealthy and inconstant husband, until she had someone new on hold. She followed Spence, her new man, to Merrivale, where his parents rented her a large house a few houses down the street from mine on Beau Cherry Lane. There is office space for her business and living space for her and Ananda at a ridiculously low rent.

She and I are easily compatible. She is a West Coast version of the women I grew up with—calmer and less brittle maybe, but we share a common sensibility. She is cultured, sophisticated, bright. She is also a knockout, which is sometimes hard to take, but we are physically such different types that it doesn't really bother me. I know I'll never be a tall blonde.

Though Kit had only been in town a month longer than I, she acted as my guide to my new surroundings. She always knows where to get the best of everything. She showed me where to buy organically grown fruit and fresh herbs, the prettiest deserted beach, the place to find deluxe linens at incredible markdowns, how to get reservations for the best tennis court, and led me to a winery where they make not only terrific wines but also creamy goat cheese and sourdough bread. For a spiritual person Kit lives in a world of sensual excellence, and always on a shoestring.

Kit even introduced me to attractive available men, though it was my mother who brought me together with Paul. And Kit had to admit Paul was eminently a find, even if she hadn't found him.

It was through Kit, too, that I met Lily, though not by Kit's design. Lily lives in a small in-law apartment at the back of Kit's house—and I'm talking serious small. Where Kit's space is lofty and light, Lily's nest is four poky rooms. With all the newcomers pouring into town, her rent is market rate and climbing. She is so happy, though, to finally have a quiet, peaceful place of her own she doesn't seem to notice its inadequacies.

Lily is one of the few people I know here who is a native. She was born in Merrivale and lived a few happy childhood years here before her parents died. Then she was shipped out to be raised in Mississippi by a neurotic and unloving aunt. When Lily's disastrous marriage ended, she returned to Merrivale with her little boy, seeking a new life in the place where she remembered she'd once been happy.

If Kit was familiar to me, Lily was exotic. I've never been close to someone like her before. I grew up in New York; my parents were professionals with a comfortable living and a fond indulgence for their only child. Lily has had a sad, hard time and any comfort she's garnered she's given herself.

Now she, like Kit, like me, has come to Merrivale looking for happiness for herself and Josh. She's at last found a tranquil home, work she loves on the village newspaper, and friendship, but still, like Kit, like me, she is not satisfied. We are all still looking for something other, something more. Maybe that's why we get so much pleasure from fantasizing.

The phone rings but I needn't get out of the tub to answer it. Expecting to hear from Paul, I've brought the phone in from my bedroom. You see, Paul, I think smugly, I've planned ahead. But as it turns out, it isn't he after all; it's Kit.

"Hi, sweetie," she says. "I've been feeling kind of guilty, have you?"

"Guilty? Whatever for?"

"Well, Spence just called and asked about my day. I told him I'd been lounging around with you and Lily, nothing special. He told me about all the terrific plays he'd made in his softball game, we chatted a bit, and hung up. But then Ananda, who was lying on my bed watching TV, says, 'Why didn't you tell him that you and your friends were drooling over some yucky made-up guys, who sounded terrible, and then you spied on some half-naked guy who moved in across the street?' Then she said she wished I was more sensible, like *some people* who appreciate Spence."

I giggle.

"It does sound a little unsavory, I suppose, put that way, but you know Ananda is very strict," I say. "Anyway, we fantasize about different things all the time. So this time it was fantasy lovers. Remember the time we all described our dream restaurants, the ones we run in our heads?"

"For sure. Mine was great, wasn't it? Handmade Italian tile, all natural . . ."

"I remember," I say hastily. "Anyway, it's the exact same thing. Everyone has a dream restaurant in their head and everyone has at least one dream lover in there too."

"I guess so," she says, "but your dream lover didn't really sound like Paul. And mine didn't sound like Spence. That worries me; doesn't it you?"

I consider. "Not really. I don't expect Paul to be my ideal man. It isn't reasonable. He probably has an ideal woman in his dreams too. And she's probably a better housekeeper with more money and bigger breasts."

"Well, a better housekeeper, maybe, but your breasts are perfect."

Wow, a compliment from Kit! She has such high standards.

"Thanks. What do you think Spence's dream woman is like?" I ask curiously.

"Oh, he's already told me that *I'm* his ultimate dream woman. His sexual fantasies are all about me." She giggles.

That figures.

"We had to cancel our day trip up the coast tomorrow. Charles's parents were supposed to take Ananda for the day, but they pooped out. So Spence will have to put those fantasies on hold. Until she goes to bed, anyway."

"I'll take Ananda tomorrow," I offer willingly. I love to spend a day with Ananda when I can.

"Oh Nell, you can't. You work so hard all week. Saturday is your only time to paint."

"Don't worry about that, Kit. I want to do this."

"Well, if you really want to, that would be great. Let me just check with Ananda."

From the happy yips in the background I can hear that Ananda approves the plan.

"I'll drop her off in the morning," Kit says. "So, have you seen anything more of our sexy new neighbor? Ow, Ananda, cut it out!"

two

"I LOVE WINDOW shopping, don't you?" Ananda asks, her arm hooked companionably through mine.

We have just had breakfast in the Last Chance Café, and are strolling leisurely along, the whole bright day before us.

"Ooh," she sighs happily, tugging me over to a shop window. It is one of the stores that have been springing up throughout the village, new, beautiful, and expensive. I've never looked into it carefully before. It is called Bébé, a white and gilt confection filled with accessories for very wealthy babies. In the window is displayed a brass and white iron bassinet, covered with billows of violet-sprigged canopy and drapery. It looks like the bed of a dauphin. Arranged around it on the floor are life-sized plush bears wearing jeweled collars. Stereo speakers in the bed's canopy are playing the Moonlight Sonata.

"I wish my mother would have a baby," Ananda sighs.

"I know," I commiserate. "I used to wish for a baby brother, too. But would you want the kind of baby that sleeps in that kind of bed?"

"Well," Ananda considers, "it looks like the bed Sleeping Beauty had when she was a baby. Everyone would stand around like they were worshiping it or something. I guess a more regular kind of baby would be better. The kind that could get grape juice on stuff."

Two people jostle past us, hitting Ananda with their glossy shopping bags.

"This street is getting more crowded every week," I complain. "I liked it better when there was just the bank, the drugstore, and the dry cleaners on this block, didn't you?"

"Nah," Ananda says. "Only grown-ups like things quiet. I like action!" She swings her hips and snaps her fingers.

I laugh. We turn the corner, past the new gourmet grocery and the old comfy bookstore. We both stop in silent accord in front of My Indiscretion, a chic lingerie shop.

My Indiscretion is infamous in Merrivale for its dramatic and naughty window displays. This week two shapely mannequins dressed in bustiers, panties, garter belts, and black stockings are engaged in a tug-of-war over a rope of pearls. The redheaded one has a black eye. A male mannequin in black tie watches in smirking amusement from an armchair.

"Weird," Ananda pronounces. Behind us, two of the older of Merrivale's inhabitants are appreciating the display.

"I'd put my money on Red," the white-haired one in the purple sweatshirt declares.

"Well, I dunno but I'd take that. A redhead is full of piss and vinegar, all right," the one in the cap and the chewed mustache agrees, "but that black-haired one looks to have plenty of fight in her. Reminds me of a gal I knew once, blacked my eye for me."

A frosty, elegant saleswoman knocks on the glass and motions for Ananda to get her nose off it. Ananda tosses her mop of curls and we march off, laughing.

"Let's go into Woolworth's and try on wigs," I suggest and Ananda agrees.

"Look," Ananda points, "there's Lily and Josh."

Lily and Josh are sitting at a table in the window of the TipTop Coffee Shop. Lily waves.

The TipTop was the only coffee shop in town when I first moved here. The locals still prefer it for breakfast, which seems to be the big meal out for them. The food is only just passable, but generously served, leaning heavily towards large doses of cholesterol.

It is jammed. We sit down with Lily and Josh. Josh is putting away a large messy jelly donut. Ananda stares at him with frank envy. Kit insists on a healthy diet, stressing whole grains and fresh fruits and veggies.

"I'll call Denise over," Lily offers.

"We just ate," I tell her, "at the Last Chance."

"Yuppie food," Lily sniffs.

"*I'm* hungry," Ananda insists. Her capacity is incredible.

"I don't know," I say doubtfully, looking at the menu board.

"I'm allowed to have frozen yogurt," she announces.

We order a cone for Ananda and coffee for me.

"The Last Chance has really great coffee at the same price," I say.

"It's narcissistic to pay so much attention to what you eat," Lily says, lighting a cigarette. The air is thick with smoke. At practically every table there is a voluble group of men or women, smoking like mad. Each new arrival is hailed by folks at different tables, and stops to chat before sitting down. Lily knows them all.

"Hi, Billy. Working on the Cotter house? I saw Andy Haggerty down there the other day. He says he's got three bathrooms to put in this month on that road."

"Yeah, I'm putting wiring in one of them for an electric *bidet*," Billy says, raising his eyebrows.

The working people of Merrivale are really enjoying their new prosperity, and the foibles of their new neighbors, as the town grows. It is relative newcomers like me who are apprehensive, who want to keep the town small and quiet, which is what originally drew us here in the first place. But men who had barely worked every winter are now busier than they can manage. The women seem happier, too, with more money coming in.

Next to us a woman our age and three older women laugh, cigarettes in their mouths and their eyes screwed up to keep the smoke out.

"Your Kelly still going out with the Hannah kid?" the younger woman asks Billy. "The soccer player?"

"The soccer player, yeah."

"It's funny how straight the kids are these days, ain't it?"

"Yeah, real squareheads. Sports is all they think about."

"They don't know how to have fun like we did, huh Billy?"

"Thank God," he says, smiling at her.

"That's Jean Fahey," Lily says. "She used to be pretty wild."

She doesn't look it now. Her short hair and plain clothes give her a tough, serviceable look. I compare her to the glossy women breakfasting at the Last Chance. There's something exotic to me about Jean and her friends. I don't fit in with them, but there's something I admire about them. They're a dying breed, I think, tough but not hard. Lily is my connection to this other Merrivale world, but she doesn't completely fit in either. She's of their stock but she grew up elsewhere. She went to Sarah Lawrence. But it's more than those things, I think. She's traded the security of knowing exactly how she fits into this little world for the more open possibilities of who she can become.

"I love coming here," she says, as if she's been reading my mind. "But it's changing too. You know who Marianne Banks is?"

I nod. Marianne is on the police force. The Bankses are one of the larger clans around here.

"She says the police don't know how to handle all the new crime they've been having. She told me they were calling in federal help to deal with drug smuggling they can't keep in check. Tons of drugs, coming in through Good Harbor. It's not just an isolated boat here and there, some local guys looking to make some cash. It's really organized, but the small-fry they catch don't know or won't say who their bosses are. There's a lot more money floating around than there used to be. I'm not sure people know how to handle it. They're getting into trouble."

I hate hearing this stuff. I want to continue to believe in the impregnability of Merrivale as my peaceful little harbor. Not Lily. She just has to keep digging, poking around to uncover whatever may be lying in the darkness.

Josh and Ananda are flicking sugar packets across the table at each other.

"That will do," Lily says. "Looks like it's time to hit the road."

It takes us about fifteen minutes to get out of the coffee shop. Lily has to say good-bye at practically every table. People rumple Josh's curls and nod politely to Ananda and me. Lily and Josh continue with us to Woolworth's.

"I want to buy a present for my mom," Ananda says, after we've tried on every wig in the aisle.

"Let's buy presents for everybody," Lily suggests.

"Yeah!" Ananda agrees. And so we do. Ananda gets black nail polish (leaving me to hope Kit will be as enthusiastic about it as her daughter is). Josh gets another truck. Lily receives a mug that says *I never make mistakes. I thought I did once, but I was wrong,* and I get a grape-flavored lip gloss, which Ananda says is really more a gift for Paul than it is for me. I decide to buy Paul a present too. Ananda finds it.

"See, it's a genius test," she says. "You have to solve this puzzle, and if you send in the right answer first, you win $13,437."

"Why such a strange amount?" Lily asks.

"That's probably a clue," Ananda says.

I have to agree it is a perfect choice. Paul loves any kind of intellectual challenge, the trickier the better. Although gentle in most respects, Paul can be a fierce competitor. And he loves money.

"They can kiss that money good-bye," Ananda exults. "Maybe he'll give me some because I got the puzzle for him."

She picks out paper dolls of Charles and Diana's Royal Wedding (a bit old and dusty) for Kit, and Andy and Fergie's Royal Wedding for Spence.

"Why don't you write 'Hint, hint' on the wrapping paper?" Lily suggests.

"I'm planning to," Ananda announces smugly and sails over to the cashier, where I surrender a surprisingly hefty sum.

It is the next weekend before I see much more of my new neighbor. I have sometimes heard his guitar when he sits playing it out on his red couch at night. I've seen the yella dog who is well acquainted now with the neighborhood pack and accepted among them. Dogs are by nature gregarious and tolerant. More so than their human counterparts. We have not done more than nod hello to the dog's master. Some of us, no doubt, are just inclined to mind our own business, content to live and let live. Some of us are shy, some unfriendly. But some of us are both curious and suspicious. I'm afraid Lily, Kit, and I are of this last persuasion.

This next Saturday finds us watching him puttering in the tangled garden, haphazardly putting it to rights. He is again bare-chested, his skin surprisingly tanned for a redhead.

"He doesn't go to work," Lily says. She is the most curious and the most suspicious. "He just strolls along with the dog, muddles about in that jungle, and plays his guitar."

"Maybe he works at home," I say.

"Or maybe he's an eccentric of independent means." The words roll off Kit's lips.

"Maybe," Lily grudgingly allows. "But if you ask me,

there's a woman somewhere who's paying for all this leisure."

We can come up with any number of responsibilities for him to be evading. A deserted wife with seven children. Widows who have made imprudent investments. A sinking business with its assets embezzled.

"He doesn't look as though he's feeling guilty," Kit points out. His gardening temporarily abandoned, The Man lies stretched out in a patch of sunlight, his dog's chin resting comfortably on his leg. He is whistling softly and seems to be watching the clouds.

"Well, he wouldn't, not if he is unrepentant," Lily persists, determinedly following her own reasoning.

"It must be nice to have no worries," I say, admiring his nonchalance.

"I suppose," Kit says, "but I think he should clean up his act. I don't like his style. Isn't he embarrassed to lie around half naked all day doing nothing?"

This seems to me a little unfair as I consider Kit lolling decoratively in her deck chair. Her own clothing is crisp and pristine, but there isn't much of it on her long form.

"And why doesn't he use the back yard?" she continues. "I guess that doesn't offer as much opportunity to check out the bodies."

In addition to his other sins, our new neighbor makes no secret of his contemplation of the women passing his door.

"The man simply has no use for a superego," I say. "Life without guilt."

"Life without guilt," Kit repeats thoughtfully.

"Reprehensible, no doubt, and yet, there could be certain compensations," Lily says.

We all fall silent, thinking our own thoughts. After a bit Kit laughs provocatively to herself.

"Yes?" Lily prompts.

"Just daydreaming," Kit says.

"Don't be shy," says Lily.

"Well, I was just imagining waking up in that big brass

bed. I see it standing alone in the middle of the floor, in this big, round room with nothing in it, just a lot of windows. The sun is pouring in."

"Umm, sounds like the cover of a white-sale circular," Lily says. Kit smiles graciously.

"He is still sleeping, but I have to get up for work. I am getting all dressed up for an important meeting—linen suit, raw silk blouse, pearls, Joan and David pumps . . ."

"Wow. A yuppie sexual fantasy," Lily says.

Kit steamrolls on. "I put up my hair. He wakes and stretches, the muscles in his chest and stomach flex. I ask him, 'What are you going to do today?' and he smiles and says, 'I'm going to lie in bed and pretend that this pillow is you, unless you jump back in here.' Then he raises the sheet and I can see he means it. I sort of swoon onto the bed, and he rips my clothes off. My pearls break, but I'm too hot to care."

"Do you lose your job?" I ask. What's bugging me?

"Yes!" Kit says happily. "While we're making love, the phone rings. I answer it, but he keeps going. It's my boss. He's very gruff and silver-haired and he says, 'Where the hell are you? We have an urgent meeting with the lawyers in five minutes,' and I say, 'Sorry, I can't make it in today, I have some important lovemaking to attend to,' and he yells, 'You're fired,' and while he's yelling, I come!" She can hardly get the last words out, she is laughing so, and we laugh with her. Now this is all rather interesting because while it is Kit who runs her own travel business, it is her father who actually owns it.

Meanwhile, as we send torrid fantasies spinning into the treetops over Beau Cherry Lane, our leading man lies unknowing across the street, placidly munching a sandwich and flicking bits to the yella dog.

The next morning, Lily comes by early to have breakfast with me before I go to the agency. She brings with her some corn fritters and a copy of the *Meridian*, the local paper. Lily and her editor, Kilby Loomis, cover all the local news. This fills most of the pages, but there is a respectable amount of regional, national, and world news from the wire services offered, too. I chew a fritter and scan the usual menu of crisis, crime, and corruption. Major security scandal rocks Defense Department. Government agents confiscate largest haul ever of cocaine somewhere fifty miles off the Good Harbor coast. Environmentalist organizations propose marine biology station and wildlife refuge on Baldur Islands; developers protest it will stifle industry. Terrorists kidnap Italian banker, killing two. And to break up the depressing news, a large photo shows a family of ducks filing along Main Street enjoying the spray from a road sprinkler as amused pedestrians look on.

After enjoying editorials on both sides of the argument as to whether Charley Bannion should be allowed to play his accordian after 10:00 P.M., I reluctantly leave Lily and Josh to linger in the kitchen as I walk off to work. Lily is rereading her sparkling prose and Josh is making vroom sounds as he chases a bit of fritter around the tabletop. Josh, though four years old, has yet to speak. Lily refuses to worry; he'll talk when he's ready to, she insists. He can hear fine, and he mimics mechanical sounds perfectly. Lily says he will start to talk, in perfect sentences most likely, sometime soon. I hope she is right.

As I leave I look at my watch. I'm not *terribly* late, I argue with myself. I can afford to let the Duchess sleep a little longer. The Duchess is my aged white VW bug. Her engine is heroically hanging on but her body is sort of rusty. I walk when I can. Today I'll walk very quickly.

I pass the yellow house and its tangled garden. The garden is still abundantly wild but is beginning to show signs of a guiding intelligence. The gardener is not out reading the newspaper and drinking coffee on his red velvet couch, as he has sometimes been these peaceful golden mornings. I breathe in a deep delicious draft. Sweet woodruff must be growing somewhere here; its soft, clean fragrance wafts out to me. Impulsively I bend to a clump of hydrangea, pachysandra, and iris to pluck a bit of the herb. With a heart-stopping jolt, I come face to face with The Man With The Yella Dog, his nose only inches from mine.

"What are you doing here?" I blurt, and instantly feel my face grow hot with confusion.

He grins widely at my question and raises a fist. I flinch. He laughs at me and opens his hand, in which he holds a bunch of pale green-and-lavender stalks, covered with moistly clinging earth.

"Asparagus. I found it growing here. Someone must have planted them once and they've gone wild," he explains, rising from the grass where he's been crouching. "Would you like to come in and have some? I'm making it for my breakfast." He is bare-chested, in the invariable white pants, leaves and wisps are entwined in his red curls and beard, but his manner is as gracious as a duke's. Although I've already had breakfast, I accept and follow him to the house.

We follow a broken stone path around to the side of the house. Overhanging leaves and delicate ferns still wet with dew brush my face and bare legs. The side door opens directly into the kitchen, which is tidy and cozy. The yella dog lies snoozing in a pool of sunlight, and can barely rouse himself to sniff politely at my outstretched hand. The Man puts on a loose cotton shirt hanging from a hook and waves me into a comfortable chair pulled up to the round oak table. He sets a thick white mug before me and fills it from a smoking pot, adding steamed milk at the same time from a small pitcher.

I taste it, then sip reverently. This is a triumph of the coffee-making art. I am especially appreciative, being congenitally unable to make good coffee. I enthuse wildly.

He smiles shyly. "An old fisherman in Marseilles taught me to brew coffee. Mine tastes like camel . . . uh, mud compared to his."

I laugh.

"I'm Will," he says from the sink where he is washing the asparagus.

At first I don't know what he means, I can't quite take it in. Of course he has to have a name, I know, but I'm so used to thinking of him as The Man.

He looks over his shoulder at me.

"Nell," I remember to introduce myself. "I live across the street," I add lamely.

"I know, I've seen you. The children, are either of them yours?"

"No, the little boy, Josh, is Lily's son."

"She's the small one?" he guesses.

"Yes, that's right. And the girl, Ananda, is Kit's daughter. She's—"

"The blond one," he finishes. Evidently he has studied us. Well, why not, I think. We've been watching him. He's always seemed, since that first day, quite oblivious, but I suppose he's just been more subtle than we.

"You called Lily the small one and Kit the blond one. What would you have called me?" I ask, surprising myself.

"You? You're the gorgeous one, of course," he says, smiling wickedly at me.

"Of course," I laugh, delighted. "So. How do you like it here?"

"I like it. This is an unusual place. Funny, pretty, peaceful."

"I know. I love it. How did you wind up here?"

"You know, it was the damndest thing. I got lost once, years ago. I was driving through to the city and I took a wrong turn. I thought then I'd like to live here one day. I never forgot it, and when I got the chance, I just came."

"I'm not surprised," I say. "It's weird, but if you ask anybody, anyone who wasn't born here, they'll tell you pretty much the same story. I was driving around myself a couple of years ago, just looking at the scenery, and I happened upon it. I walked on the bay beach by the harbor, had an unbelievably good piece of peach pie in the café—have you eaten there yet?"

"No, I don't go into town much."

"Oh. Well, it's great. Anyway, I just fell in love. The place haunted me, until I couldn't stay away. I was living in New York City but I just packed up and moved myself here. Where did you live before?"

Now I may be imagining this, but he seems to shift gears, it's almost like a curtain coming down. He's smiling but he looks distant. Maybe I'm being oversensitive. I really want him to like me, I realize.

"Oh, here and there," he says breezily. "I've moved around a bit. I was out of the country for a few years, a bunch of different places, working."

"That sounds exciting," I say.

"No, not really, it's actually very nice to be settled somewhere." His face is hard to read.

"And you don't miss it?"

"What?" he asks.

"The excitement? Wandering about?"

He laughs and looks into my eyes. "This is about as much excitement as I can handle right now."

"Well, you've made the house really nice," I say.

He looks around the kitchen as if it's someone else's, as if he's seeing it for the first time. "It *is* nice, isn't it? I'll show you around after we eat." He goes back to his work at the stove. "Don't talk to me for a second. This is a very delicate operation."

I sip coffee contentedly. What an interesting morning I am having.

"There," he says. "Now we'll just let that warm through."

He smiles at me. His smile is kind of wonderful. I notice a small gold hoop in one of his ears.

"What kind of work do you do?" I ask, a little huskily.

"Whoa!" he laughs. "Who says you get to ask all the questions. It's my turn. What do *you* do?"

"I'm the art director at an ad agency," I answer, pushing

away the thoughts of all the work waiting for me in my office.

"Do you like it?" he asks.

"Yes. That is, it's not bad. Well, I guess it's not exactly what I meant to do when I came out here."

"And what is that?" he asks, looking up from his pan.

"I'm a painter," I say shyly. Usually I can't even think those words without panic, but somehow they come tumbling out.

"You look like an artist," he says seriously, studying me.

Careful, Nell, I tell myself, this guy is smooth.

"I'd love to see your work sometime, if you don't mind."

"Sometime," I say cautiously.

He's looking at me intently; I feel uncomfortable. He's not flirting exactly, but he's acting like a man who's, well, *interested*. I have to regain control of this conversation.

"So what do you do, Will?"

It is effective. He turns back to the stove. The sunlight shows the outline of his shapely back through his loose white shirt.

"Oh, I'm just getting settled in. I putter around this place, walk with Shiloh there, play my guitar a little. And as a matter of fact, I do a little artwork myself."

Uh-oh, I think. "Do you paint?"

"No, I'll show you, but eat this first." He puts a beautifully arranged plate before me. Pale green-and-lavender asparagus stalks lie below a perfectly poached egg, the whole covered by a creamy hollandaise. We eat in companionable silence, except for my rapt eggy murmurs of congratulations.

He leaves the kitchen and I look around the sunny room, sipping my coffee. I get up to inspect a wall of photographs. There are pictures of boats, a number of different boats I think, and group shots of rugged, wind-blown laughing men and women. There are none of Will; no, wait, there's one—he is wearing a woolen cap, squinting into the sun between two bearded men. All three are wearing plaid shirts and Will has his arm around one of the men's shoulders. We are three jolly fishermen, I hum to myself. He looks younger.

On the counter below the wall of photos is a shoe box filled with more pictures. I pick up a few. One is of Will and a tall, cool blonde. The next stops my heart a moment, though I can't quite make it out at first. Then I realize the red oozy mass is gore. It is a pile of bodies, animal bodies—seals maybe?—battered and bleeding. Ugh. I drop the photos and hurry back to my chair disturbed.

Will comes back in, smiling shyly, a hunk of wood in his hands. He hands it to me. It is a carving of a whale, stiff, crude, but with a sense of life in it.

"I'm just about finished with this," he says proudly. "Not too shabby for a beginner, eh? Think I'll be able to sell it?"

"It's very strong," I say.

He laughs. "You little liar. Fortunately I have other ways of scraping together a living. Listen, why don't we finish our coffee and then you can show me your paintings at your place?"

"Sorry," I say. "I'm already way too late for work as it is."

"Some other time then."

I rise and collect my bag and my paper. "Thank you so much for the lovely—"

He grabs my wrist. His grip is shockingly powerful. Startled, I look at him. His face is red. He is staring at the newspaper in my hand.

"Can I have it?" he asks.

I let the paper drop to the table. My wrist burns where he holds me tight. Slowly he releases my arm and I rush to the door.

"Good-bye," I say, tripping down the stairs.

"Sorry," he says. "Good-bye."

I walk quickly through the garden, where once again I catch the faint scent of woodruff. From the street I turn back to the house. I can see him in the open doorway, looking at the paper. Suddenly he crushes it in his hands and throws the wadded mass to the ground. Looking up he catches my eye and scowls. I hear the door slam as I hurry away.

three

ALL DAY MY work is disturbed by my thoughts. They return insistently to The Man With The Yella Dog, to Will. Kit, Lily, and I have built an entire fantasy world based on his air of carefree calm. Now I am haunted by the image of his brow contorted with rage and his powerful hands violently twisting the newspaper. At lunchtime I run out to buy a *Meridian* to try and figure out what enraged him so. I scan it cover to cover but can't come up with anything conclusive. Is it terrorists in Paris, drug smuggling in the harbor, environmentalists, developers, baby ducks? It's hard to say. Now that I've met him he's more of an enigma than ever. I've learned almost nothing about him. Nothing, that is, except that his eyes are a golden green, and that a fierce rage lies buried not too deeply beneath his smooth surface.

I throw the paper down in disgust. Then, lying there upside down, something in the photograph leaps up at me. Can this really be all there is to it? Standing among the crowd watching the column of ducks is Shiloh, the yella dog, wearing a foolish tongue-lolling doggy grin. Why should Will mind his dog being photographed? Is the dog stolen, I wonder. I don't even think he's a thoroughbred.

Late that afternoon when I return home I am agitated as I near Beau Cherry Lane. The thought of seeing him again makes my heart contract with anxiety. I am both relieved and disappointed to find that he is not out on his porch. I decide to enjoy a cool drink on mine. I sit out in the slanting sunlight, my tape player infusing Billie Holiday's smoky yearnings into the atmosphere.

I see Lily hurrying down the block towards me, her over-sized glasses perched on her delicate features, a pencil tucked behind her ear. Lily Brown, ace reporter. As she hustles towards me, Will ambles down his walk, yella dog in tow. I can't wait to tell her my news. They pass each other and nod in a friendly manner. Unseen by Lily, Will's glance follows her as she passes on, subtly yet certainly appraising the rear view.

Just wait until I tell her, I fume indignantly. Then, for the hell of it, I stand and try to assess my own behind in the reflection of the window beside my front door. I can't tell much.

"What *are* you doing, child?" Lily asks. Her cheeks are very pink.

"I thought I heard something rip."

"Oh. Want to go inside?" she asks. I don't really, but she seems so purposeful. She plants herself at the kitchen table. Does she want coffee? No, thanks. Iced tea? No. Beer?

"Nell. No drinks. Just listen please."

"Oh, OK. You don't have to get so upset."

"Who's upset?" she snaps. Then sighs. Why are we having so much trouble?

"Um, you know The Man With The Yella Dog?" she says warily. She is staring fixedly at her sandals.

"Yes?" I answer with some trepidation. I should have known. Lately all weirdness springs from his general direction.

"What do you really think of him?" she asks.

Oh, no. I'm not about to be put in this position. "Lily, we've been discussing him for weeks. What do *you* think of him?"

She is certainly interested in those sandals. She mumbles something.

"What?" I ask.

She looks up at the ceiling in a kind of desperation.

"I think I have a crush on him," she announces wretchedly. She looks at me, silently willing me not to laugh. I don't. Well, well. Lily-the-impervious, Lily-the-suspicious, Lily-the-mocking has fallen for The Man With The Yella Dog. I am amazed.

"How amazing," I say. "What are you going to do about it?"

"Do? I'm not going to do anything. I'm going to lie down with a cool compress and wait for it to go away. I don't know what *to* do. I've been away from this kind of thing so long, I can't remember. I just have a hazy memory that it's dangerous."

"Oh, Lily, that's ridiculous. Why not go for it?" I say, perhaps more enthusiastically than I feel.

She looks at me helplessly. It's painful to see her like this.

"OK," I say, "the first thing you do is let him know you're interested. Then you find out if he is."

"How do I do that?" she asks sullenly, her lower lip pouting. "I hate this, I really do. You know that Goethe quote? Something like, 'So what if I'm in love with you; what business is it of yours?' "

"Stop whining, Lily, forget Goethe, and listen to me. I've had more experience. You don't come right out and say, 'Are you attracted to me?' You just act a little flirty and see if he flirts back. If he's interested, you'll be able to tell. If not, he'll let you know in a nice way, without hurting your pride. Unless he's an asshole, in which case it's no loss."

I fight off the image of myself prattling away in his kitchen while he tries to read my newspaper upside down.

"You make it sound so easy, but I feel stupid," she says.

"That's part of it, feeling stupid. You have to be brave."

Lily nods her head like a dutiful child. I feel sorry for her. In many ways she's the bravest woman I know. She went straight from an unloved childhood into a lousy marriage. She wrenched herself out of the marriage with a tiny baby, no resources, no help from anyone. She fought a dirty, expensive custody battle, got herself an education. Now she's found some security in her self-sufficiency, raising her boy alone, working at her reporting job with skill. No wonder she's knocked for a loop by the prospect of a relationship. She hasn't had much luck trusting in other people. But she can trust me.

"Let's plan your outfit," I say. Lily laughs. She knows I'm into it.

I enjoy looking across the table at her. Her eyes are light blue, with long downswept lashes. The delicate skin around her eyes is violet and breaks into fine lines as she smiles conspiratorially at me. Her fine straight hair is light brown; it sweeps away from her smooth round brow in two soft wings. Her heart-shaped face is lightly tanned and freckled. On the table in front of her rest the glasses she really doesn't need; she thinks they give her credibility when she does interviews. A white blouse with the sleeves rolled up is tucked into a short denim skirt the same faded blue as her eyes. She's small but strong. She looks like a woman with experience, a woman who has wrestled considerably with life, been down but not out, scarred but not vanquished.

"Well, I have some interesting things to tell you about him," I say.

"What?" she demands.

"OK. First, I just saw him staring at your ass, as you passed by."

"You're lying!" she says.

"Uh-uh. He looked quite appreciative."

"Yeah, he looks at everyone that way," she scoffs, but she looks as if she might be pleased.

"And," I say, ready to drop my little bomb, "I had breakfast at his place this morning."

"Nell! How'd that happen?"

"Oh, I ran into him and he just asked me in," I say breezily, skipping over the Certs encounter in his shrubbery.

"Unbelievable. You see?" Lily complains. "I'm just not cut out for romance. These things never just fall into my lap, like they do for you and Kit."

"What are you talking about? He didn't invite me in for romance. I came up on him gathering his breakfast. What else could he do? I'd practically invited myself in and tied a bib on."

She waves a dismissive hand at me. "Sure. He's probably been admiring you from afar. 'Who is this ravishing creature with the wild black hair and perky bosom?' he wondered to himself. 'I must have her!' So, what's the scoop? What did you find out?"

"His name is Will. I didn't get his last name."

"Pengryth," she supplies promptly. "I looked at his mailbox."

I laugh.

"What else?" she asks.

"I have no idea," I shamefully admit. "I didn't really find anything out except his first name. Oh yeah, the dog's name is Shiloh."

"What a wasted opportunity," she shakes her head at me sadly. "Still, I don't suppose artists can be expected to be very linear. On the other hand, you *are* supposed to be observant."

I am stung. "Well, I could draw you a sketch of his kitchen," I offer coolly.

"Good," Lily says, and gets up to fetch me paper and pencil. As I sketch, Lily restlessly prowls about the house (no doubt stirring inquisitively through my papers and drawers).

"How is Josh doing in preschool?" I call out.

"Well, one of his teachers really likes him a lot. He still fights with some of the boys, but he's made a friend, Jamie Denadio. I love to say his name. He still kisses the girls, but some of them are kissing him too. He won't make anything but trucks in arts and crafts."

I hand Lily my sketch.

"Looks nice," she muses. "Sunny, very trim."

I look over her shoulder. It's surprising how much I remember. There's the yella dog lying in his patch of sun, the photograph of a boat hanging on the wall next to the railed plate racks. Will, at the round table, his well-shaped arm reaching for the newspaper, with its lines of type and photos of captured boats and ducks penciled in. The newspaper. I must find out what it means to him. I must tell Lily.

"You're really good," Lily enthuses. "Can I keep this?" I nod.

"Something sort of strange . . . ," I start to say, when Lily interrupts me with an enormous sigh.

"Even a sketch of the back of him is attractive," she breathes longingly. "What were you saying?"

Oh, Lily, I think, you've got it bad. "Eh, nothing, I don't know. So, you really are kind of interested in him?" I ask.

She nods shyly. "I like the way he walks with his dog," she says.

I know what she means. He makes Beau Cherry Lane seem like it runs through some gentler century, some more leisurely time, as he strolls by. There is something rather Belle Epoque about him that radiates the clarity and ease of a Renoir afternoon. I can understand how that appeals to Lily. She can use the clarity and the ease. I wonder if I should warn her about his other, fiercer, newspaper-crumpling side, but I don't like to. It's been so long since she's expressed interest in any man and her distrust is so great; she could be talked out of the whole thing in a moment. Considering my own ambiguous feelings about him, the way my blood fizzed like ginger ale when I sat across the table from him, I'm not sure my motivation for telling her would be completely clean. I'll wait and see what unfolds, I decide. Let her draw her own conclusions.

"Well, then," I ask, "what if you invite him for dinner?"

"I just march up to his house and invite him?"

"Why not?"

"I just can't imagine myself doing it. The long, lonesome walk from the street to the porch. I'd pass out by the time I reached the house." This from the woman who waylays officials and inquisitively assaults criminals and hotshots. Then she turns to me horror-stricken. "And everyone would be able to see me walking up to the house. Kit! No, I can't do it. I'd never live it down."

Though she's found new confidence, the old doom-ridden Lily lives close to the surface.

"Oh, Lily. Don't give up so easily. You can do it another way. Watch for him to start walking the dog sometime. Then you go out too and meet him along the way. You strike up a nice, neighborly chat, and it will all seem very natural."

"Except I'll be wearing something absolutely stunning," she giggles.

"Exactly."

"All right, I'll do it. But not a word to Kit. I don't want her to torture me, or worse, commiserate with me when he turns me down."

"He won't turn you down, you're too adorable," I say, almost comfortably. "But don't worry, I won't say a word."

Then my kitchen door swings open. It is Kit, radiant in a crisp white tennis dress. She comes in so quickly she almost falls into my lap. Once in, she does a little pirouette in her spotless white sneakers.

"I have news, ladies," she announces.

"You're engaged again," Lily guesses.

"Not quite. Spence and I have decided on a parting of the ways."

"Not again," Lily complains.

Kit waves away my expressions of concern.

"No, I really feel OK about this decision. We just can't get it together to make a commitment. It's our karma. We're just not meant to be. I am a teensy bit afraid to tell Ananda. She is going to be upset. She told me last time we got back together that if we didn't get married this time, she was going to move in with her father."

"Poor baby," I say.

"I know, but I can't marry him just to please Ananda. She'll have to live with this. Besides, you know they'll still spend time together. He's going to see her on Sundays. Anyway, that is not the interesting part of my news.

"To take my mind off all this, I've come up with the most fantastic distraction. You'll never guess what it is. This is really delicious—get ready to faint, ladies—I'm going to have a petite flirtation with someone *wild*. Now don't tease me—oh, you're guessing, I can tell! Tee hee, yes, it's The Man With The Yella Dog!"

She squeals with delight and falls into a chair.

I turn to Lily, speechless. She fires me a strict warning with her eyes.

"Kit, you're amazing," Lily says. "You just are."

"I know," Kit purrs. "Isn't it awful?"

I try to control myself, but I lose the battle. I just have to laugh. Lily helplessly joins in. Kit sputters indignantly.

"You two are mean. I know we made fun of him, but it's not like he's really awful or anything. I just bet underneath it all you both think he's sexy too. And if one of you wanted to go out with him, the other one would be all supportive."

The truth of this stings.

Helpless, Lily explains. "Don't be mad, Kit. It's just such a ridiculous situation. Before you came in, I was just telling Nell that I, well, I'm interested in him too."

Kit covers her open mouth with her hands.

"Oh my God," she says in delighted horror. She looks from Lily to me, her eyes sparkling with mischief.

"What do we do now?" she says. "This hasn't happened

to me since *high school*. My friend and I, into the same guy. It's like the *classic* dilemma in adolescent ethics!"

"What would you have done in high school?" I ask.

"Oh, go all out for the guy probably. Wash my hair every night. Wear my most devastating outfits. Flirt. Join his clubs, make friends with his friends, whatever was necessary."

Lily laughs. "And I would retreat. Wait to see if she got anywhere, or wait until they got tired of each other. Then there I'd be, laid-back, not trying too hard, mysterious."

"Oh, I'd be mysterious, too," Kit adds.

About as mysterious as a tank, I think.

"But that was then. Now we can't compete for a man. It's too undignified *and* politically incorrect."

"So are you ready to back off?" I ask.

"Um, that wouldn't be exactly fair to me. I suppose we should both step back, for the sake of our friendship."

"I suppose," Lily says. "Actually, the whole subject is starting to make me nauseous."

"No, dear," Kit says pleasantly. "It's the idea of competition that's nauseating you."

Lily smiles sourly.

"That man!" I say. "I knew he was trouble a mile away."

"Oh, I don't know," Kit says. "He's still very cute. We can solve this. Of course, there is a *leetle* complication I haven't told you yet."

"What's that?" Lily asks.

"I've already invited myself to dinner at his place. Tomorrow night. Want me to cancel?" she asks pathetically.

Lily laughs. "No, Kit, you go. I want you to. Really. Just tell me all about it. I'll dance at your wedding."

"Really, Lily? That's so generous of you! I promise it will only be this once. Even if we fall deeply, madly in love with each other. Even if he crawls to me on his *knees*, I will sweetly but firmly—"

"Go out with him, go out with him, just spare me the histrionics," Lily says.

"OK, thanks," Kit says.

She can be magnificently obtuse. Lily just snorts.

As they sit at my table, seemingly resolved, I'm left once again with an uneasy feeling, and once again it is an uneasy feeling raised by Will, damn him.

That Kit, I think to myself later on, as I get ready for dinner with Paul. As Lily said, she really is amazing. No agony for her; she wants to fool around with Will, she just walks over and invites herself for dinner. And, I think, if there *is* a competition between her and Lily, though Lily may have more depth, may actually be the prettier in her quiet way, I have no doubt that Kit will get the goods. She always does. She's the golden girl.

She grew up in Northern California, the only daughter of a prosperous family. She was popular in high school, a cheerleader. When she went off to college she designed her own program, a combined major in Philosophy/Religion/Nutrition. She was a pretty, blond hippie princess, and when she got pregnant her handsome hippie prince (heir to a bottling plant empire) married her. Together they pioneered the home-birth movement in Hawaii.

A couple of years later Charles told her he was blocked. He needed to further his spiritual development in an Indian ashram and was taking off for a while. She wangled the money from his parents for her and their daughter to go along. So two-year-old Ananda, whose name in Sanskrit means "that joy in existence which holds the universe together," was cared for by the temple caretakers, who also cooked, served meals, washed clothes, swept floors, and otherwise made it possible for the devotees, including the two handsome young Americans, to meditate without distraction. I like to imagine Ananda as a toddler in the cool, sanctified hush of the mountain temple, playing with a leaf that floats to the stone floor of an inner courtyard. Now she's a happy, savvy American child, her clothes and hair as nifty as Kit's.

I wonder how she will react to this latest development in her mother's romantic life. As I've said, she's devoted to Spence, Kit's on-again, off-again love. It's been quite an eventful courtship. Every so often, Kit and Spence announce their engagement. I am shown innumerable pictures of wedding gowns, menus are discussed, flowers chosen. Then the inevitable occurs. One of them decides what they really want is to walk the Appalachian Trail, or become an anthropologist, or move to the Caribbean and start a skin diving school, and the wedding is off. They split. They talk and talk and talk to their friends. They go out with their secret-flirtation person who turns out to be a disappointment. They discover they can't live without each other, get back together, and go into couples' counseling. Soon they're getting married again, and we're off on another cycle.

I don't mean to sound snide. After all, I can hardly claim any prizes for consistency or intelligent choices in the love department. *Au contraire.* I've gone to the wall all too many times myself with love gone wrong. Thank heavens I've finally found some peace. I've chosen a man with my head this time, not just with my hormones.

Not that I actually chose Paul or he me. We were brought together by Chance, wrapped in the outer guise of two older, somewhat plump but chic urban matrons. In other words, we were fixed up by our mothers.

Of course, I had doubts, serious doubts, when my mother suggested a blind date.

"Ma," I said, "I'm twenty-eight years old. I've been married twice. I'm too old for my mother to choose my dates."

"Who's choosing?" she said. "I never met the man. All I'm suggesting is that you give it a shot. Meet him for lunch. If you don't like each other, at least you've had lunch. And if you do, fine. He sounds like a nice man and his mother is a fascinating person."

"Yeah, Ma. That's another thing. His mother is your client." My mother is a psychiatrist in New York. Her clients are mostly women artists. This client was a former opera diva. "How together can a man be if his mother is still in therapy?"

"That's nonsense, Eleanora. Therapy is for healthy people too. I sometimes think they're the ones it helps the most. You don't want to meet him, so fine. Constanzia and I merely thought since you're both in the same area . . ."

After all, what did I have to lose? I'd done riskier things. There was the time I flew to San Francisco with a stranger I met in the airport. And that weekend with my cousin's fiancé. So I took a chance. He turned out to be rather sweet. We met in a café downtown. He had soft, myopic blue eyes. They looked sleepy and sexy when he removed his tortoise-shell glasses to read the menu. His silky blond hair fell into his face, his lips were biteable; he reminded me of Michael York. He was amusing, with surprisingly far-ranging interests for a microbiologist. Things have been very nice for us the past couple of years.

I put on a pink sundress I know he likes. He works in a lab all day where the colors are muted and the surfaces slick. He appreciates color and texture.

Both only children, we approach each other with a respect for personal space. It's OK to leave suddenly without a lot of explanation. Sometimes we don't see each other for a week or two. Kit and Lily find this strange and dispassionate. I think it's why we get on so well together.

The bell. He's on his way in. He has a key but he always rings to let me know he's coming. Thoughtful. I hastily pick up a pile of newspapers, some shoes, and a wet towel and throw them into my studio. An artist's studio, Paul knows, is a creative sanctum and therefore exempt from ordinary standards of housekeeping.

My housekeeping is one of Paul's reservations about me. Our thoughts here differ widely. I say that if Buzz, my neighbor's cat, licks leftovers from one of my dirty dishes, it makes that dish easier to wash. He feels this is incorrect. He, while seemingly indifferent to passing trends, states that paint smears on one's clothing do not make a fashion statement. I feel they are optional. Learning to tolerate the opinions of others is an important aspect of self-growth, I tell him.

Paul walks in. One of the loveliest things about him is his glow of health. His hair is shiny, his cheeks pink, his teeth and eyes sparkling. His kiss tastes like spring water. He is wearing the cornflower blue sweater I gave him. He hugs me.

"Hi, little Nell. Been doing some painting?" He sniffs inquiringly for the smell of turpentine.

"Not in the last few days," I say quietly. I don't want to be hassled about it.

"Eleanora, whom I adora, you've owed me a painting since nineteen ought foura." He's trying to play this lightly, but I don't want to play at all.

"At least I'd hang it. Proudly. Expensively framed. At any rate, I wouldn't leave it to molder with its face against the wall."

These are my crimes according to Paul:

1. Too messy.
2. Doesn't paint.
3. Doesn't hang or show paintings.

"Paul, please stop brooding over me like a mother hen. You should develop your own interests."

"Nell, you wound me. It may be I have some interesting hobbies you know nothing about. I like to think of myself as a Renaissance man, varied, devious, adept."

"Uh-huh. Well, the painting I'm working on now is for you. You can do whatever you want with it, including parade down the street naked, carrying it. If you and my mother didn't hound me so much about painting . . . ," I trail off.

"You wouldn't even paint as often as you do now. I've tried saying nothing. It doesn't work. I don't want to fight with you, but you need that finely sculpted ass of yours kicked occasionally, and I'm just the man for the job. You get depressed when you're not working."

"Yes, but I get even more depressed if the work's no good."

"It *is* good. Your standards are too high. You shouldn't be so tense about it. Loosen up. Have some fun. Isn't that what you painters are supposed to be about anyway? Stuck in the anal phase? Just smear that nice gooey stuff all over the place. Don't worry about going outside the lines."

I am laughing now. "I'm not that kind of painter," I say, "but I get your drift." Reaching into the refrigerator for some iced tea, I am suddenly inspired. "Here, let me smear some nice gooey stuff all over you." I hold up a can of whipped cream.

He looks uncomfortable. "What are you going to do?"

"I'm being loose. I'm going to paint you."

"I don't think so." He sees my face. "OK, OK, but let me take my sweater off." He lays himself down on the floor, passively offering me his smooth golden back, a lamb to the slaughter.

"Turn over," I command.

He flips over, sunnyside up. I shake the can and make cat's eyebrows arc from his eyes and decorate the tip of his Slavic nose. He is detached, his long body lies there, but he's taken his thoughts somewhere else, leaving his elegant skin for me to play with. I put a stripe of cream on each collar bone, and start to lick it off. He opens his eyes suddenly. He looks like a mountain lion.

"You're punishing me for bringing up your painting. This isn't being loose. It isn't sex either, lady. This is aggression."

I bite my lip. "All right," I say. "I'm sorry." I should have known he wouldn't like it. I feel contrite. "Go wash it all off and I'll take you out to dinner."

He looks somewhat mollified, but he's still sulking.

"I'll treat you to *Ma Table Provençal* and feed you a bourride," I wheedle.

"Great," he says, and he means it. All is forgiven, the storm cloud has passed.

A little later as we pass out the door into the summer

night I catch a faint whiff of whipped cream. I can't help but regret what might have been.

Dinner goes beautifully. We are seated in the courtyard. The bourride is scrumptious, the rich garlicky sauce perfect over the delicate white fish. The wine is wonderfully dry, like biting into ashes. We follow tiny cups of chocolate mousse with espresso and cognac. We are feeling distinctly mellow as we ride back to Beau Cherry Lane with the top down.

A little silly, more than a little tight, we are quite amorous as we waver across the lawn with our arms about each other's waists. From the porch across the street comes some dreamy jazz guitar. Will is enjoying the balmy night air, evidently. As we mount the steps to the porch the music changes abruptly. My brain easily supplies the lyrics, though it's been some time since I've heard them:

> *Lay lady lay*
> *Lay across my big brass bed*
> *Stay lady stay*
> *Stay while the night is still ahead....*
>
> *Stay lady stay*
> *Stay with your man awhile*
> *Until the break of day*
> *Let me see you make him smile....*

Is it meant for me? I burn with resentment. How dare he spy on me? Mock me? Unaware, Paul hums along. My hand is unsteady as I finally find the key I'm groping for. Well, I think, I'll give him something to really gawk at! I pull Paul to me and kiss him feverishly, moving my hands hungrily all over him. Paul, though startled, responds. Not for a long time have I been so demonstrative, so insistent. Paul swings me up into his arms and (staggering only a little) carries me through the door and into the house, closing the door with his foot.

What does it matter that some of his urgency might be his dislike for public display? His style is dashing and makes a fabulous statement to anyone who might be watching!

four

I WAKE EARLY the next morning, despite the wine and brandy, feeling great. While Paul still sleeps as pretty as a child, I slip from bed. A fresh morning breeze is blowing through the house. This early coolness is especially delicious since it will soon be eaten up by the heat of the day. Bird song trills in the treetops. I have sheer white curtains hanging in every window. They billow gently into the rooms as I wander happily from bedroom to kitchen, living room to studio. My house is beautiful to me. Every corner and table-top is lit with sunlight, every dish and chair possessed of a happy anima, like Disney furniture. When I leave the room they will start to dance about and sing.

The studio is the chapel of this sunny world. The air is pungent with the exciting smell of oil paints and mineral spirits. Unfinished paintings in various stages of work surround me like a cocktail party full of people I am happy to see. It is only other people who are hung up on my finishing my paintings. While I am working on one, it is alive to me.

We wrestle with each other, I learn from it as I change it and it changes me. It is a relationship.

I pick up a brush and quickly lay in some paint, working into the slightly wet surface. I am filled with a busy happiness as I stand naked, painting rocks in a streambed.

Gradually I am forced to acknowledge that I can feel the day heating up, which means it's getting late. I look at the clock in the kitchen. Damn! It is eight-thirty. I am going to be late, and damn, I don't want to stop painting.

I'm still so filled with residual affection from the satisfying love we made last night that I take special care not to wake Paul as I dress. He can go into his lab anytime and will, in fact, be happy to do so.

In less than an hour I am in my office. The board for the ad I completed yesterday is on my drawing table with a yellow note attached.

Without putting down my things I read the note. It says: *Design good, but too boring. Less abstract?* I am not happy.

We are doing a poster for the city's libraries. It is a coup for Hal, my boss, to have gotten the job, as we are a small out-of-city agency. My job was to provide the art. I had given Hal a stylized black book, seen dead-on from the bottom, its pages spread like a fan, the copy in fuchsia against a yellow background. It is beautiful, but Hal hates it and Hal is the boss.

I chew on a pencil as I sit at my table and doodle. Something less abstract. A drawing of the main branch in pen and ink? Too predictable. A close-up of a kid, smiling as he reads? I pencil in freckles and a gap-toothed smile. Hal would probably love it. I shudder in revulsion. I pencil in a title on the book's spine, *Sex Goddess of Planet V*, and make the kid's smile into a leer.

"That oughta send the kiddies scurrying to their local branch."

Looking over my shoulder is J.J., the sales rep. She's my

main buddy in this joint. She's also having a hot affair with Hal.

"Oops," I say, smiling at her. "How's it going?"

There's an ominous silence. Her face crumples and she starts to sob. J.J. is a big woman and uninhibited. Her sobs are loud. I quickly close the door. J.J. takes up her customary seat on my settee. Her ample cleavage heaves as she cries, her Cupid's bow mouth quivers, blue mascara leaves tracks on her cheeks. I sit next to her and pat her back while she cries it out. We both have our parts in this routine down pat. After five minutes or so, the sobs turn into sniffles. I hand J.J. a paper towel. She blows her nose into it vigorously.

"Stacey came into the office last night, after you left," she says. Stacey is Hal's wife. Supposedly they are divorcing. J.J. has been sleeping with Hal for two years now. He has been promising her a home and a baby. Two months ago he moved out of his house, which we all know he loves more than life itself.

Now he and J.J. are squeezing past each other in her tiny apartment with its ruffled chintz pillows and china-animal-covered tables. Meanwhile, Stacey, the small and chic, is rattling around in the postmodern renovated beach house, where the floors are bleached as blond as her immaculate hair. How long J.J. can hold on, with all this architecture against her, she doesn't know.

"She came in waving fabric swatches, and said she was re-covering the couches. Nell, I could see him salivating. *Then* she said she'd had a guest for the weekend, and *he'd scratched the floor in the living room.*"

"That was really low," I commiserate.

"Hal turned pale. I don't know if it was the floor or the overnight guest."

"It was the floor," I assure her.

"He was preoccupied all night. I made Cajun barbecued shrimp and he had no appetite. I wore my peach silk camisole and garter belt to bed and all he did was pat my bottom."

That sounds serious. Hal pursued J.J. for her opulence, her cooking, her ripe sensuality. She resisted for months, capitulating only when her generous heart could no longer hold out against his desperate declarations. One day Hal cornered her in the sales office, fell to his knees, buried his face in her lacy hem, and pleaded, "Oh please, J.J. She's so dry and you're so juicy."

Practically swooning, she says, she fell down on the couch, at last allowing Hal access to her size 15 charms. Now she needs comfort.

"Well, maybe he was just upset by seeing her. An ex can be very disturbing, you know. That doesn't mean he wants to go back to her. The sight of her might just have put him off his feed, so to speak."

"Well, maybe," J.J. says doubtfully, "but on the way in, he stopped off to buy *Architectural Digest*, *Metropolitan Home*, and *HG*. Now he's alone in his office mooning over them."

"Can't you redirect that energy? Talk him into buying a house with you. Then he can obsess on it to his heart's content. The *two* of you can pick out fabric together."

J.J. looks at me incredulously. "Hal pay mortgages on two houses? Get serious."

I see her point. Hal is rather tight. Tighter than a bull's bunghole in fly time, Lily would say. He doesn't eat lunch if he can't write it off. I have to pistol-whip him to get him to order art supplies.

At that moment the doorknob of my office rattles viciously. I open the door. There is Hal looking grumpy. He stares down at my dirty little boy and gives me a disgusted look.

"Can't you at least draw something useful while you gossip?" he complains. "I'm not paying you to sit around and bend J.J.'s ear with complaints about your love life." I bite my lip. He points his finger at J.J.

"My office," he orders. She flicks his finger aside but she follows him as he marches out. I wonder what she will have to do in there to cheer him up. At least his office is carpeted. From the hallway comes Hal's voice. "Just because the library can't afford to pay more than peanuts doesn't lessen our responsibility, Nell. Try to think of this job as your civic duty."

Patience, I tell myself, patience. I start to doodle. I try to concentrate on something with a reading theme. I think of the pregnant woman Renoir painted, serenely reading on a bench in a sun-dappled garden. I start to draw, looking for the same sense of solitary content and endless afternoon. All of a sudden I know I'm on the track of something good. I sketch steadily, then take out my colored pencils. An hour later, I am done.

Lying on his side in the grass is a man. In one hand he holds a book, in the other he props up his head. Next to him sleeps a yellow dog. The cuffs of the man's white shirt are rolled up over muscular golden forearms. His leonine head is red-bearded and shaded with a straw boater. You can't see his eyes, which are downcast on his book, but he wears a mysterious smile and an air of infinite leisure. In one earlobe there might be the suggestion of a gold ear-ring. I feel the buoyancy of having created a beautiful thing.

I take a short walk in the sun to reward myself. As I walk past the small shops and flower-covered houses of Merrivale Centre, I confront myself.

Am I upset that I just used Will in my poster? I decide that I feel good about it. Now I can make sense of my whole obsession with the guy. It's just been aesthetic. See how much progress you've made, I tell myself. All I have to do is use him as a model for a painting, not get involved with him. In this same situation in the past, I made some big mistakes. I mean I probably married my second husband because he had such a beautiful jawline. Now that I've drawn Will, used him, I can forget about him. I feel lighthearted. Let him lie about on that red couch day and night. Let him make love to every woman in the neighborhood, Lily and Kit at the same time, it don't make no never mind to me.

I am just about whistling when I get back to the agency. To my surprise, my office is rather full of women. Suzi, the receptionist, J.J., and a copywriter named Anne are all standing around my drawing table. They look up as I enter.

"Wow," sighs Suzi. "He's great."

"Is he real?" Anne asks wistfully. "Or is this just a daydream?"

"This will be the hottest campaign we've ever run, Nell. They'll have to put on extra staff at the library to handle the hordes," J.J. declares.

"What are you talking about?" I ask them, annoyed. "It's just a picture of some guy reading, for Pete's sake. What's hot about that?"

"He's sexy," Suzi giggles. "This picture just oozes afternoon delight."

"Well, it's not supposed to," I say firmly. "I'd better put glasses on him, or make his nose crooked."

J.J. blocks the drawing table with her sizeable butt. "No!" all three women protest.

"Don't you touch him," Anne commands. "I'm bringing him into Hal right now."

Hal loves it.

He calls me into his office. "Gee, kid, this is terrific." He puts the poster up on his easel and stands back admiring it.

"I love it, I really love it. I really do. You know what's the matter with it, don't you?"

"No, Hal. I don't."

"It's too good. Too good for the library. They pay crap— what do they expect, masterpieces? I think we should adapt it for one of our big clients. Let's lose the earring, though. No, huh? Yeah, maybe you're right. It's good just as it is, damn good."

His eyes start to bug out as they do when he's really thinking. You can see the wheels turning.

"Yes!" he slaps his desk. "We'll give it to Madora Vineyards. We'll sell them a whole concept. You could paint a wine bottle and a loaf of bread in there."

He picks up his phone.

"No, Hal," I say.

He dials. "Vic? Hal Slater. Listen, I've got a terrific new concept for you. I'd really love to show it to you. . . . Yes, well, I was at the museum for an opening, I got a terrific notion for you." My mouth falls open. Hal squeezes my upper arm. "Tomorrow, for lunch? Beautiful. You're going to love this, Vic." He hangs up and winks at me.

"No, Hal," I say. "No wine bottle."

"Why in hell not? It's great. What's wrong with it?"

"This is the library's poster, Hal. I made it out of my civic duty."

"Screw your duty. What do you care what we use it for?"

"I don't want him selling something. He's, you know, reading a book."

"Look, sweetheart, this is an ad agency. That's what we do here, sell things. Anyway, wine is classy. It's as high-culture as books. They call it *viticulture*," he protests.

"I won't do it. No wine bottle," I say.

Hal thinks desperately. He's confused. "All right," he says, slapping his desk. "I've got it. This is really, you'll love this. Close your eyes. Come on, closed. Imagine this. Back cover of the Sunday magazine section. Davio's! It's the slickest men's shop in the city. We could put some suspenders on him. They'll fall for it like a ton of bricks. Baby, we could make a bundle."

"Forget it, Hal. You have obviously not listened to a single thing I've said. I made this for the library, and if you make me change it, I'll quit. Come on, I'll do something better for Madora."

Hal gives in, but he's hurt and puzzled. He won't actually

step on my toes, but he's disappointed I didn't catch his enthusiasm. I've put out all his fizz.

"OK, but you'll *never* do anything better," he says spitefully.

"Don't sulk, Hal," I say. "I did you a terrific poster. It'll be on walls and shop windows all over town. Maybe you'll win a prize."

He starts to brighten. "OK. Now go do me something for Madora. And make it snappy. We can't be chitchatting all day here. We need something by lunch tomorrow."

five

WALKING TOWARDS HOME I see two figures waiting for me on my porch. Even at a distance, with no detail visible, these two figures are unmistakable. Both heads are very fair. The long body lounging under one blond head can only belong to Paul. The tousled mane on the small body is unquestionably Ananda's. They are sprawled on the steps, talking companionably. How nice to come home to, they are.

"Nell," Ananda shouts warmly when she spots me, and rushes at me head-first. As she burrows her hard head into my ribs, I smile at Paul over her curls. He smiles back lazily. He looks very attractive.

"Nell," Ananda says dramatically. Everything is urgent with her. "You have to save me! You just have to."

"Save you from what, Mopsy?" I ask.

"SHE is going on a date tonight. SHE has arranged, without even asking me if I wanted to, for me to go to Mrs. Miller's. I hate Mrs. Miller. Can I stay with you tonight? Please, oh please. You won't even know I am puh-resent."

"Maybe your mother wants you to go to Mrs. Miller's for

a reason. We can't make arrangements without her permission."

"SHE wants me to go to Mrs. Miller's because she thinks I'm so awful to be with, the only way someone will agree is if she *pays* them. SHE has to have dinner alone with that new guy. You know, El Baldy Nudo."

"Ananda!" I protest, but I am laughing too much to be convincing. "You know your mother loves being with you. All grown-ups need some time to themselves. Of course you can stay here if your mom agrees." I look at Paul, who is nodding his head. He also is laughing. "Why do you call him that?"

"Well, he is bald, practically, and he's always walking around with his bare chest showing." Ananda struts in parody of a macho swagger. "I wish I was grown up. I'd marry Spence and live in a nice house like a real family, and never send my kids to stay with gross babysitters. So what are we going to do tonight? Can we get YoBurgers and go to the movies?"

"I've got a better idea," Paul says. "YoBurgers to be sure, but let's take them up on Nell's roof and look at the stars instead."

"Outrageous. I'll get the binoculars. Hey, Nell, we can spy on my mother and El Baldy, like you did when he moved in."

Paul shakes his head in disapproval, and goes on making plans. "And we can stop off at a video place and rent some movies. Three Stooges, Laurel and Hardy."

I groan. Paul has a weird passion for old slapstick and he's grooming Ananda to be a fellow aficionado.

"Great. I'll go call my mother and tell her I'm staying." She trots off happily.

"The kid was telling me about this guy before you got here. She is not too fond of him. What's the deal? Anyway, I thought it was Lily who always manages to fall for the wrong 'uns."

I laugh. "To tell you the truth, she *has* fallen for him too.

And you're right, that alone is enough to finger him as a suspicious character. Kit and Spence are on the outs again and I guess Kit made quick work of finding a diversion."

"At least she doesn't have to try to find a Buddhist nunnery that takes kids this time."

The evening unfolds as Paul and Ananda planned. We ride to pick up our YoBurgers with the radio blasting. Ananda rides in the front seat with Paul, who loves being her partner in crime in her foray into junk food. They are both wearing punk sunglasses from her collection and she has her hair screwed up under a hat with false black bangs attached so she won't be recognized. I am scrunched into the small back seat, the wind whipping my hair. Back at my place we take our food out onto the flat roof balcony that overhangs the porch below, along with a blanket, a bottle of wine, and the binoculars.

"Ladies," Paul announces, "the show begins. Please refrain from any unnecessary conversation that might annoy your neighbor." He points grandly to the west, where the first pinks and peaches of the sunset are beginning. Spellbound we watch as each minute brings a shifting hue or configuration of clouds, a dance of light and shadow. Each moment seems as if it must be the pinnacle of beauty, unsurpassable, and then the next moment unfolds some new wonder.

As the last purples and oranges are fading into twilight, Ananda draws my attention to the street below, where her mother, curiously small and far away, walks with a bottle of wine towards Will's front porch. Daughter and I share a look of apprehension.

"It's Venus, the evening star," Paul says, pointing.

It is the first star, delicately shining in the blue dusk.

"Star light, star bright . . . ," Ananda begins the wishing poem, and though she keeps the important part to herself, as she must, Paul and I look at one another ruefully. We know she is wishing for a wedding, a wedding for which the prospects at present seem fairly ephemeral. But who knows? She is wishing on Venus, star-goddess of love, and in the jewel-like twilight above the trees, such a wish must have a peculiar potency.

Kit comes quite late to fetch Ananda, and despite the child's wishes, I can see the mother is sparkling. She looks great, her skin tanned, teeth white, fluffy blond waves of hair attractively mussed. Both Paul and Ananda are asleep, sharing a quilt on the couch in front of the TV where I watch the end of an old movie.

"Did you have a good time?" I mouth.

Kit nods her head. We go out to the kitchen where we can talk. I persuade her not to wake Ananda. She can get her in time for day camp in the morning.

"It was so much fun to be with someone new," Kit enthuses. "He is so funny."

I can see that Kit has had quite a bit of wine. He wasn't so funny the other morning, I think.

"Why didn't he walk you home?" I ask.

"He walked me to your door. He didn't want to come up. I think he must be shy,"she confides fondly.

I knew it! He doesn't like me! Well, screw him!

"Look what he gave me," Kit says. She holds out a smooth, pale object. It is a carved bird, its form sleek and curved like Eskimo sculpture. It sits nicely in the palm, surprisingly lightweight. Kit slips it back into her pocket. We sit in silence, my unasked questions heavy on my tongue.

"We'll talk more tomorrow," she promises, stretching luxuriantly. "I have to sleep."

The next morning I wake to the delicious fragrance of French toast being cooked in my kitchen. Paul is sleeping next to me, it must be Ananda cooking. I pad into the kitchen where Ananda is standing at the stove, a pancake turner in hand. The radio, volume turned considerably low, is tuned to a talk show.

"This is neat," Ananda enthuses. "The guy talking spent a week on an alien spaceship, *he says*, and other people are calling up and saying he's crazy or they were on spaceships too."

"Neat," I agree. "You're pretty neat yourself. This looks delicious."

"Do you like how I set the table?" The table is extravagantly spread with wineglasses, my good china, and what look suspiciously like my neighbor's cream roses, still wet with dew.

"What time did you get up?" I ask.

"About six, I always do." Evidently her mother is also an early riser. I see through the window Kit striding towards the house.

"Here comes your mom," I tell her. Her annoyance with her mother must have evaporated because she runs out the door and down the stairs to meet her. I see her run full speed into Kit's midriff in her customary headfirst manner.

Together they walk into the kitchen.

"Ananda has to hurry," Kit says. "She's going sailing with Spence."

"That's great, but you'll miss your nice breakfast," I say.

"No I won't!" Ananda shouts joyfully, and stuffs a whole piece of French toast into her mouth. "And I don't have to go to camp!" she mumbles happily.

"Don't you like camp?" I ask her.

"Nah, boring. Swim, volleyball, arts and crafts. Swim, dodgeball, arts and crafts. Are you coming, Ma?"

"You know Spence and I are spending some time apart," her mother reminds her.

Ananda shrugs. "Well, can I go now?" she asks, edging out the door.

"Change your clothes," Kit calls after her. "Take a sweater." Ananda is gone.

"That's nice, they're spending time together," I say.

"Umm," Kit is noncommittal.

"Did he say anything pertinent?"

"No, but he looked kind of cute. He was wearing the sweater I crocheted for him."

Kit may not realize it but this is definitely a gesture towards her. She is not a great needlewoman and the sweater is lilac, far from Spence's more conservative style.

A shrill whistle pierces the air. I lean out the window. Lily is below. What a busy morning.

"Don't let her say a word till I get up there," Lily hisses. "If I miss anything I'll do bloody murder."

With studied casualness Lily drifts into the kitchen and pours herself a cup of coffee. She shimmers over to the table, arranges herself, and lights a cigarette. Kit makes a moue of dislike and waves away the smoke with eloquent fingers. Lily's expression is detached but attentive. Kit's is half nervous, half defiant. I try to keep my own face neutral, like a patient kindergarten teacher who will hear both tots out before administering justice.

"Well," Lily prompts, "did you make it?"

"Really, Lily," Kit says, "how vulgar."

"Yeah, I'm crude," Lily answers, her plantation accent becoming Tobacco Road. "But you have to remember I'm just poor white trash, and we don't have the advantages you-all picked up in dancing school. 'Podden me, dahling, I was on my way to the tennis courts and I thought I'd drop in to borrow a cup of tennis balls. Do you have any balls for your little blond neighbor?' "

I can't help laughing, but Kit just directs a frosty look of derision at Lily and gets up to go.

"No way are you leaving, Kit, sit down," I command. "And Lily, you be quiet. Now, Kit, tell us everything that happened."

"He made a delicious dinner," Kit says. "His place is really rather nice. It has a serene atmosphere. I was kind of surprised to tell you the truth. And he is simpatico, such a good listener. He just kept drawing me out. My life, my business, my friends. He asked lots of questions."

"What about your friends?"

"Who did I know in town, what were their stories, you know."

"What did he want to know about us?" Lily asks.

"Oh, you know, what you are like, what you do." She giggles. "Your love life."

"What did you tell him?" we say together.

"The truth, of course, as I see it." Lily and I look at each other, aghast.

"Be more specific," Lily says grimly.

"Well, I said you'd both found your share of Mr. Wrongs, and that you, Lily, were compensating for that by avoiding men, even though that nice Kilby Loomis at the *Meridian* is obviously pining away for you."

Lily is silently horrified.

"And me?" I ask nervously.

"I told him that you were going along forever uncommitted to Paul, who is no Mr. Wrong, but whom you don't love, either."

Now it is my turn to be horrified.

"Is she right, Nell?" Paul asks.

For Paul is standing in the doorway, his hair rumpled, his rangy form covered only by a sheet he's wrapped saronglike around him.

I spring up and go over to hug him.

"I never said that," I say.

Kit removes her hands from her face. "I'm sorry, Paul, but sometimes it seems like you and Nell only stay together out of comfortable habit."

"Oh, Kit," Lily says venomously. "You're just so unstable you can't understand two people being quietly happy together without all kinds of agonizing scenes, storms, and hysteria."

This is getting more nightmarish every minute. I don't know what to say or do. Paul comes to my rescue.

"We've all got our different styles," he says calmly. That's all, but it seems to be enough. All three of us nod.

"I'm sorry, Paul," Kit says. "I'm sure Nell really does love you, as well she should. Why you two don't get married . . . I might marry you myself."

"I'm sorry too, Kit, that I was nasty before. I told you it was OK to go out with the guy, and I shouldn't have tortured you." Lily sounds contrite.

"I wasn't tortured," Kit says.

"Well, did you make love or not?"

"I don't kiss and tell," Kit says. "Now, I've got to run. I'm arranging for an entire prep school to spend a month at Oxford. The details are excruciating."

Paul, Lily, and I stand around silently for a bit, then Paul sits down and starts to eat Ananda's French toast. Lily joins him. I go off to the shower and ponder Kit's answer.

I don't have such a great day. I wearily capitulate to the persistent Hal. He's like a jackhammer. My reading man will be the star of a new campaign for Madora Vineyards. He will even read in the grass on the label of their new Chardonnay. The library will get my original effort on their behalf, a nice gesture towards me, Hal thinks.

When I finally arrive home, rumpled and grouchy, I find Ananda once again waiting for me on my front porch. This time Lily and Josh are waiting with her.

"How's it going?" I ask, trying to sound up.

"Terrible," Ananda answers. "Mommy had a 'delightful time,' and she can't wait for me to meet him. Ugh! I'm going to Hawaii to live with my Dad. They can be delightful together alone."

Lily rubs Ananda's shoulders consolingly.

"Don't you think you're overreacting a little?" I say.

"No! And I stole the present he gave her, too. See?" Ananda holds out the white carved bird. I examine it in the daylight. It is, like his whale, a crude, funny little thing—a seabird asleep, its long curved bill resting on its puffed breast.

Ananda stares at me defiantly, waiting to see if I insist she return it. I just hand it over. She snatches at it angrily, it slips from her and falls to the paved walk. It hits the pavement and cracks in two.

We bend down together. I take the pieces in my hand. Ananda's face is white.

"Don't worry," I tell her. "I can glue it easily. What a funny way for such a thing to break. It's hollow, not solid. It was like a shell and the two halves were joined with glue. No one will ever know. But you see why it's not a good idea to take things that belong to someone else?"

She nods. Lily takes it from me.

"I wonder why it's made like this? Just a cheap figurine, I guess," she says.

Ananda rolls her eyes. "Don't you guys see it's to hide something in? He must be some kind of bad guy. I knew it!"

I laugh.

"The jewels or poison, or whatever goes in here, where it's empty. *Will*, that's probably not his real name either, has already gotten them out. We've got to catch him and save my mother from being the girlfriend of a bad guy!"

"His moll," Lily offers helpfully. I frown at her.

"We'll be detectives and spy on him," Ananda enthuses. "We can call ourselves the Black Widow Spy Factory, and this will be our first case."

"What do you mean spy on him?" Lily asks.

Oh God, I think, she sounds interested.

"You know, follow him, look through his garbage, peek in his windows."

Lily is grinning wickedly.

"We'll have to tell your mother," I warn.

"NO!" Ananda shouts. "You *can't* tell her, she might already be in his power. We have to maintain absolute secrecy."

"We can't go behind her back," I insist.

"How can I be a detective if I can't make a move without my mother on my tail?"

"How about if we make a deal?" Lily says. "We let your mother know we're spying, but not how or why. We won't tell her what we find out either. OK?"

"OK," Ananda reluctantly agrees. "But Josh can't be in it, it's too dangerous for a small child."

Josh starts to cry. Lily cuddles him, pushing his dark curls off his face.

"He might come in useful," she says. "He could wiggle into small spaces we couldn't reach. You know Sherlock Holmes hired little boys to help him solve his cases."

"He did?"

"Uh-huh, they were called the Baker Street Irregulars."

"OK, we'll be the Black Widow Spy Factory and Josh can be the Beau Cherry Lane Irregular."

And so it is settled to the satisfaction of all, except perhaps me. Ananda rushes off for supplies to make badges, codes, and other necessary paraphernalia. It is only a little girl's game, I console myself.

Six

THE MADORA VINEYARDS campaign kicks off with a big splash. The vineyard invites us to a lavish party at the winery. Bottles are lined up along the long polished granite bar they use for wine tastings, my red-bearded man reading on their label. Paul studies the label closely but says nothing.

Soon posters and magazine ads are all over. Kit and Lily are unmerciful, to say the least, and suddenly all sorts of people are interested in my work. Arch women asking me where I get my inspiration. Earnest types asking about my paintings. I've done some nice little things in the past and there's never been such a fuss. It's like the bloody thing is under some awful spell. Hal is delighted but I wish I'd never drawn the damn thing. I feel like Gelett Burgess:

> *Ah, yes, I wrote the "Purple Cow" —*
> *I'm sorry, now, I wrote it!*
> *But I can tell you, anyhow,*
> *I'll kill you if you quote it!*

I know how he feels.

It is Lily who comes up with the first bit of news for the Black Widow Spy Factory. She calls me at work, but mindful of Ananda we make a date for tonight. I am free to indulge in all the foolish pleasure we can come up with. Paul called me last night to cancel all our plans for the next few days. Some kind of business stuff he needed to take care of. A little silly malice with Lily and Ananda is just the ticket.

When I get to Lily's, Ananda is there watching cartoons with Josh.

"Just out of the blue this morning," Lily tells us, "I had a very interesting talk with Margie Salomina."

"Who is Margie Salomina?" I ask. Although Lily knows everyone in town, their children, their lovers, their pet canaries, she forgets that I do not.

"She's the head teller at the Merrivale Cooperative Bank. She was grilling me about our new neighbor. It appears that she too has fallen victim to the seemingly irresistible charms of Mr. Pengryth."

"What does that mean?" asks Ananda.

"It means she has a crush on him."

"ICK! I don't get it. He's not even cute. He looks like a pirate."

"Maybe it's his cologne," Lily laughs. "Some kind of ancient Egyptian—"

"Never mind that, Lily, did she give you some info?" I say.

"Well, actually she did," Lily says, looking smug. "I can't believe she told me, it's *so* confidential, and she blabbed without blinking an eye. I almost feel guilty."

"You do?" I ask. "I always thought you'd sell your grandmother for a hot tip."

"I operate strictly within journalistic ethics," Lily maintains.

"Get to the juicy part," Ananda urges.

"Will Pengryth opened a new account a couple of weeks ago. He made the largest deposit the bank's ever seen."

"Wow! How much?" Ananda asks. "I knew he was a bad guy."

"She wouldn't give me an exact figure. I guess that's too unprofessional even for Margie. But it's in the six figures. *And* that's just the money market account; there's a checking account too."

"Incredible," I say. "But it doesn't prove he's a criminal. Actually it has to be money he got legally or he wouldn't dare deposit it. Kit must be right. He's just an eccentric millionaire. Ananda, your mother has uncanny instincts," I say.

"*Stinks* is right. I still say he's a bad guy and if you don't want to be in the spy club anymore, I'll be in it myself."

"Who says I don't want to be in it? I'm recording secretary," Lily says.

"Who says I don't want to be in it? I'm sergeant-at-arms," I say.

Josh walks over to Ananda and shows her his badge, pinned to his striped tee shirt.

The telephone rings. It's Kilby Loomis, Lily's editor. When Lily gets off the phone, she's pink with excitement.

"You know My Indiscretion, the fancy undies store run by that pal of Kit's? It was ransacked last night," she says.

"Is that big news?" I ask. "It's just a robbery."

"Burglary, Nell—robbery is when the victim is present. Anyway it *is* exciting. You see, Claudia, that's the owner, her house was broken into a couple of weeks ago. It looks as though someone's out to get her. I've gotta run down there right away. Will you watch Josh for me? I shouldn't be gone more than an hour or so."

"That will be fine, won't it, Josh? We can go in the wading pool."

Josh nods happily at me and starts to remove his shirt.

"Whoa, bunny. We have to get your bathing suit on and fill up the pool first."

Now he's really happy. Josh likes squirting the water from the hose even better than splashing in the pool.

"I'm going to do some scouting," Ananda reports. She pats her utility belt, which she made for the club. She has a notebook, pencil, binoculars, rope, and various mysterious items hung on loops attached to an old belt of Lily's. I feel uneasy watching her prowl away, but Kit has OK'd it.

"A healthy, creative way for her to deal with her hostility," she said. "You simply must encourage children to be open with their feelings. Ananda is not at all inhibited, thank goodness. And it's not as if there's any real danger. Will is a little rough around the edges, but he's no underworld mastermind." She had giggled knowingly. "Actually, he's rather a pussycat."

Lily takes off and I prepare to get very wet.

I never get to hear Lily's report on the burglary at the lingerie shop. All lesser news is eclipsed by that of the arrest of Daq Fahey, a local boat builder. Daq was apprehended by Marianne Banks and her partner, caught in the act of unloading packets of cocaine from his boat into a dinghy in Petticoat Cove. I remembered admiring Jean Fahey, who had seemed so happy that morning in the TipTop. I suppose it is a coup for the Merrivale police, but I feel terrible for Daq's wife.

"The whole thing is a tragedy," Lily is saying as we stand cooling our toes in Josh's wading pool. "It's not as though they were desperate for the money. Daq's been working overtime at the boatyard. They have more orders lately than they can handle. I think he did it for the excitement, for God's sake. Jean is always saying that Daq hates working 'for wages.' I guess this made him feel big. Some big. Jean had to go to her mother and all their friends, and she still couldn't raise the retainer and the entire bail. I asked Kilby if we could do anything. He's going to try to get a community fund together."

"What about Marianne?"

"She's excited about having made the arrest. It makes her look good, especially with state and federal agencies sniffing around. But I can tell she's worried about something. She won't tell me, of course, but I think it has something to do with Daq withholding information. She hinted that the Drug Enforcement Agency wants to make an example of Daq, trying to force him to spill the beans about whoever is arranging the whole shebang.

"Ooh, there's Kit, I want to ask her about Claudia McKee."

"Hi, children." Kit kicks off her shoes and joins us. "What a day I've had. The senior's group that's going to study Urdu in Pakistan went to get their shots today. The women were fluttery but rather stoic, but the men! They all needed quarts of TLC and hand-holding."

"You know Claudia McKee, don't you?" Lily asks.

"Yes, why?"

"What's your take on her?"

"She's *very* successful. I hear she's coining money from the shop and investing in real estate. I met her in my women entrepreneurs' group."

"Might she have any enemies that you'd know about?"

"What? God, I don't know. Do people have enemies anymore? It seems so overdramatic and old-fashioned."

"Let's say someone out to get her. Someone vengeful?"

"I really don't know. She's terrifically chic, of course. I could murder her myself for the slubbed silk suit she was wearing at the last meeting."

"Seriously, Kit."

"What's this all about anyway? She hasn't been really murdered, has she? Because I was only kidding."

Lily visibly struggles for patience.

"Someone has broken into her shop *and* her home and torn both places apart. I'm wondering if it's someone who's angry, out for revenge."

"Ooh la la, let's see. She can be awfully bitchy. I think she's funny, but some people can't stand it. But it would have to be more than that, wouldn't it? Something like stealing someone's husband, or screwing them out of money. There's her business, she could have done something there, though I doubt it, it's not really the kind of business for that. Maybe she fired somebody? I don't think she's the most simpatico person to work for. Then there's her real estate development. Maybe someone forced out of their home or something? And she attracts an awful lot of male attention. At parties men are always falling over each other to get to her. But she freezes them. I've never known her to be linked with anyone. I think she's one of those women who are too bitter and angry for a relationship. Evidently her marriage was devastating."

"Yeah? What happened?"

Ananda, who has wandered back, is sitting extremely still, trying to remain inconspicuous so she won't be ejected from the juicy stuff to follow.

"Um, let's see. I think he was some kind of professional, a doctor or something. He'd been in graduate school for eons and Claudia had supported them. Then, just when he graduated and she was ready to enjoy a little hard-won luxury, he insisted on taking off for some godforsaken spot, Antarctica or something like that, to do volunteer work. She had no choice but to go along.

"She left absolutely everything behind, her job, her friends. They went to live in this horrible poverty-stricken little fishing village, where her husband went off for days at a time and left her with nothing to do. Needless to say, the marriage didn't work out. Then she fell in love with someone but somehow the husband destroyed the guy. Finally she left, but not before he cheated her out of some money. I probably have the details messed up, but that's the gist of the story.

"Of course, it doesn't fit with what you need. She's the one who got screwed over. That's all I know. She's fairly tight-lipped. You say they broke into her house *and* her shop? She must be dying, that store is so exquisite, completely done in genuine Art Nouveau. And I hear the house is fabulous too."

"Very interesting," Lily says. "Thanks, Kit. That was helpful. The real estate stuff sounds promising. I think I'll nose about. I am going to try to see Daq Fahey, too."

This is all gravy for Lily.

When Paul drops in unexpectedly that night we discuss the Fahey arrest.

"I feel so bad for his wife," I say.

"It's tough on the family, of course," Paul says, "but the guy must have realized what kind of a risk he was taking. He knew he had a wife and kids—he probably thought he couldn't get caught. Like so many of these small-time operators, he just wasn't smart enough."

"Aren't you being kind of harsh?"

"Maybe it sounds that way, my Nell, but people have to accept the consequences of what they do. This guy saw a way of making a lot of money and he grabbed it. But a thing like this is a gamble. A gamble means maybe you win, maybe you lose. He obviously didn't think about the loss, or he would have made better provisions to cover himself. And even then it's a gamble. Otherwise everyone would do it."

"Not everyone," I protest. "You and I wouldn't do it. Do you really think most people would smuggle drugs if they were positive they wouldn't get caught?"

"I think most people don't have the nerve, or the brains. If they knew they could get away with it, yes, I guess I do believe most people would. Of course, if it was a sure thing, the ones who do it for the challenge would have to find a new game."

"But, Paul, what about it being wrong?"

"Wrong? Everyone takes drugs. You certainly took plenty of recreational drugs in your time. We drink alcohol, people take tranquilizers. Lily smokes. They're all mood-altering drugs, including, I may add, the caffeine you can't live without. Cocaine just happens to be illegal. But is the cocaine smuggler worse than the guy who owns the Wine Flagon in the village? More people die from alcohol than from cocaine."

I hate arguing with Paul.

"What about kids getting all screwed up on crack?" I ask.

"Losers," Paul says.

"Paul, they're children. They don't realize what can happen."

"It's too bad that kids do stuff that's harmful to them. But you can't stop people by making it illegal."

"But I'm not talking illegal. I'm saying it's immoral. People who make a profit out of others' weaknesses are wrong."

"In that case, my dear, you just made an eloquent argument for locking up Daq Fahey and throwing away the key."

He's so exasperating. I start to hit him with a sofa cushion, when I remember I have to be nice to him.

"Oh, by the way, Kit invited us for dinner Friday night," I say.

"All right."

"Yes," I say casually, "she's also having our new neighbor over."

"Having him over what? Over a barrel? Over toast with cream sauce?"

"She's also invited our new neighbor to dine with us at her abode."

"That aging hippie?"

"Please, Paul? I want to go."

"What Nell wants, Nell shall get. And now, how about if I get a little of what I want, for a change."

"And what is that?" I ask coyly.

"Some peace and quiet. I want to listen to my new *Don Giovanni* on CD. I just bought it."

Oh. I thought he meant sex. And I hate opera.

seven

IT'S EMBARRASSING TO admit how carefully I am dressing for
the dinner at Kit's tonight. I left the agency early so I could
dry my hair with the diffuser and put in hot rollers, too. I
have laid out my new white minidress and my turquoise
earrings.

I am painting on my lipstick when my doorbell rings.
Damn, Paul's early. But it is Ananda. She comes in slowly,
giving me the evil eye.

"Yes?" I probe.

"You are an unbelievable traitor," she says.

"Why?"

"A double date with Mommy and the bad guy? Can't you
see that you're just encouraging her?"

"What do you mean?"

"So she thinks it's just normal and fine for her to be invit-
ing him to my house. Just like you and Paul used to have
dinner with her and Spence."

"Ananda, I can't just drop her and refuse to be her friend."

"You would if you took this seriously. You don't have to

stop being her friend, but you could tell her you don't want to socialize with him. Just like I'm supposed to do if any of my friends smoked or something. Which they wouldn't, because kids don't do as stupid things as grown-ups. I don't think I want to be a grown-up. I'm going to sleep over at Sara's. *Her* mother doesn't have a boyfriend."

"Ananda, don't be mad. Life is more complicated than you can understand right now. Besides, maybe I can get him to say something incriminating."

She looks at me doubtfully.

"You look pretty sexy," she says. "If he lays a hand on you, tell Paul to beat him up."

I laugh.

She fires her parting shot as she trots out the door. "And for your information, you're having pasta with yucky green pesto sauce. I hope you all get sick and barf!"

I return to my makeup. Oh, Ananda, how horrified you'd be if you knew how excited I am.

A little later Paul and I walk through the last of the blue evening to Kit's, where the front of the house is festive in its blaze of lights. Upstairs around the back where Lily lives it is dark but for a single window. It is eight-thirty. Josh will be in his bed. Lily will be working at her kitchen table, the steam from her cup of tea rising to meet the blue smoke from her cigarettes, the table cluttered with her typewriter and notes. Dear Lily, I'm sorry. Sorry Kit and I are here sparkling for Will in our lipstick and high heels.

Don't be sorry for me, I can hear Lily answer. What about that poor schnook ringing the bell?

Paul looks very handsome tonight. He's wearing a black cotton sweater that's striking with his pale hair. I give him a squeeze and kiss his shoulder.

Kit welcomes us, elegant in a mocha-colored jumpsuit. Some spacey New Age music is playing. Her house looks as perfect as it always does—glossy floors, her grandmother's beautiful cherry furniture, plush ivory orientals, flourishing greenery, and paintings on the walls, including two of mine.

Will is sitting on the couch. I can't believe my eyes, he looks so stiff, and what *is* he wearing? I've never seen him in anything but work pants, hardly ever with a shirt on. He looks strange. He's wearing shiny black pants, a little tight, a white-on-white shirt, and a royal blue tie. The curly red sides of his hair look like he tried to slick them back to lay flat. He looks like a pimp whose stable has been down with the flu for months.

Kit introduces us. "Nell Styles, Paul Varensky, Will Pengryth."

Will stands and shakes hands with Paul.

"Hi, Nell, you look wonderful," he says, taking my hand. "Nell and I are already friends," he tells Kit. She and Paul look surprised.

"I have a bottle of Sauvignon Blanc open, would you like some?" Kit says. Paul and I accept. Will says he'll stick with beer.

"What is that, Wiibroe?" Paul says. "I haven't had that in years. I'll have one of those. I didn't know they sold Wiibroe in this country."

"They don't," Will says, fetching Paul a bottle and a glass. "A friend brought over a case for me from Denmark. I used to drink it all the time over there."

"You did? This is the first beer I ever drank. I was thirteen and a friend of the family brought me to the Café Sommersko. Best beer I ever had."

"Oh yeah, I know the Sommersko. That's on Kronprinsensgad. You ever go into the Hos Karl Kik near there?"

Satisfied that they are getting on well, I offer to help Kit with the hors d'oeuvres.

In the kitchen Kit starts to giggle. "Nice outfit, huh?" she asks me.

"He's not a great dresser."

"You should have seen the jacket—royal blue to match the tie. I suggested he'd be more comfortable with it off."

"You're more comfortable with it off, anyway."

"Yes, well, I'd like it all off."

"Kit. Have you been with him yet, with it all off?"

"This is only our second date, Nell. But I'm working on it. Tacky clothes or not, there's something so warm and male about him. Do you know what I mean?"

"Oh, I think I can see it."

We carry in trays of caponata and bagel chips, and little baked potatoes hollowed out and filled with caviar and tofu sour cream. Something must have happened in the short time we were in the kitchen. We can hear the tension in their voices from the hall.

"You've got to admit the man was a brilliant sailor, a strategist. He eluded the Danes, Interpol, the Brazilians. What he did takes a certain amount of genius. And flair."

Paul is pacing passionately back and forth in front of the seated Will, who is watching him warily.

"A modern-day Scaramouche?" Will suggests.

"No, no. You're deliberately missing the point. Rolfsen wasn't some kind of hokey romantic scoundrel. There was none of the do-gooder in him. He was just very tough and very smart. More of a modern-day Henry Morgan, if you like. And they say he made a buccaneer's pile, too."

"Who are we talking about?" Kit asks.

"Henryk Rolfsen. He made a fortune in transporting illegal and exotic goods. Things people want and can't get. Rare live birds from the tropics, tortoise shell, ivory, rhinoceros horn."

"Rhinoceros horn?"

"Chinese herbalists grind it for sale as an aphrodisiac."

"Really?"

"Oh yeah," Will says, "walrus tusks too. Whale teeth. Certain furs. There's a lot of illicit money in wildlife."

"What happened to him?"

"Who knows?" Paul says. "He was captured in a Costa Rican jungle bagging parrots. The Costa Ricans say he committed suicide in jail, but some people say he escaped or bought his way out. I wouldn't put it past him."

I take a long, speculative look at Will.

"He's dead," he says. "That other crap is just wishful thinking from misguided people who think he was some kind of hero. He died in the can."

"I didn't say he was a hero, Pengryth, I just said he was clever," Paul says hotly. "Let's drop it."

"Fine with me," Will says and walks restlessly about the room. He stops in front of a painting.

"Nice painting," he says.

"It's one of Nell's," Kit tells him.

"Really? I like that light."

I join him in front of a large painting of some rock outcroppings, wild grasses, and a stone wall.

"Very, very nice," he tells me.

"Thank you. I like to paint rock and stone."

"Why?"

"Well, you know, people think of stone as just being a rough mass of grey, but really it's incredibly varied in texture and color. If you look, something that appeared to be neutral can be peach, purple, green. It's so common but so beautiful if you look closely. And it's so lovely to touch or hold in your hand, so I try to put that in too, so that you want to touch it."

"I like the way the natural rock is juxtaposed against the stone wall," he says. "You really get to see that though the wall was made by human hands, it remains true to its natural form and was influenced by the material as well as by the builder."

"That's right," I say, excited that he is getting my painting. "And that's why I like to paint stone and rocks next to water. It's another interesting contrast. Stone wants to keep its shape, water is continuously changing. Stone channels water and gives it form. Water slowly changes the form of stone."

Will smiles at me. Paul comes over to us and puts his arm around me.

"Yes, Nell is a remarkable artist," he says.

"She is indeed," Will says and walks on to the next painting, a jetty.

"Dinner is ready," Kit announces.

We take our seats in her dramatic dining room. The oversized window looks down onto the village and the harbor, lights winking through the branches of the trees. The room is full of candles.

Throughout dinner I can't deny what is happening. Will is practically ignoring Kit and Paul, directing all his remarks to me.

"I finished my arrangements for the cooking tour today," Kit says. "I'm taking six couples on an extended tour of the lake district in Italy and Switzerland."

"That sounds fabulous," I say. "Who's going to be teaching?"

"The master chef in each of the hotels will be teaching right in the hotel kitchens."

"I've never been to Italy," I say wistfully.

"You're lucky," Paul says. "Everyone's constantly on strike, the mail is impossible, telephones go out in the middle of calls."

"Paul hates Europe," I tell them. "He grew up in hotels there, longing for hamburgers and 'Have Gun Will Travel'."

Paul frowns. He doesn't like his childhood discussed.

"Well, you should go anyway," Will tells me. "You should paint in France. In the countryside all the farmhouses are built from this incredible yellow stone. And in Paris there are the bridges of carved stone crossing the Seine."

"It sounds wonderful," I say, smiling at him.

"It would probably be raining, and your hair would get all curly and glistening, the way it was the other morning."

"I could lend you my blow dryer, Nell. It adapts to European current," Kit offers.

Paul laughs.

"There's also the marble of Tuscany, and in Greece," Will

goes on, "everything is white, against an incredibly blue sea."

"Maybe she could get hit by a wave," Paul says.

"Yes," says Kit, "you could do a tour. It would be like 'Lifestyles of the Wet and Famous.' In Ireland there's the Blarney Stone and all that mist."

"And in Nepal there are the stone Buddhas. And mountains covered with nice wet snow," Paul offers. He and Kit are having a blast. Will and I smile at each other.

Kit brings in the dessert, a beautiful platter of fruit and cheeses. I pick up a mango and am having trouble opening it with Kit's dainty fruit knife. Will takes it from me and neatly slices it with a pocketknife into quarters. Then he scores the fruit and pulls back the skin so that cubes of orange flesh spring up to be deftly sliced from the peel. He spears one with his knife and feeds it to me.

"Kit, cara mia," Paul says, "peel me a grape."

It's all very juvenile and embarrassing, but at the same time I have to admit I'm enjoying it.

After dinner the conversation is not going well. Paul and Will are glowering at each other and Kit is trying too hard.

"I've got a big day tomorrow," Paul says. "Have to go create slavish life-forms for the capitalists. Need lots of sleep for that kind of work."

"Knock it off, Paul," Kit says. "Don't go yet. It's still early. Come on, Nell," she appeals to me.

"How about if we play a game, Paul? We haven't played cards in a while."

"Yeah, OK," he says. "How about poker? You play poker, Pengryth?"

"Oh, I play a little," Will says, his eyes glinting. "Set it up." He begins to roll up the sleeves of his shirt.

"Uh, let's see, Ananda has poker chips, I think." Kit digs around in a cupboard and takes out a kid's poker set. She empties it—there are about nine chips.

"Oh well, we can use pennies. Now cards." She finds a deck and hands it to Will to count. Some are stuck together. "Grape juice, I think. I'm not too sure it's a whole deck anyway," she says apologetically.

"Go borrow some from Lily," Paul says to me. He's hot to play.

"NO!" Kit and I shout together. That's the last thing we want.

"There must be something here we can play," Paul says, flipping through the game cupboard. "Do you have Risk?"

I mouth "No" to Kit. Too deadly.

"How about Sorry?" Kit suggests.

Paul looks doubtful. Will laughs. "Sure," he says. Kit sets the board and pieces on the coffee table.

"I'm blue," Paul says.

Will claims red. Kit and I are yellow and green.

"How do you decide who goes first?" Paul asks. Kit reads the rules.

"It says the players decide."

"OK, I'm going first."

"Be my guest," Will says.

Paul draws a five.

"No go," Will says cheerfully. "Sah-ree. C'mon, baby," he croons as he draws a card. "Two!" he shouts exultantly and moves a man out. His next card is a four and he deftly steps his man backwards to the edge of his safety zone.

Neither Kit nor I can start a piece. Paul draws another five, throws it down, and frowns as he opens another beer. Will puts his man into the safety zone. Kit is soon on the board, too, and in an incredible stroke of luck I get two pieces out. Paul draws again but remains stuck in start. He crunches macadamia nuts and tries to look unconcerned. I pat his leg lovingly and he gives me a murderous look.

Will gets an eleven on his next move. He examines it craftily. He could switch places with my piece and have another man almost home. Instead he smiles at Paul and moves the red piece eleven slow paces, stopping temptingly in the square where Paul must enter. Paul looks determined. If he is successful he'll knock Will's man back to start.

"Ooh, isn't that dangerous?" Kit asks.

"Skill, darling, and balls. You can't get anywhere without skill and balls."

I nervously sip more wine. Will sticks a long, slim chocolate pirouette in his teeth like a cigar, and winks at me over it, his eyes narrowed.

Paul draws a one disdainfully and knocks Will's man back to start. From thereon in he is sheer murder, drawing Sorry cards and driving pieces back to start, splitting moves to slide through a phalanx of rival men.

I am steadily inching three men around the board when Kit splits a move and bumps two of my pieces. In a hot spurt of righteous indignation I join the warfare. From thereon we are recklessly pursuing and destroying each other, no quarter asked and none given.

Eventually, despite the most careless disregard for progress, Will has one man in home and two more lined up in the safety zone. The fourth and final man stands at its edge. One more lucky draw and he will be beyond our reach. Paul is playing the most desperate game of all. He has not even tried to get pieces home, using every move to bump others. He will need incredible luck to get all his pieces in before Will does.

"Two," he chants, and gets it. It is enough to place a man in the safety zone. He draws again and gets a seven that will allow him to put two more within striking distance. Instead he goes forward and zaps Will's piece back to start. But I thought that move needed an eight. Did he miscount?

Kit looks at me, shocked.

"Sorry, old thing," Paul says languidly.

"Think nothing of it," Will says. "Would you mind getting me another Wiibroe?"

"Not at all, not at all. Anything for you ladies?" But we have our bottle of wine with us on the table and have been refilling our glasses frequently. Will reaches for a strawberry. His arm nudges Paul's piece back into start. I look at him and he smiles sweetly at me. This definitely was no mistake.

Paul comes back and studies the board. Will smiles pleasantly. The game now deteriorates into unabashed cheating. Kit and I are giggling madly as I move two pieces backwards towards home. The doorbell rings.

"Who can that be?" Kit wonders, tottering uncertainly to the door. It is Lily.

"Oh," she says, peering over Kit's shoulder into the living room. I go to the door.

"I came by to see if you could keep an eye on Josh for a bit, but it looks like bad timing. I'll see you all later," she says, and turns to go.

"No, Lily, I'll do it," I say. "You wouldn't mind, would you, Kit?"

"Of course not, but I'll stay with Josh. She came to ask me."

"Don't fight over me, you can both stay with him."

"What's up?"

Lily looks over our shoulders into the living room, then speaks swiftly and quietly.

"Daq Fahey's out on bail. Kilby just called—an anonymous donor slipped an envelope filled with cash through Kilby's mail slot. FOR FAHEY'S BAIL was printed on it. He went down to bail Daq out. He doesn't know what to do with the envelope, if he should turn it over to the police. He wants to talk to me. Also, Daq asked Kilby to set up a meeting with Marianne Banks and his lawyer. He wants to cooperate with the locals rather than deal with the state police. Kilby says Daq saw something queer out in the harbor. He says boats—" she breaks off. Paul and Will are crowding in back of us in the entryway.

"Hi, Lily," Paul says. "Going to join us?" He is smiling rigidly. He must still be wound up from the game.

"Lily's got to run, Paul," I tell him. "We're going to stay

with Josh. Never mind, Kit. I'm leaving you with the dishes."

"What's up?" Paul asks Lily.

"I've got to run down to my office for some notes I forgot."

"Thanks for dinner, Kit," I say. "It was delicious." I pick up my bag.

"Sorry to break up your evening," Lily apologizes.

Kit brushes off her apology. "Don't even think about it."

"I'll walk out with you," Will says. "I've got to go too." Kit looks disgusted as she fetches Will's jacket. We all step outside, lingering a moment on the porch. Paul puts his arm around my shoulders.

"See you around, Pengryth. Maybe we'll get around to that poker game some other time."

Will laughs. He gives Kit a kiss on the forehead which she receives coolly. He winks at me and walks off into the dark.

We follow Lily around back, where she lets us in and leaves us at the door.

"He shouldn't wake up. I'll be back pretty soon."

I sit on Lily's couch. Paul paces restlessly about the room, staring out the window at the night.

"Are you mad at me?" I ask.

"Mad at you? Why would I be?" he asks. "Oh, because you liked having that trained orangutan play footsie with you? I don't take that phony joker seriously and I can't believe you or Kit do either. But I do have a lot of work tomorrow, Nell. I want to go back to the city tonight so I can get an early start tomorrow. Would you mind?"

I tell him I don't. He kisses me quickly and leaves me alone with a book. I wonder if Will bothered him more than he admits. I try to read, but my mind keeps slipping back into reminiscence of the more interesting moments of the evening.

Lily wakes me some time later.

"How'd it go?" I ask.

"I should stick to small-town zoning disputes," she says

dispiritedly. "This kind of stuff is beyond me. The Faheys won't see any reporters, including me. Marianne won't talk to me either. She's all hyped up. This is the biggest case the Merrivale police have ever handled and it's all her baby.

"Tomorrow the big guns from the city papers and TV stations will be on it. I guess she thinks the *Meridian* isn't big-time enough for her now. She's playing the publicity game like a pro. Daq won't deal with anyone but her. Everyone's treating her like a queen bee. Well, at least *her* career is taking off. And I still have my exclusive about the girl's volleyball team going to the championships."

I put my arm around her. "Don't be down, Lily. Wait and see how you feel tomorrow. Things always look brighter in the morning."

In the morning, Marianne Banks is dead.

eight

A DARKLY HANDSOME visitor, elegantly dressed, is sitting in Hal's pigskin suede chair. I've never seen him before.

"This is Eleanora Styles. She designed the Madora Vineyards campaign and, as I told you, produced the artwork."

Hal is unusually formal and subdued. I feel as though I've been called into the principal's office.

"Miss Styles, I'm delighted to meet you," the man says. His voice is deep and rich, like cognac. His manner is slightly amused, self-deprecating. His smile shows even white teeth to great advantage in his darkly tanned face.

"Please call me Nell," I say, holding out my hand. "Mr. . . . ?"

"I'm Donald Dugan, and I'm very interested in your drawing." He holds a bottle of Madora Vineyards Chardonnay in his hands.

"Thank you, I enjoyed doing it." Donald Dugan smiles appreciatively. The smile is so dazzling I can hardly keep my eyes on his clothes. They ride richly and elegantly on his racy form. I try to hide the scuffed toe of my flat behind my other leg.

"That's nice," he says. "I'm so glad you enjoy your work."

What the hell does this guy want, I think. If he's a potential client, Hal sure is lying down on the job. Ordinarily he would be choreographing the whole situation, talking up the agency, handing drinks around.

Suddenly Dugan leans towards me. His expression is serious.

"Nell, I'm hoping you can help me. I need your help badly."

I sit quietly waiting.

"I'm looking for someone." He hands me a photograph. It's a black-and-white snapshot of a man with a head full of wind-tousled curls and a mustache. Despite the obvious differences it is undoubtedly a picture of Will Pengryth. My heart starts to pound wildly.

"Is this the model for your label, Nell?"

"No," I say quickly.

"His name is William Trevane. Take a minute to think. It's very important."

I don't know why I lie. I'm just feeling panicky.

"I'm sorry, Mr. Dugan. I didn't use a model. I just painted out of my head, here in my office."

"I told Don that, Nell, but we thought perhaps it was based on someone you had seen." Hal speaks for the first time. I wonder if he is intimidated, as I am, by the beautiful Mr. Dugan. He is so obviously everything Hal aspires to be —suave, handsome, rich, sophisticated.

"That's right, Nell. Perhaps a face you saw on the street, or on a beach."

I almost hold my breath. Here is another chance, but I don't take it. I continue as if my life depends on convincing Dugan and Hal I am telling the truth.

"I'm really very sorry but I can't help you. I just made it up, my idea of a Renoir subject."

Dugan shrugs philosophically, Cary Grant losing a fortune at roulette.

"Well, that's that then. So I needn't call this a wasted trip, will you both be my guests for lunch?"

I see Hal leaping to accept. "Sorry," I say, beating him to the punch. "We've already had our lunch."

"Too bad. I seem to be striking out consistently. Thank you for your time, both of you." He gets up to go.

"I'll see you out," I offer.

The interested eyes of my co-workers follow us to the door. His hand on the door, Dugan stops and looks into my eyes.

"What did he do," I ask, "this man you are looking for?"

Dugan raises an eyebrow and looks at me appraisingly, his head to one side.

"He's a very nasty fellow," he says. "My friends and I like to keep an eye on him and he's dropped out of sight. When I saw your wine label I thought perhaps we'd gotten lucky. You know, I don't think I'll go right back to town. I'd like to have a look around your charming village. You're very lovely, Nell. Would you have dinner with me tonight?"

"Thank you," I say, a lot more breathlessly than I would have liked, "I already have plans for dinner."

"Tomorrow night, then?"

"Sorry," I say. "Busy."

"Some guys have all the luck. Invite me to the wedding." Abruptly he's gone.

I slump against the door with relief.

I try to reach Lily at the *Meridian*. I call again and again, but the number stays busy. Why is he looking for Will? Who is Will? Why is he using a false name? Ananda has been right all along. Out of the mouth of babes . . . Will Trevane, William Pengryth, The Man With The Yella Dog, or whoever he is, is not just an attractive enigma. There is something wrong, something very wrong here.

I go into Hal's office. Hal is looking out his window, frowning.

"Who was that guy Dugan?" I ask. "Where was he from?"

"Hold on a second, he gave me his card," he says. He hands me a thick white card, embossed with a globe of the earth.

DONALD DUGAN
Chief Officer
International Compliance and Security

I hand it back to him.

"I wonder what that was all about," Hal says. "What do you make of him? An interesting sort, I think."

"You're much cooler, Hal."

"Get out of here. Go work on the jewelry ad." I laugh.

I leave the agency late that evening after trying repeatedly and unsuccessfully to reach Lily. I decide to go down to the newspaper office. It is not far. I catch Lily just as she is leaving. She looks terrible.

"Lily, what's wrong?"

"Marianne Banks is dead. She never showed up for the press conference this morning. Her partner, Tom, went to her home and found her. The back of her head was bashed in. And Nell, it's so awful. Her body was sprawled on the floor . . ." Lily covers her face with her hands. "She was in her uniform, and there was a banana peel draped over her boot. Whoever murdered her made it look like some kind of a sick practical joke. I just can't bear to think of it."

"I'll take you home," I tell her. "Where's your car, in the lot?"

She calms down as we drive.

"Is there any information? Do they know who did it?" I ask.

"It has to be connected with the drug bust. Daq Fahey's disappeared. Jean doesn't know where—he wouldn't tell her. She just says he flipped out when he heard about Marianne and took off. His boat is gone. The Coast Guard is searching for him. Jean's just destroyed, they questioned

her for hours and she's terrified about Daq. She doesn't
know what he told Marianne and neither does anyone else.
The Faheys' lawyer instructed him to wait until the morning to meet, but you can't tell Daq what to do, he got together with Marianne alone.

"Oh, Nell, she was so happy, and I was jealous of her."

I try to soothe her. I want to tell her about Donald Dugan,
but I'll wait until she's in better shape.

We pick Josh up from his preschool. Unfortunately there's
more upsetting news for Lily.

She is fuming when she comes out. Josh looks dark and
hunkered into himself.

"Some new kid came to school a couple of days ago. He's
been picking on Josh. His teachers told Josh he'd catch holy
hell if he ever hit anybody again. They made me get on him
too, you remember? They threatened to kick him out if he
hit anymore. So it turns out this kid has been beating on
Josh for three days, and the poor little guy's just been taking it."

Josh sits looking out the window and kicking the back of
my seat.

"They found out today. One of the other kids finally told
the teachers. Don't you worry, Josh, no one's going to ever
beat up on you again. Mommy's going to teach you how to
fight."

She begins as soon as we climb out of her car in the driveway. With all her pent-up rage—the unholy combination of
her pain over Marianne's death, her fierce determination to
protect Josh, the slings and arrows she herself endured as
an unwanted kid in an unkind world—Lily teaches her
mute little son to fight. She is a good, tough instructor, I
think, though I know nothing of the art. Josh is certainly a
willing pupil. He stands slightly crouched, his fists near his
face, his small pretty, bare back to me, biting his lips with
intense concentration.

"That's right, always keep your eyes on the other guy, and
keep your arms up. Keep moving, keep moving, don't stand

still. Now jab, good, up with the left. No, no, that's your left. See, one, one, two. Right!" Soon mother and son are sweating and laughing. I decide I can leave them to their blood-thirsty pleasures.

At home, I wonder what I should do. I think about Marianne and about Will. A cold lump of iron sits in my stomach. I try to reach Paul, but there's no answer at his lab or at his house.

Will. I try on the picture of him as a drug smuggler. I can see him pushing a boat onto the sand of a dark shore, silently unloading his cargo. The role fits him, I'm afraid, like a glove. Then the scene in my head changes. I see him waiting in the dark, in Marianne's apartment, a club in his hand, see him arranging the body with its grotesque adornments, his green eyes cruel with the sick joke. I push the picture away. I just can't believe it.

But how many women have been taken in by cruel men with gentle manners and lying, handsome faces? I don't want it to be true, but it may be. It may be.

Marianne was confident, even cocky, Lily said. She thought she was smart playing a lone hand and now she is dead. And what kind of dumb trick have I played? Why didn't I tell Donald Dugan about Will? Did I lie to protect him? I don't think so. In some crazy way I felt like I was protecting myself. Maybe I can't admit anything about him because in a way he's my guilty secret. But he's a stranger, and as Ananda said, a suspicious stranger. Ananda! My heart jumps. Where is she and what is she up to? If he is dangerous, we can't allow her to continue spying on him another moment. I've got to find her right away.

I run to the door and almost collide with Paul. "Hey," he calls and gathers me up. I wrest myself from him.

"Paul, I need to find Ananda right away. I'm worried about her, please come with me."

"Honey, I just saw Ananda walking down the block holding her mother's hand. What's the trouble?"

I am relieved. Relieved to know that Ananda is with Kit

and also that Paul is here. All of a sudden things seem ordinary and safe. I relax against his reassuring bulk, let him hold me and stroke my hair.

"You heard about the policewoman, I guess," he says. I nod.

"Did you know her?"

"No, but Lily did. She's very upset."

"It's upsetting. What kind of creep would do that, leave her that way, I mean?"

Then I tell him everything. About Dugan. About my fears concerning Will. He listens silently and he looks anxious.

"Well, I know one thing. Whatever else he may be up to—and I wouldn't put much past him—Pengryth, or whatever his name is, didn't murder the policewoman."

"How do you know that?" I ask him.

"The newspaper says that she was killed before 1:00 A.M. The woman upstairs says she heard something and stayed awake listening."

"Even if she's right, Paul, we all left Kit's together by midnight."

"Yeah, but I was with Pengryth until after two."

"You were?" I am surprised.

"Yes. After I dropped you off, I saw him out on his front porch and I went to talk to him."

"What about?"

"Oh, this and that. I didn't like to leave things on such a negative plane."

Paul never ceases to surprise me. I wouldn't have thought he'd care one way or another how things were left between him and Will.

"Well, that's a relief, I guess. Now what about Dugan? Should I try to reach him and tell him about Will?"

"You say he didn't tell you why he was looking for him? He didn't say anything about drugs, for instance?"

"Nothing."

"Never volunteer information about anybody, Nell. Let him do his own work if he wants to track the guy down. I'm not saying Will is Mr. Clean. He's probably dirty as hell. But you don't have to point the finger at him."

I never do know how this man is going to react.

"Paul, do you think he *is* the drug smuggler?"

"Forget about it, little Nell. I hate to see you so upset. I've been worried about you. You seem so nervy lately. I think we should get out of town for a while, take a vacation. In fact, that's why I came by—to ask you how you'd like to go to France for a few weeks."

"France? Are you serious? I thought you hated—"

"I realized last night it wasn't fair for me to be so rigid—you're dying to go—Pengryth's not the only one who'd like to see you with Paris rain in your hair," he laughs.

I laugh excitedly. "When were you thinking of? I don't know what Hal will say. I just took a week in May."

"Let's be spontaneous for once. I think this weekend would be good. By Saturday night we can be eating trout meunière in a Parisian bistro."

I am thrilled.

"I have nothing to wear. I don't even have a passport."

"Go shopping right now. It's better not to take a lot. One bag, Nell, I mean it. And we can get twenty-four-hour emergency turnaround on a passport. Oh damn, I forgot the visas. Another way for the French to hassle Americans. . . . How about London, then, or Florence?"

"No, you said Paris," I insist. "Please? You see how quickly we can get them, and I'll call Hal."

Paul paces while I try to reach Hal. Paris, I think to myself as the phone rings and rings, Paris. I've always wanted to be the kind of person who flies off to Paris on a whim and now I'm going. I'm about to hang up when J.J. answers.

"Yes? Hello?" Her voice is husky. Uh-oh.

"Hi, J.J. It's Nell. Am I bothering you?"

"Oh, no," she says, but with J.J. you can't tell, she's so polite.

"J.J., I'd like to talk to Hal for a sec."

"Wait a minute, Nell. I'll see."

I hang on, listening to whispers and laughter in the background. Damn. With these two you can never be safe.

"Hal!" I hear J.J. protesting, then a string of giggles. I start to count to ten. If he doesn't pick up soon, I'll hang up.

"No!" J.J. protests, not too convincingly.

"Ha, ha," Hal laughs. Finally he says hello, his tone resentful. I haven't caught him at the best of times for my purposes.

"Hal, is there anything particularly big coming up soon at the agency?"

"Why are you calling me now to talk about this? You know what's on board, Pizza Piazza, Journal of Orthodontics mailer, the Davios proposal, and Topaz is ongoing."

My heart sinks. I forgot about Topaz Computer—I can't go.

"Right. Just trying to stay organized."

"Why can't you keep a little black book like everyone else? Now if you're through, I'm getting off. I'll see you later. Tell your boyfriend you'll get some time off in September."

I hang up slowly. Paul is looking like a thundercloud. "I don't even want to hear it," he says. "Why can't you ever be there for me when I need you?"

"That's so unfair!" I shout. "One time I can't just drop everything to take off with you and you make it stand for our whole relationship. I want to do things for you. I want to be there for you. This is just about the only time you've ever asked me."

"All the more reason then, Nell. Please do this for me. It's important. Please, Nell, come with me this weekend."

"I can't. I'm the only one Hal has to finish this project. It will be over in a month—we can go then."

"Forget it, Nell. Just forget it. Hold Hal's hand, hold Lily's hand, hold Ananda's hand, and screw me!" He storms out the door.

nine

THE SUN HAS set. I am crying in the dark in my unmade bed when the doorbell rings. Paul! Relieved, I rush to the door. I am dying to make up, but it is Kit and Ananda standing there looking delighted with themselves.

"I can't talk right now," I say, trying to hide my tear-stained face behind the door.

"Why are you crying?" Ananda asks anxiously.

"It's nothing, baby. I just want to be by myself a little bit."

"Are you sure, Nell?" Kit asks.

"Uh-huh," I say. "It's nothing important, I'll see you later."

"OK, honey, feel better." Kit turns away.

Ananda sticks her head in for one last try. "But Nell— Mommy joined the spy club! Isn't that great? We're gonna go spy on him right now. Don't you want to come?"

"I can't, Mopsy."

"All right. We'll tell you all about it later, OK?"

"OK," I say and close the door. I go back to my bed, but

my mind is no longer on Paul. Just what have they got in mind? I have to stop them. I splash cold water on my face and hunt for shoes. Outside, I see no sign of them in the dark street. Unsure of what to do, I walk towards Will's house, but the night is still and dark, nothing's stirring. I am wandering aimlessly back and forth when I hear it.

"Hssst!" I whip around. "Hssst!" Then I see them, two dark shapes crouched in the shrubbery near Will's kitchen window. Oh no, I think to myself. I beckon to them, trying to draw them from the window, the only one lit in the house, but they don't respond.

As quietly as I can, I join them. Ananda mimes her excitement and pleasure at seeing me. Kit holds a warning finger to her smiling lips, her eyes are mischievous and bright. The sound of voices within carries easily out to where we hide.

Kit and I can just see over the window sill. Ananda tugs on my shirt. I try to hold her up but she is too heavy. She kicks my foot once in protest when I put her down, but keeps quiet.

Three men are sitting closely together at the round oak table. One is Will himself, who has some kind of map or chart unrolled on the table before him. He is pointing something out to the two strangers. One of them is an enormous man with a rough blond head and beard and a red face. His eyebrows are like two fierce white caterpillars. The other is a thin black man with an elegant goatee and a spiritual look. His long hyperextended fingers follow Will's pen along the chart. He seems familiar to me, but I just can't place him.

"Some is hidden here and here," Will says, "but the bulk of it, the really killer stuff, is kept here in a small man-made cave in the cliff side, which is unapproachable except by sea."

"You are sure it's still safe?" the black man asks.

The towheaded giant grunts. "We are checking every night." His voice is guttural and heavily accented.

"Good," the black man says. "I think I can promise you we will be ready to move by next week."

"Next week might be too late," Will says. "What's the holdup? We can be discovered at any time. Then I'm dead, or as good as, and you've got nothing. If you're not interested, say so, and I'll find someone who is. It will all slip through your fingers, Teague."

Teague, I think. Do I know that name?

"Don't threaten me, Trevane. You know I'm interested. You overestimate my resources. We are not as powerful as you might imagine. I have to assemble men, money, equipment, without attracting too much attention from my white friends who'd love to grab everything for themselves. They might even have just the connections you wish to avoid. Let me take care of my end of the business my way. It takes . . . finesse. That way we all protect our investment."

The blond man laughs. "Yah, yah. So we sit on it."

"Just a little while longer. Now, you said you had some samples for me?"

Will nods. "I'll get them."

He rises. Suddenly I realize he is headed out here. I flatten Ananda and myself against the house. Kit's fingernails are digging into my wrist. I endure it silently.

As Will comes down the stairs past us we hold our breath. He is bearing a flashlight, and walks through the grass and unlocks a chain fastened across the door of an old gardening shed. He soon comes out carrying a box. As he climbs back to the kitchen he is no more than three feet from us. He stops and sniffs the air experimentally, like a wolf, and listens. The flashlight's beam misses us by inches. Will goes inside. Too soon, I release my pent-up breath in relief.

"Shiloh, Shiloh!" To my dismay I hear him call to the yellow dog. He turns on an outside light. "Get up, you lazy hound. Here, damn it."

I drag Ananda and tug on Kit. We run for the street. It is a short but breathless sprint to my front porch. Clinging to one another, we watch from across the street.

"Get out there, you good-for-nothing," we hear. Will is

pushing the unwilling Shiloh with his foot through the doorway and down the stairs.

The yellow dog looks resentfully over his shoulder and lopes down the stairs, Will behind him. Will plays the flashlight over the garden, and looks around as Shiloh sniffs urgently at the spot we fled moments before.

"Good boy," Will urges. "Get 'em." The dog lifts his leg and anoints the bushes.

"You dumb dog," Will says disgustedly. Ananda laughs, as dog and master climb back into the house.

We have a conference in my living room. First we have to describe everything Kit and I saw through the window to the impatient Ananda. I'd like to leave her out of the whole discussion, but it's clearly too late for that. Kit and I are subdued and frightened, but Ananda is thrilled.

"First of all, Ananda," I tell her, "this is the end of the spy club."

"Are you crazy? This can't be the end," she protests. "We just found out something important. We're supposed to find out stuff and we did. We're real detectives."

"This is too dangerous, honey," Kit says. "I thought it was just going to be a game. Now listen to me, Ananda, you have to promise."

Ananda is sulky and silent.

"Do you promise?" Kit grabs Ananda by the shoulders, hard. Ananda looks shocked. Her mother has probably never laid a rough hand on her.

"Do you?" Kit asks fiercely, giving her a shake.

"OK!" Ananda yells, and throws herself onto the couch, face down.

"I'm sorry, sweetie," Kit says, rubbing the child's small back. "I just don't want anything to happen to you. These are very dangerous men and we can't fool around. Do you understand?"

Ananda silently nods her head, crying into the sofa cushions. Her mother scoops her into her arms and rocks her.

"I'm not a baby," Ananda sobs.

"We know that," I tell her. "We're scared too. Now the three of us have to decide what to do."

Ananda sits up.

"May I have some iced coffee?" she asks, snuffling. I look to Kit. She agrees to the forbidden beverage, wisely knowing when to give in, just as Ananda knows when to press an advantage.

Ananda and I sip coffee while Kit drinks spring water, putting the cold, beaded glass to her forehead.

"Should we go to the police?" she asks.

"And say what? We just happened to be looking through this guy's window and heard him say something that sounded fishy."

"Umm, I see what you mean. Well, we should tell *some-body*," she says. I think of Dugan.

"I think we should tell Lily," Ananda says. She is right. Lily will know what to do. I make the call.

Lily soon arrives, a sleeping Josh in her arms. We put Josh on the couch and fill Lily in. She is as excited as Ananda. Her delicate nostrils flare and her grey-blue eyes are thoughtful as she listens. She smokes two cigarettes while the three of us give her details.

"What do you know about that!" she says finally, expelling smoke daintily from her nose like a miniature dragon. "We did it, we really did it. Now the question is, how do we nail them?" She twists the cigarette out remorselessly in a plate. Kit fans the air in front of her face, while Ananda gazes adoringly at Lily.

"We talked about going to the police," I say.

"Are you crazy?" Lily echoes Ananda's earlier question. "This is our story. We can't just hand it over to that bunch of stiffs and let them ride the glory train on our tickets." Ananda's admiration swells visibly.

"We're onto this and I say we stay on it. I'm made! I'll show everyone in this little town, *and* the city reporters, *and* the bitches from school, and maybe even the hicks back in

East Bumfuck, Mississippi. Oops—sorry, Kit. Don't mind me, Ananda honey. I've got a dirty mouth." She laughs. "And shabby clothes and a little boy who can't talk, but no one is ever going to feel sorry for Lily Brown again. This is my story, do you hear me, Nell? Don't you go running to any men with it."

Dugan, I think. Paul.

"Lily, can't you hear yourself? You sound like Marianne," I say.

"I'm smarter than Marianne," Lily says. "And the real beauty of the thing is, no one knows about us. We're a dark horse. They don't even know we're looking. Everyone knew Daq talked to Marianne. That's one place to start. We *have* to find Daq Fahey and find out what he knows. And we have to get our hands on that chart somehow, find out what they've got hidden and where. And find out what was in the toolshed. Kit, you take that. Go on romancing Mr. Pengryth and dig around Mata Hari style."

"What's Mata Hari style?" Ananda asks.

"I'm afraid that won't be possible," Kit says coolly. "Mr. Pengryth and I are no longer on romantic terms. You'll have to call on Nell for that. It seems he prefers her charms, and from what I can tell I don't believe she'll exactly mind that assignment."

Yikes.

"But I hope she won't help you. Ananda and I are out of this, and Nell, you should be too."

Fresh tears from Ananda.

"I have to agree, Lily. You're talking crazy. It's just too dangerous," I say.

Lily looks frustrated. "You know, Kit," she says, "your trouble is you've never had to fight for anything in your life. Everything you ever wanted has been handed to you on a platter. You don't know what it means to take a risk. And that goes for you too, Nell. I know you think you had a wild and reckless youth, but let's face it, going to art school in the Village instead of college ain't it. Not with Mommy and

Daddy swarming around to pay the rent and buy the groceries. And yes, I know you romanced a few fellows you shouldn't have, but that's not really the right kind of risk, is it?"

I'm absolutely stung into silence.

"The trouble with playing it safe is it gets to be a habit. You're both afraid to take a chance so you don't recognize a good and necessary risk when one comes along. But I do. I'm sorry you won't take it with me, but I'm not going to let you spoil it for me."

"I'm taking this child home," Kit says. "She's already overwrought. You have to do what you think best, but I think you might reconsider." She looks meaningfully at Josh, curled in sleep upon my couch.

"Don't worry about us," Lily says fiercely.

After Kit leaves, we sit in silence.

"You mad?" Lily finally says.

"I'm hurt, I guess, but I suppose what you say may be true. I've always admired your guts." She's made her own way and always fought her battles alone. I wish I could join her now.

"I just don't want them to find you with your head bashed in," I tell her.

"Don't go to the police," she says.

"I won't for now, but if anyone gets hurt, it will be on my shoulders."

"Trust me, Nell. I really do know what I'm doing. Do me one favor. Will you draw the two guys at Will's tonight for me?"

"Sure," I say. "That art school education comes in handy at times."

She smiles.

Quickly, admiring my adroitness, I sketch the big rough blond and the dapper black man. I draw each of them twice, full face and profile.

Lily stares at the paper with a strange, catlike expression.

"What?" I say. "Do you recognize someone?"

"Never met either of these gentlemen in my life," she says firmly.

There's a grin hiding somewhere that's making me very uneasy.

"Relax, honey," Lily says. "Everything's just fine."

But it isn't, I say to myself after she's gone. Everything's just awful. I remember the hurtful things Paul said before he slammed out, the painful denunciation from Lily. I think of Ananda's tears and the way Kit looked at me when she talked about Will and me. I love these people and they all feel I've betrayed them, just by being who I am. And then I think of Will himself, attractive and deadly, plotting in the dark.

ten

I WAKE FEELING blue. To cheer myself, I put on my favorite comfort clothes—a huge rose-colored sweatshirt with dolman sleeves, black warm-up pants, and ballet slippers. At least my hair looks good, I think contentedly, pushing forward a glossy black wave. Lots of mascara and pink gloss on my lips help to console me.

Walking down Beau Cherry Lane the wrong way to avoid running into Will, Kit, or Lily, I take additional comfort from the perfect day. The birds overhead in the leafy canopy must agree, as they're singing their heads off. Paul once told me that bird song means the birds are fighting, not happy, but I don't believe it. I'm starting to feel OK, looking forward to losing myself in the Topaz Computer project. Then I see him.

It's just like those newspaper features I used to see when I was a kid, "What's Wrong with This Picture?". Same high leafy trees, same sunshine, same tipsy Victorian houses, and then on the corner a tall, dark, and handsome Donald

Dugan, leaning against a low-slung sports car parked on Beau Cherry Lane.

He's got his hands in the pockets of a charcoal grey linen suit, he's wearing a white shirt, a pale pink tie, and the bone-melting smile. The smile is aimed right at me. I have to fight the impulse to run in the opposite direction. Instead I force myself to walk steadily towards him. Does he know about Will (and therefore that I lied to him) or is he just here because my perfume stayed on his mind?

The car he is leaning on is the same dark grey as his suit, and so gleaming and racy and expensive that it might as well have his name on it.

"I thought I'd offer you a ride to work," he says.

"I like to walk."

"I do too. I'll walk with you." He falls into step beside me. He smells costly and wonderful.

"He lives in that yellow house back there, doesn't he?"

"Who?"

"Come on, Nell. Why are you fencing with me? I'm the good guy." He smiles. I first notice his dimples. "My mother told me to beware of beautiful women who tell lies. What's going on, Nell? Are you in some kind of trouble?"

"No," I say. "You should listen to your mother."

"I should. And didn't *your* mother tell you to stay away from short ugly bad guys? This guy is not someone a woman like you ought to be mixed up with. Whatever kind of line he's been laying on you, don't you believe it."

"I'm not mixed up with him, and I don't think he's ugly."

"No? Really? There's no accounting for tastes. Still, you should have told me about him. Of course, I didn't have much trouble locating him, once I figured he was here in Merrivale, but it's not a good practice to fall into; helping a criminal hide out can make you an accessory, you know."

"An accessory to what, exactly, Mr. Dugan?"

"Just Dugan, please. To whatever it is he's up to now. Did he tell you he was in prison? He was up for murder, but he managed to beat those charges. He may not be so lucky this time. And he'll drag down with him anyone involved."

"I'm not involved with him. Are you a cop?"

"No, I'm private." He opens his jacket and shows me the silk lining. "But see? No gun, nothing scary."

We walk in silence. When he takes my arm as we cross the street, I let him. His touch has me feeling well cared for and tingly. He knows exactly what he's doing, his lead is assured but gentle. I bet he's a wonderful dancer. When we reach the other side he keeps my arm.

"Will you have lunch with me later?" he asks at the door to the agency. "I want to ask you a few questions, and tell you some things as well."

"Meet me at the Last Chance Café," I say and get a warm, intimate gaze as a reward.

"One o'clock," he says, and walks off.

I drift into the office in a fog. Paul is standing just inside the door. He looks as though he hasn't slept in a week.

"Jesus Christ, Nell. Who was that?"

"Paul, what's the matter with you?"

"I'll tell you. You turn me down for Paris, you accuse me of being cold, I can't stay with you, I can't go home. I sleep in my car. The next morning you show up hanging all over some guy I never saw before, purring like a kitten."

I quickly steer him out of the office and into the street.

"I wasn't hanging on him, Paul. That's Donald Dugan, the guy who came to the agency yesterday about Will. He's a private detective and he just wants to talk to me."

"Oh my God," Paul says. "What did he ask you? Did you tell him anything?"

"I haven't told him anything yet. But what are you so upset about?"

"I told you not to answer any questions about *anybody*, didn't I? *Anybody*. He's not the police, you don't have to talk to him. I mean it, Nell. Neighbors informed on my father, people he knew for years."

I'd forgotten about Paul's father, who'd killed himself in a Soviet work camp when Paul was a baby.

"I'm sorry, Paul. I didn't say anything. Please calm down. I'm sorry we couldn't go this weekend. Let's make plans for later—Paris in September, doesn't that sound romantic?"

"Forget that. What I really wanted to say to you—uh look, Nell, can we sit down somewhere?"

We cross to the little park and sit on a bench. Paul looks terrible. He is pale and rumpled and his hair is sticking up.

"Nell, we're going to get married. I love you. You love me. We should be together."

I am totally stunned.

"Damn it, Nell. You're not going to say no—I can't take it. I know I'm acting weird. I had a terrible night. I'll calm down. Say we'll get married and we'll start all over—a new life. I talked to the Praeger Institute. They want me to direct my own laboratory, in Luxembourg. Want to live in Europe, Nell? It's a fabulous opportunity, for both of us. You won't have to do ads anymore, you can paint full-time. Say yes. We can be so happy."

I'm very confused. I start to laugh, nervous laughter. Poor Paul.

"Paul, don't get upset. I have to have time to think about this. Can you let me just think about this calmly for today? We'll talk tonight. You're making me so nervous, staring at me like this."

"OK, you're right. I'm behaving terribly. I know that. OK. But I love you. You know I love you, don't you?" He strokes me imploringly.

I do know that in two years Paul hasn't told me he loves me as often as he has in these past fifteen minutes. I nod my head.

"We'll talk tonight, all right?" I say.

He agrees.

"Go get some sleep. Please, Paul. You look terrible. Get some rest and I'll call you tonight."

He kisses me fiercely and walks off to his car, turning his head to watch me, as if afraid I'll disappear.

I sit on the bench after he drives off, my feelings jangled. The worst part is, I'm not happy about Paul's proposal. I feel panicky and pressured.

I go into my office and close my door. I start to work on the layout of a brochure. While I work I try on my options. I try to paint a picture of married life with Paul that I can be excited about—a tiny fairy-tale country, a sunny loft above the tiled rooftops, walking with a basket among market stalls, a picnic in a field of flowers by a storybook river and a turreted castle beyond. Paul laughing by the river with a straw hat on his golden head opens a bottle of wine.

Donald Dugan steals into my thoughts. I see myself riding beside him in the low grey sports car, his tanned hand coming teasingly close to my leg as he shifts gears. We climb a twisting road up a mountain overlooking the sea. We are going very fast. A table on a terrace in an open-air cafe lit by paper lanterns, sweet dance music as he takes me in his arms and spins me about the floor, my body perfectly, thrillingly following his every nuance. We glitter like stars in the night.

Or me alone and unattached in my little house on Beau Cherry Lane. Peacefully chaste sleep in my white bed. Long unstructured days in my studio. Work. A meal eaten out of a bowl and a book in my bed, or lively dinners with my friends. I buy a dog. A free and happy life.

Then, unbidden, another scene forces itself on me. Will Trevane, his green eyes sleepy, laughs and gathers me up in his arms. His arms are warm, his breast is hot, his lips burn me. I fight against this picture, push it from me, but I am stirred to my depths. A murderer, I say to myself, but my loins are meltingly aflame. I jump up from my drawing stool and pace around my office.

"Damn!" I shout.

I stride into the hall and out the door. I walk down the street, agitated, very fast. I walk without knowing where I am going. I have some thought of cooling my burning cheeks in the clean wind off the harbor, I try to steer my steps in that direction, but I am drawn irresistibly towards Beau Cherry Lane. I can't work. I can't meet Dugan. I have to see Will.

eleven

IT STARTS TO gently rain as I walk with a kind of fatal dread up the path to the yellow house. I don't know what I'll say when he opens the door. What if I just ask him straight out, "Are you a murderer?" I knock.

When he sees me, he unchains the door and steps back into the living room. I haven't seen this part of his house before. I get a quick impression of books and comfort. Seated deep in one of the big armchairs is the foreign blond man, who leaps to his feet.

"It's all right, Benno. This is Nell, a neighbor," Will says. "This is my friend, Benno Jikki."

"Hi," the blond giant says stonily and glowers at me. "I stay here now," he tells Will.

"No, I tell you, it's all right. Go along on your errands."

Benno leaves unwillingly. He turns at the door. "Be careful," he says, looking at me suspiciously.

"You be careful too," Will tells him, laughing.

"Yah. I'm always careful." He shakes his head and walks out into the rain.

"Benno is Nordic," Will says. "Naturally dour."

"Yes," I say. "Will?"

He smiles at me.

"Is there a reason someone might be looking for you?"

He studies my face. "Yes," he answers simply.

"Why?"

"Your damn wine label. As soon as I saw you, that first day on your porch, I knew you'd be trouble for me."

"But *why* is he looking for you?" I persist.

"He and the people he works for seem to think I'm dangerous. I've got things I've got to do and they have to try to stop me. I can't tell you more than that." His voice is gentle but firm.

"He knows where you are," I say. "What will happen now? Will you stop?"

"No, the game has changed a little, that's all. I've lost one advantage, they've gained one. I have to be more careful. They've found me, but they haven't got me."

"What kind of game?"

"A deadly game, for them and for me. You should keep away."

"And if you lose?"

"Who knows? They almost had me once or twice. They're ruthless bastards who fight to win, but so am I. And I've got some moves they've never dreamed of."

"Do they include murder?" I have to whisper and keep my eyes on my hands to ask this.

"Is that what Dugan told you?" he asks gently. "You look like you believe him."

"I don't know what to believe," I say. "I'm asking you. Who are you?"

"I'm not a killer. Who did Dugan tell you *he* is? I'll tell you this much. He and I are both in this up to our necks. We're both on the edge, both desperate. I can't say more. I've already said too much, and there are others, I'm not in this alone. It's dangerous for my friends and too dangerous for you. Stay out of it. Stay out of it and leave me alone."

The rain starts to fall in torrents. Outside the trees are groaning as they bend in the wild wind. All of a sudden I am afraid. He doesn't know that I know about the drugs. If he did, would someone get rid of me like they got rid of Marianne Banks? Even if it wasn't he, someone—Benno?— bashed her skull in. I start to shiver.

"It's cold in here," he says. "I'll light the fire." He puts a match to wood laid ready in the fireplace and hands me a glass.

It is Irish whisky and it feels warm going down. He sits next to me before the fire. There is an awkward silence. I glance sideways at him and find him watching me.

Then he reaches for me. I roll into his arms. We kiss, first hesitantly, then surely. His beard is much softer than I thought it would be. His lips are soft, too, and warm. His clean male scent envelops me. We pull closer and closer, locking our legs around each other. I run my fingertips over his shoulders and down his arms—I need to feel more of his flesh. I slip my hand under his shirt, his back is smooth and silky over the hard muscular frame. He takes off his shirt first, then mine. I rub my cheek against his chest. He is warm and so sweet.

He pushes me back onto the pillows and looks at my breasts and then into my eyes. He moans and I am faint with desire. He takes me in his mouth and my back arches. I want to give him anything, everything. Quickly we are naked. He is so beautiful! But I can't stop long enough to explore him. We both need him to be inside me.

The pleasure is so sharp I am lost. Nothing matters, nothing exists but to fill myself with this sweetness, to arch and sway beneath him. Every movement unlooses some fierce new delight. Let this be forever, I pray inside. His cries of passion echo mine.

Afterwards he holds me on his chest and I drift in blind content. All I want is to be held by him, all I need is here. I don't want to come around but I do. Suddenly we are separate and I fear what may come next. But he smiles at me and doesn't say a word. Tenderly he kisses my forehead, my eyes. He strokes me, my cheeks, my breasts, my buttocks, my belly, my thighs, with his warm, rough hands and my body awakens to his again.

This time we are slow, we are curious. We taste every curve and rise. I drink in every golden plane of him and worship his magic maleness in its fiery bush. He enters me slowly, slowly, every millimeter leaves me breathless and I open for him like a flower unfolding. I please him and he pleases me. We are gleaming and wet and the earthy fragrance of our lovemaking fills the room and makes it our kingdom.

Through the windows the sky is black. Now we should have time to light the lamps and laugh and talk and multiply our pleasures. Instead he says, "Benno will be back soon." We dress.

He holds my face in his hands. "Nell, you are so beautiful. There's nothing I can say to make this easier. This has to be a one-time thing. I should never have let it happen. I have nothing to offer you. Not even an explanation. You don't know who I am or what I'm about. I don't want to let you go, but I can't let you stay. And I can't walk out on what I'm doing either."

"I haven't asked you to," I say coldly.

"Nell, please, I know I have no right to ask this, but don't shut me out. We both know if things were different we'd be together. It's not over because we don't want each other, it's over because I'm living a life I can't ask you to share. But let's not lie about it. I'd give you my heart if it was mine to give."

I can't say anything. I can't look at him. I just have to get out as quickly as I can. I pull away from him and stumble out into the rain.

Once upstairs in my own bedroom I can't even cry. My bones are still liquid and my loins warm from him, but my heart is like a stone, sitting coldly in my chest.

"You fool, you fool," I tell myself.

. . .

Much later, I call Paul. He answers on the first ring.

"Nell? I tried to call you all day."

"I couldn't work. I needed to sort things out," I say. In a way it's true; I have sorted things out. "I want to marry you, Paul," I tell him. "I hope I'll make you happy. And I do want to go to Luxembourg. I'll go as soon as we can."

"Little Nell!" he says gladly. "You make me very happy. I'm on my way there. I can't wait to see you. It will be so wonderful not to have to travel an hour every time I want to hold you. We must have been insane to live apart all this time."

"No, I'll come there," I say. I want to get far away from Beau Cherry Lane.

"What? You're going to actually drive the Duchess? This *is* a red-letter day. I'm going to go out now and buy champagne. Then I'm going to take off all your clothes and pour it all over you and we'll—"

"—do no such thing," I must interrupt. "We're going to drink that champagne. Buy lots of it, the very best they have. I'm going to be a very expensive wife. We'll drink it all, then we'll call my parents and your mother. I think we should get married in New York."

"Whatever Nell wants," he says.

I'll be very, very good to him, I promise myself.

twelve

I SPEND THE weekend at Paul's. Our parents are thrilled to get the news. Constanzia and my mother call a thousand times a day with new wedding arrangements. Paul is busy making lists of all that we have to do before we leave. He helps me write a letter of resignation and dictates one for himself. Everyone is completely happy. Everyone except me. But I am so busy it is easy to bury my feelings in details. I just have to forget that afternoon in front of the fire. The memory will fade away and I will be involved in my new life far away.

Monday morning early we go to apply for my passport. Despite the bureaucratic green walls and the long lines, the room is filled with a common jocularity. Everyone is happy and excited to be getting away. I drive right to the agency without even going home to change. Hal first explodes, and then very genuinely congratulates me and warmly wishes me well. J.J. sobs and Hal looks haunted.

That evening I go home. It seems a long time since I've been here. I walk nostalgically around my house, patting the walls and sitting in the chairs. Then I permit myself to stare out the window at the yellow house for a long, long time. I see no one.

I go to tell my news to Kit and Lily. I'm dreading this. How can I say good-bye? On an impulse I walk past their house and up the hill. I sit under a wind-twisted juniper and look down on the village and the harbor. I cry as I say good-bye in my heart to the beloved place I came to so hopefully, with all my best dreams in my hand.

When I get to Kit's, Spence is sitting in the center of the couch like a king. Ananda screams out, "It's Nell!" and almost knocks me over as she runs into me headfirst.

"Where have you been?" Kit demands. "Nell, Spence and I are getting married! The wedding is this Saturday. Why are you laughing?"

Ananda is dancing around the living room. "I made them promise to do it right away. Even they can't change their minds that fast. Wasn't that smart? I'm going to be maid of honor. Do you want to see my dress?"

"Yes, darling," I tell her, "that's wonderful. Oh, Kit, I'm so glad. How will you ever get ready in time?" I rush to kiss her and Spence.

As they tell me their plans, I wait longer and longer to reveal my own. Ananda glides into the room in stately splendor, looking like a wood sprite in her pink silk gown.

"It will look even better when I have my hair up and flowers in it." She twirls and accepts my admiration of the way her skirt bells out.

"Go change now, Ananda. I mean it," her mother tells her. "I'm having trouble keeping her from sleeping in it. We bought it Saturday and I only hope it makes it until the wedding. You should see mine. It will be ready Wednesday. Claudia McKee, you know, my friend who owns My Indiscretion, has her seamstress making it for me. It's stunning —off the shoulders and a ruched skirt."

"I'm wearing this," Spence says, indicating his rugby

shirt and khaki shorts. "With tulips in my hair and a rose between my teeth."

"Whatever you want, darling," Kit says blithely. "You can walk down the aisle buck naked if you want."

"With a li'l black bow tie around your neck," Lily chirps from the doorway. "Hiya, stranger," she greets me. She looks happy too.

"Let's leave the lovebirds to feather their nest. I want to talk to you," she says.

I look to Kit and Spence.

"Yeah, get out of here if you value your sanity," Spence says. "My mother and the caterer are coming here in five minutes, the floral designer at seven, and Kit's folks are calling every five minutes. The only thing holding me together right now is a cold case of Moosehead and I can't spare you any."

Kit just waves a hand at him. The phone rings, and Lily and I leave as Kit pounces on it.

"Looks like they're really going through with it this time," Lily says as we walk around back to her stairs.

"I'm so glad! Ananda is absolutely bonkers and they look pretty pleased too."

"So what's up with you? Something, I can smell it."

"Paul and I are getting married too."

"Really? Incredible. I wonder if they're putting something in the water. Oh, Nell, what's the matter?"

She turns and looks at me. I'm sort of crying.

"Nothing. I don't know. I'm just crazy. Don't mind me. It's just—we're leaving, Lily. We're going to live in Luxembourg."

"*Luxembourg?* Why?"

"Paul has a new job there."

"You don't want to go?"

"I guess so. No."

"Then tell him."

"It's very complicated, Lily."

"All right. Come have a nice cup of tea with Lily and tell her all about it. We'll figure out something."

Lily's living room is full of unfolded laundry and toys. The kitchen is full of dishes and toys. The table is covered with the typewriter, ashtrays, stacks of papers, and notebooks. Josh is in his room, which is packed with clutter but has a loft bed, a fish tank, and a rope swing. He maneuvers spacemen, robots, and horrible creatures over piles of stuff, all the while emitting whistling, crashing, beeping sound effects. He acknowledges my greeting with a shy smile, then gets down on all fours and kicks his feet up like a donkey.

I follow Lily into her room, a tiny sanctum of peace and order. At the round chintz-covered table, she pours tea from a flowered Spode pot that rests on a lace doily in a china tray. Here are the few treasures she has from her mother. I pick up a photograph of her parents in a silver frame. They are a young and handsome couple, laughing, dressed in white, their heads crowned with the hazy halos of light the long-dead somehow acquire in photographs.

"So, why do you have to go to Luxembourg?" Lily asks. "And is that really the only reason you're unhappy?"

I hesitate. How can I explain my impulsive acceptance of Paul without revealing the sticky truth about my experience with Will? Do I want to tell her or not? Her phone rings loudly beside me.

"All right, I'll come right down," Lily says after listening. "It's no trouble, just wait for me."

"Shit," she says, "I have to go let the cleaning woman into the office at the *Meridian*. Kilby lost his keys and borrowed hers and he's not home. I'll be back in twenty minutes. You can stay here with Josh or I can take him with me, or we can all go."

"I'll wait here," I tell her and she dashes out. I wander into Josh's room but he's happy by himself, so I go into the living room and start folding sheets and pillowcases for Lily. I'm matching socks when the doorbell rings. At first I don't recognize the woman on the stairs, then I remember Jean Fahey from the TipTop.

"Hello?" she says uncertainly. "I'm looking for Lily?"

"She'll be back in a moment, Jean. Won't you come in?"

"My kids are in the car," she explains, pointing to a small van in the driveway. There seem to be a dozen kids in there, shouting and climbing over seats.

"Have we met?" she asks. "You're Lily's friend, but I don't recall your name."

"Nell." I want to tell her I am sorry for her troubles, but I'm not sure I should bring them up.

She sits on the steps and lights a cigarette. "I just came to tell Lily good-bye. She's been so kind. I'm taking my kids to my mother's. I can't stay around here anymore. You know about Daq, my husband?"

"Yes," I say.

"Of course you do. Everyone knows. The police are driving me crazy and these men keep coming around asking me questions. I don't know if they're from the government or what. I'm having a breakdown."

"I'm sorry," I tell her. She smiles. It would still be a very pretty, a young woman's smile, but she needs work done on her teeth.

"He's not a bad man. Anyone in town will tell you. Lily knows. He just got scared when Marianne was—died. He loves me and those kids."

"Of course he does," I say.

"People are saying he's gone for good, but he isn't. He'd never desert us. You don't believe me."

"Of course I do."

"No, no you don't. I can see it in your eyes. You feel sorry for me. No one believes in him but me. Look, don't tell anyone, but he sent me word." After years of marriage, five kids, and all this trouble, her eyes still shine.

"I'm going to join him. When things cool down we'll send for the kids. You look kind and you're Lily's friend. I know you won't say nothing. After they catch the guy that killed poor Marianne, he'll come back and do his time for the smuggling. When he gets out, we'll start again. He can always make a living with his hands. Nothing he can't do around a boat."

"That sounds wonderful," I say.

"Nicole, you let go of her hair. Now!" she yells towards the van. "I got to go. Poor kids are all upset. Don't tell what I told you. Just tell Lily I went to my mother's and I said bye and thanks for all her help, and I'm sorry people lost the money they put up for the bail. We'll pay back every penny, you tell her I said so, when times are better. Nice meeting you."

"You too. I hope everything works out for you."

She smiles and shrugs. "You never know," she says. She looks almost like the reckless, cheerful young girl Lily described. And she is happy because she's going to join her man.

Back upstairs, I continue to straighten up and I think about Jean's shining eyes, of the pride in her voice as she talks about him. Is she just a fool? Her husband is a small-time drug smuggler who's left her to deal with five kids, their savings wiped out, their house mortgaged, and their friends in debt. The police are dogging her and her life may be in danger. The whole town thinks she's been abandoned but she believes in him. She's ready to leave her home, her friends, even her children to follow him, who knows where, into hiding. And me? I'm waiting for Lily to come home to talk me out of following Paul across the seas.

Could any man light a glow in my eyes like the one in Jean's? That's what we were describing, after all, that day weeks ago on my front porch. A love we'd follow anywhere under any circumstances. Now Kit is marrying, does she feel like that? Have her doubts been supplanted by certainty? And mine? I'm rushing into Paul's arms, despite my doubts, because I'm running away from another pair of arms, aren't I? Strong arms, covered with a golden glint, arms that first pulled me close, then pushed me away.

I put down the pile of towels I am carrying. Could I feel that way about *him*, about Will? Could I leave everything behind to accompany him down whatever dark path he may be following? Even if it is he who tempted Daq Fahey with easy money, who tumbled the walls of Jean's life around her? How shamefully my heart leaps at the memory of the firelit room, despite what he's done, despite the fact that he kicked me out of it.

Damn Lily, why is she taking so long? The last thing I need is to be left alone with my cursed memory, my conscienceless heart. Then I remember Marianne. Can I forgive even this? He said he didn't do it, but what do the promises of a murderer mean? A man who killed would not stick at lying. My heart argues with me. Paul said he couldn't have done it. Oh, Paul! I am such a coward. I can't take back the promises I've given you. I've made my bed. When Lily gets back, I'll tell her I will lie in it.

When Lily does get back, she looks worried. I give her Jean's message.

"I'm glad," she says. "Her mother will help her with the kids and take care of her. She looks like hell lately. Now, Nell, when did Paul get this new offer? You never mentioned anything before. Was he looking?"

"I just found out about it myself," I say.

"Ummm. Something funny just happened. I ran into Tom Waite—you know, he used to be Marianne's partner. He told me the police had a new lead. It seems they traced the money that was anonymously dropped off at Kilby's, for Daq's bail."

"Yes?" I wait breathlessly.

"Nell, Paul paid the bail."

"What? My Paul?"

"How many Paul Varenskys could there be?"

"I don't know. A lot. Look in the phone book." She opens the fat city directory. There are three Varenskys and a Varens. There is only one Paul. Mine.

I call him. There is no answer. I dial his lab.

"I'm sorry," the receptionist tells me, "he doesn't answer."

"He must be on his way to my house," I say to Lily. "As soon as I hear from him, I'll call you."

"You don't have to call me," Lily says. "I just thought you'd want to know. It *is* kind of funny. So much money. Maybe it's a mix-up, or he was just sorry for the Faheys and embarrassed to let you know. Is he the kind to be shy about his good deeds?"

"Definitely," I agree. As I walk to my place it seems to me to be the explanation. He can be surprisingly generous on a whim. And it would be just like him to keep quiet about it. He expected to get the money back, after all. But he doesn't even know the Faheys.

I remember the words we had over Daq's arrest. Maybe I moved him after all, in spite of his unsympathetic statements. He has been more incomprehensible than ever lately. He's almost forty. Is this midlife crisis?

I walk into the bedroom. Paul is sitting on the bed, in the dark.

"I let myself in. I hope you don't mind?" he says.

"Of course not. But why are you sitting here in the dark?"

"The better to eat you, my dear," he growls and lunges for me, pulling off my clothes.

"Stop it," I say. But he doesn't stop. He pushes my skirt up around my waist and tears at my panties while I try to fight him off.

"Stop it, Paul, you're scaring me."

"I need you, Nell. Take off your clothes."

He is frenzied and quickly spent. Afterwards I hold him. I don't know anything anymore. Not even myself. When he used to be so cool and self-sufficient I felt locked out. Now he wants too much.

He jumps up and goes into the shower. He comes out of the bathroom with his wet hair combed and his pants on.

"You paid Daq Fahey's bail," I say.

He sits on the bed. "Only part of it."

I look at him. "I felt sorry for his wife and kids. What's the matter, Eleanora? You don't like inconsistency? So I talked like a hard-boiled egg. I'm really just a marshmallow, you found me out."

"The police might think it means you're involved in the drugs," I say.

He laughs. "I guess they better run me in then. But they'll have to act quickly. Dr. Weber wants me to come out right away. That's why I'm here, to tell you."

"You don't mean right now?"

"They're reorganizing the staff at the Institute and they want my input. I'll have to leave immediately, and you can join me as soon as your papers are ready. I'm sorry about the wedding, sweetheart. We'll be married there. Don't be too disappointed. We'll fly the folks over for the ceremony and we'll have the most romantic honeymoon—Paris, Florence, Venice, whatever you want."

"No. Things are happening too fast. Every day it's something new. I can't handle it."

"Yes you can. Don't let me down now. I have to tie up loose ends at my lab here. Come with me and then we'll have dinner. My flight leaves at 6:00 A.M., you can drive me to the airport. I sold my car. Maybe I'll buy a Volvo over there."

"You're leaving tomorrow morning? Paul, what about your building?"

"I'm all packed. My apartment is rented and the tenants downstairs are staying. Don't worry so much. I know I'm leaving you in a mess." He looks around the room and shakes his head disapprovingly. "But this will give you a chance to learn how to organize in a hurry. Go on, get dressed and we'll be on our way."

"And what about the police?" I ask.

"If they want me, they can find me. Come on." He tosses my clothes to me.

thirteen

AT THE LAB, Paul fills box after box with papers, leaving some for his co-workers and putting aside others for me to ship overseas. He shreds countless other papers. I nervously sip coffee made on the Bunsen burner, expecting the police to knock on the door any minute. Paul is tightly wound up and efficient. When he is done, it's very late. An all-night restaurant in Chinatown is the only place to eat. I'm not hungry, but Paul orders with his usual precision. We drive to the airport as the sky lightens. We make out in the waiting area of the international terminal like teenagers. And then they call his flight and he is gone. There's no place lonelier than an airport terminal at 6:00 A.M.

It is too late for sleep and too early for work when I drive back to the cliffs of Merrivale. The day is sparkling and fresh, but I feel rumpled and used up. I park the poor tired Duchess and go into the Last Chance Café for yet another coffee. Donald Dugan is breakfasting at a window table, immaculate in a crisp olive suit and light blue shirt. He has company.

I slink towards a table in the rear, but I needn't fear he will see me in my disrepair. He's head-to-head with an absolutely stunning woman and shows no sign of coming up for air.

His companion is probably the only woman he could have found more beautiful than he. She's tawny and sleek and showing about a mile of elegant leg between her beige silk skirt and high-heeled beige slingbacks. Her honey-colored hair is glossy and straight and has been cut by someone who knows his way around a sliderule.

The Last Chance isn't going to sell many of its famous pastries as long as she sits in the window. The expensively dressed ladies come in, push up their sunglasses the better to study Dugan and pal, and look sour. "Just coffee, black please," is written all over them.

Dugan and the woman are oblivious to the attention. Maybe they're used to it, maybe they're too engrossed in one another. I am surprised then when Dugan looks up and, catching my eye, excuses himself and comes to my table.

"Did you stand me up Friday or are you just very, very late?" he asks.

I laugh. "At least you haven't been pining away," I say, inclining my head towards the window table.

"Yes, Claudia is very decorative." I realize that Dugan's companion is Kit's friend Claudia McKee. "It's just business, though. You were my date." I look over at her. She is glaring coldly at me.

"Sorry, something came up," I say.

"Something on Beau Cherry Lane?" He's smiling. Is he just teasing me or does he know where I spent Friday afternoon?

"Your business breakfast seems to be breaking up," I tell him. Claudia is getting up angrily and twitching towards the door.

"All work and no play," Dugan sighs. "Can I call you?"

I nod and he hurries after her. I watch him pay the bill and catch up to her on the street. I can see them through the window. They seem to be arguing. She is almost as tall as he is. She looks back thoughtfully through the plate glass window. I don't like the nasty smile on her face.

That evening two policemen come to the house. I am apprehensive when I see them in my doorway, but not surprised.

One of them does the talking. He is very pink with a black mustache, and good-looking, if a little too beefy. He introduces himself as Officer Waite, Marianne Banks's old partner. His new partner is small and thin and sad-looking.

"We want to ask you some questions about your . . . ," he hesitates over his choice of word, ". . . about Paul Varensky."

"He is my fiancé," I say, helping him out.

"Your fiancé. He's left the country?"

"Yes. I dropped him off at the airport this morning." The thin, sad cop walks around the room, studying my paintings.

"I see. You heard from him yet?"

"No, I don't expect to, not until tomorrow morning."

"Where is he headed?"

"Luxembourg. He is head of a research laboratory there."

"Isn't this rather sudden?" He consults a notebook. "I have here that he works for Whitton-Huxley Research Corp."

"This is a new job. It came up suddenly and he had to put together an entire staff. Why are you questioning me about him?"

"Are you aware, Miss Styles, that your fiancé paid the bail for Daq Fahey, a suspected drug smuggler who jumped bail?"

"Yes."

"He paid out over fifteen thousand dollars. Anonymously."

"Yes. Paul knew I was worried about his wife and children. He wanted to help."

"You know the Faheys well, then?"

"No, not well." I don't know if it's better if I know them or not. "In fact, I never met Daq. Jean I know only slightly."

"Mr. Varensky knows them?"

"No."

"So he pays out fifteen thousand for the husband of a woman you only slightly know, because you felt sorry for her?"

"Paul is an unusual man. He does things spontaneously."

"I see. Was he upset when Fahey skipped? It was a pretty expensive gamble to take and lose, someone he didn't even know."

"I—yes, he was upset." I wonder what Paul feels about it.

"And you? Were you upset when you found out fifteen K had gone down the tubes?"

I don't want to say that Paul paid the bail without telling me. I shrug.

"Your fiancé, is he a very wealthy man?"

"It depends on what you mean. He has some family money in trust and some real estate. He's very well paid in his profession."

"We've ordered his bank records. We're going to go over his finances with a fine-toothed comb. Think we'll find any surprises?"

"I have no idea what you mean. I'm sure everything will be very correct. Paul is an orderly and upstanding person." I sound so pompous. "I don't know anything about his finances."

"But you are engaged to get married?"

"We don't talk about money. I assumed I'd be comfortable."

"Yeah, Tom," the skinny partner calls from my studio, "she's an artist. They don't care about money."

Tom gives him a look of disgust.

"Your fiancé, Miss Styles, uses drugs?"

"Paul? Never! He's the only person I know who's never even smoked marijuana. He'd never destroy brain cells."

"No cocaine? Lots of your clean-cut professional types go in for that extra juice."

"I'm positive Paul has never touched cocaine."

Finally I explode. "What are you getting at?"

"What I'm getting at, Miss Styles, is that we think Mr. Varensky is the guy behind the drugs that are pouring into this area. We think he hired Daq Fahey and that he may be behind the murder of police officer Banks and that he got the wind up and left the country. Maybe he gave you the slip too. I bet you never hear from the guy."

"This is totally outrageous!" I say angrily. "Paul would never do such things. You have a lot of nerve saying such horrible things about an innocent person. Don't you dare repeat anything like this to anyone or I'll make sure you're sued for slander."

"You tell your fiancé, when and if he calls, to contact us right away. We want to ask him some questions. If he's clean, I'll come over here personally and beg your pardon. But if he's guilty, if he killed Marianne, I'm going to fry his ass."

"Tom!" his partner protests.

"If I upset you, Miss Styles, I'm sorry, but I'm pretty upset myself."

Then, to my horror, he breaks down. He cradles his head in his arms on the top of a bookcase and sobs. His partner comes over and starts patting his back.

"That's right, Tom, you go ahead now and get it all out. I told you, man, you shoulda stayed out longer."

Still patting his partner's heaving back, he turns confidentially to me.

"He's been keeping it all bottled up inside. He didn't cry at the funeral or anything. He's the one found her body. Sorry he yelled at you, but he feels so guilty, you know? He blames himself, he didn't make Banks tell him what she knew. I'm sure you understand, artists are sensitive too. This is beautiful, he's finally getting in touch with his rage and grief, know what I mean?"

I nod numbly.

"Hey, you know what would be great, if it's not too much trouble? Do you think you could make him a cup of tea? He takes it with milk and sugar."

fourteen

DESPITE TOM WAITE's predictions, Paul does call. He tells me he is wiped out from jet lag, that Luxembourg is cold and wet, but lovely, and that he loves me. He is delighted by my third degree, as he calls it, and promises to call the Merrivale police and confess to all kinds of dark deeds as soon as possible. I promise to join him in two weeks, as I have things to take care of and I've promised to have Ananda stay with me while her mother is on her honeymoon.

In the next week I'm very busy. I try to produce as much as I can for Hal at the agency. I even finish my painting of the stones in the streambed. It will be my wedding present to Paul. The fair Claudia must have tightened her reins on Dugan; I never get his call. And though I've passed Benno hulking in the garden and seen Shiloh trotting busily along, I've seen nothing of Will Trevane. And I've looked.

Saturday shines as brightly as it is meant to for Kit. I go over early to dress with Lily. She and I are bridesmaids. I can't believe my eyes when I get to the top of the narrow steps. Her apartment is spotless.

"Kit had the cleaning service do my place too," Lily says. She is wearing her midnight-blue kimono and has electric rollers in her hair. She's lounging on the sofa with a cigarette.

"Where's Josh?"

Lily laughs. "Mrs. Anglund is giving him a bath downstairs. I think she's afraid I wouldn't wash behind his ears." Josh is to be the ring bearer. I take it Kit's mother doesn't approve of Lily.

Lily sips from a mug.

"Want some?" she asks.

"Of course."

"It's not coffee," she warns. "It's brandy." Then she starts to sing, "Wedding bells are breaking up this old gang of mine . . ."

"Do you mind?" I ask her.

"Well, I do and I don't. Kit's moving into Spence's house. You're off to Neverland. Beau Cherry Lane just won't be the same. Still, the evil Mr. Trevane remains and I'm hot on his trail, so to speak." She laughs lewdly. "But if you mean do I mind that I'm not getting married too, I don't. Marriage is a disease I don't intend to catch again. Honey, I been inoculated but good. Still, I wouldn't mind a little lovin'. Do you realize it's been over a year since I messed with anything? I'm getting rusty. Need a lube job."

"Lily!" I throw a pillow at her.

"Hey, don't you spill my good brandy."

"Maybe there'll be a sweet young thing at the wedding," I say.

"Yeah! One of Spence's preppy friends, like William Hurt wearing glasses. I can feature that."

It is time to dress. I'm wearing something new—pale celadon-green satin with a fitted bodice and a swingy skirt. A short matching jacket with tightly fitted sleeves makes it modest but chic for the ceremony. Then the jacket comes off and it's sexy for dancing. Kit has ordered me a pale green orchid for my hair.

Then Lily comes out of her bedroom and takes my breath away. She's wearing a lavender organdy dress with a sweetheart neckline and a long ballet skirt. Crinolines rustle as she walks. Silk violets nestle at her tiny waist. Her hair falls in a sexy wave over one eye and is caught up in a purple orchid above her ear on the other side.

"Where did you get that dress? I've never seen anything like it."

"It was my mother's," she says happily. "My father bought it for her right after they were married."

"You look lovely, like a flower," I say.

"And you. You're so beautiful, Nell. And so luscious." We kiss each other.

"Come down and see my mother," Ananda calls. "Wow, you both look so beautiful."

Ananda is radiant. Her blond curls spill down her back under a circlet of pink rosebuds and baby's breath. She looks like a Rosetti angel walking cautiously so as not to displace her halo.

"You belong in a fairy tale," I tell her.

"Don't be afraid to move, gorgeous," Lily says. "Nothing will fall off."

Ananda guides us solemnly into Kit's bedroom. Pride in her mother and anxiety lest we outshine her are mixed in her face. She needn't fear. Kit's never been more lovely. Her gown is regally simple and her face is aglow from within. She looks like a goddess.

Ananda relaxes as we ooh and aah. Lily rushes forward with affection.

"Don't you kiss her!" Kit's mother shouts. Lily looks shocked.

"Don't want to get lipstick on the bri-ide," Mrs. Anglund sings. "Don't you both look lovely? What an unusual dress, Lily. Is it an antique?"

We settle for squeezing Kit's hand. Mrs. Anglund is petite and expensive. Spence's mother is here too, big and breezy. She hands Kit a heavy gold chain and locket.

"This was my mother's," she says proudly. "I want you to have it."

Mrs. Anglund is about to object as Kit replaces the pearls she is wearing with the locket, but Kit flashes her a look so fierce she is squelched. She consoles herself by pulling a wet comb through Josh's curls, parting them neatly to the side. He looks to Lily for help. He is scrubbed and fidgety in his miniature suit. As we file out to be photographed, Lily surreptitiously restores his curls.

The caterers are running between the kitchen and the lawn, where the reception will be, as we drive off to the Vedanta Peace Garden for the ceremony.

The Peace Garden is wonderful, completely secluded from the outside world by its high trees and old stone walls. Gravel paths and little wooden bridges crisscross the mossy grounds which are dotted here and there with fountains or statues, tucked into corners and surrounded by the cabbage-sized roses.

At the very farthest reach of the Garden is a cleared circle of emerald grass, backed by an altar, and beyond that, only the sea and the sky. It is here that the ceremony will be.

The guests sit in folding chairs. A surprisingly young and Celtic-looking man in a soft white cotton suit and turban beckons to us from the flower-filled altar. We set out in procession from the Meditation Barn, surrounded by some of the permanent residents of the community in their saffron robes, who giggle like children and pelt us softly with sugar-coated Jordan almonds.

At the end of the procession, Lily and I sit down on a stone bench but Ananda stands waiting for Kit and Spence, who walk towards us together, holding hands.

"Welcome Sister and Brother!" the young man in white booms jovially, and puts one long necklace of flowers around them. "Don't they look beautiful?" he asks the guests, turning Kit and Spence to face them. "I think they must be in love."

Some guests laugh nervously. The priest, or whatever he

is, laughs too. "Some music, please!" he calls out, and from somewhere behind the hedges comes an unearthly Indian music, with cymbals, flutes, and drums. The priest hums along casually, as he pours water from a pitcher into a bowl, washes his hands, and holds the bowl for Kit and Spence to wash in. He hands Kit a white towel, which she drops.

"Help her," he instructs Spence, who picks up the towel and dries Kit's hands and his own.

"Are you full of joy?" he asks Kit.

"Yes," she answers clearly.

"Good. And you?" he asks Spence.

Spence is unintelligible. "Tell him to speak up," the priest instructs Kit, "or these people will think he didn't want to marry you." Kit and Spence are laughing now too.

"Yes, I am. I'm full of joy," Spence says loudly.

"Great," the young man in white bellows, and claps Spence on the back.

"May all the spirits of the earth and of the air, of the waters and in the dancing flames, bless you in the hour of your joy and wait upon you in the chambers of your love. More than the shores are teeming with grains of sand, more than the heavens are filled with limitless spinning stars, the universe is teeming with life. And all these beings are one, all our joy is complete. Bring the rings."

Josh gets up from his seat with the rings on a silk pillow. Halfway to the altar, he stops to look at the guests who are murmuring to each other and laughing because he is so solemn and small and cute. He stares a minute, then rushes back to his seat.

"Don't mind them, little brother. They're silly people. Bring me the rings here, and I'll give you some candy." The priest holds out a handful of Jordan almonds. Josh walks stiff-legged to the altar. The priest picks him up.

"They look pretty silly, don't they?" he asks, pointing to the guests. I hear Mrs. Anglund gasp. Josh nods and munches candy, while the priest goes on, keeping Josh in his arm.

"With these rings you symbolize your devotion, and the never-ending circle of your love." He turns to Ananda. "Step up here, little sister. Don't you belong with these people? Come into the circle of love."

Ananda shyly steps into the circle made by Kit and Spence's necklace of flowers. "Enjoy each other, take care of one another. Be kind and make each other laugh, keep your hearts pure. Will you do those things?"

"Yes," they all say.

"Then you will be happy. No one can ask for more. Go ahead, kiss each other." The young man kisses each of them, puts down Josh, who rushes to his mother, and walks back to the barn. Slowly the guests realize the ceremony is over and rush to congratulate Kit and Spence.

Walking around on the grounds, I am amused to see Claudia McKee, with Donald Dugan in tow, among the guests. Dugan is gallantly helping Claudia along the gravel paths, where her spiked heels keep sinking into the ground and sticking. She's wearing crocheted cotton lace and a heavy primitive gold necklace. I wonder if all her clothes are beige. When they reach the more solid footing of a wooden bridge, I wave gaily to Dugan.

Back at Kit's house for the reception, musicians are playing the music of the big bands as waitresses carry round trays of drinks and appetizers. Kit's father, a heavyset white-haired man, is explaining to his friends that the vegetarian menu is healthier for them.

I accept a stuffed mushroom cap and a glass of champagne and am about to locate Lily when a cool hand delicately takes my wrist. I look up into Claudia's catlike amber eyes. She is even more devastating up close—the Lauren Bacall eyes and about a thousand white teeth.

"I don't think we've met," she says.

"I'm Nell Styles," I say.

"I'm Claudia. So happy to know you. Kit looks marvelous, doesn't she?"

"Lovely."

"I believe you know another friend of mine," she says.

"You mean Donald Dugan. I don't know him very well."

"No, I don't think you do. I wouldn't become better acquainted," she says.

"Really? Why not?"

"He's not a very nice man. He's a terrible liar, for one thing." She laughs. I realize that though the party has just started, she's already had too much to drink.

"You brought him to your friend's wedding."

"Well, I'm not very nice either. We like to keep an eye on each other. No doubt he thinks he's keeping me out of trouble." I look at her.

"How funny. You think I'm jealous. Well, you must look after yourself. Don't say I didn't warn you." She slinks off.

It is time for the toasts to the bride and groom. Spence's brother Roger stands before us.

"If you're like me, you've probably pinched yourself a few times to make sure you're really here today," he says. The crowd laughs. "I've wallpapered a small room with defunct invitations to Spencer and Kit's weddings. However, this day has definitely been worth waiting for. I finally get to wear the tux I rented two years ago.

"When Spence and I were kids he always had the most incredible luck. Sometimes I'd get to school, unpack my lunch, and there'd be no Twinkie in there. When I complained to Spence he'd say, 'Really? That's weird. I had two in mine.' And then when we got older the McGregor twins moved in next door. Some of you, I see, remember the twins. Well, I thought we were all going to double-date one night. Then I found out they were both going out with him. Today he's done it again. He's married the two prettiest women in Merrivale. I don't know how he does it." There are cheers, everyone drinks champagne to Kit and Spence's health, and couples begin to fill the dance floor.

Donald Dugan appears out of nowhere to lead me out onto the temporary wooden dance floor. He's very graceful. I wonder how Claudia will take this, but I see her glide expertly by in the arms of one of Spence's friends.

"Your girlfriend warned me against you. She said you weren't a nice man."

"I'm very nice to the people I like. You wait and see. I'm going to be very, very nice to you," he says.

"I won't have a chance to find out, I'm afraid. I'm getting married next week."

"Nell, how tragic! Who's the culprit? If you say Trevane, I'll have to break your neck right here on the dance floor."

"Stop nagging. It's not anyone you know."

"How long do I have to change your mind?"

"About two minutes. Talk fast."

"I'll do better than that." He threads us through the dancing couples and leads me by the hand away from the party. He picks up two glasses and a bottle of champagne as we pass the bar. He leads me around to the far side of the house, where roses are climbing the crumbling stone of ancient garden walls. We lean against the sun-warmed honey-colored wall. He pours out some champagne.

"Drink this up. I'm going to kiss you," he says. We clink glasses and drink. He puts his arms around my waist.

"Kiss me," he says.

It is completely enjoyable.

"Again," he says. We kiss for a long, long time.

"Am I changing your mind?" he asks.

"Uh-uh," I say, trying to clear my head, "try harder."

He loosens his tie. Just then we are joined by a teenaged couple on a similar mission. They go into a clinch.

"Do you mind?" Dugan says.

"We don't, if you don't," the girl says, and giggles.

"Go ahead, man," the boyfriend says. "We're not lookin'."

We retreat.

"Just when I felt I was beginning to get on. I don't suppose you'd like to go for a ride?" Dugan asks wistfully.

"I really couldn't," I say.

"Hello, hello. What's this?" Dugan says, and pulls me through the hedge into the next garden. It's deserted. The residents are next door at the reception. There is a padded sun chaise beside the pool. Dugan leads me to it.

"Now then," he says, "where were we? Am I making any headway?"

"None," I sigh.

"Well, I'm not getting discouraged," he says. "Try, try again."

We're just settling into a rather convincing moment, when we hear raised voices.

"Now what?" Dugan frowns. He bends to his task again, but I recognize one of the voices. I get up and cross the yard to the other side and peer through the high wooden fence. I look into the junglelike growth of Will's garden.

"Stop playing games, Claudia. Do you have anything or not?"

I can't see them, but I can hear fine.

"How much are you willing to pay? Yes, go on, you've always been good at contempt. Look at me any way you want. I don't care what you think. I only care about the money. Half that money belongs to me by rights anyway."

"How do you figure? You bedded Lewis's murderer, so you're entitled to part of his blood money?"

"I didn't kill Lewis, you did. You wound up with that fat little bankroll all to yourself, didn't you? You should have been on the boat that night. If you weren't such a weakling, always running to him to prop you up, you'd be dead, not him. You know it's true."

"Shut your mouth now, or I'll shut it for you."

"I'm not afraid of you. We both know you're gutless."

"I've changed. I'd be happy to strangle you right now if I knew for sure where you had those papers."

"I'm leaving. If you change your mind, you know my price and you know where to reach me. I know it was you who paid those slimy little calls on me."

"I don't know what you're talking about. And I'm not about to make any deals with you. I'd rather trust a shark."

"Then you can go fuck yourself."

I feel sick. Dugan is beside me. He looks angry. Murderous.

"I guess we could both keep better company," he says softly to me.

"How do they know each other?" I ask. "What's this all about?"

"Oh, just your average domestic dispute," he says grimly. "Didn't you know? She's his ex-wife."

fifteen

DUGAN LEAVES ME there, no doubt to go after Claudia. I walk back through the hedge to the reception. Lily waves to me from the dance floor, where she is dancing with a very attentive and attractive young man with horn-rimmed glasses. Kit is floating about like a queen bee. Everyone seems to be having a good time. Then I see someone who looks as forlorn as I feel. It is Ananda.

"What's the matter, bunny? Why aren't you with the other kids? Don't you feel well?" I ask her.

She shakes her head no.

"Let's go in to your room. You can lie down."

Ananda walks into the house and flops on the bed, careless now of her dress.

"Did you eat too much cake?" I ask.

"They're going away without me," her voice comes muffled from the pillow.

"But you knew that. You're staying with me. We always have fun, don't we?"

"Yes. But it's not how I thought it would be. I wanted the three of us to be together."

"Oh, honey, you will be. Newlyweds need a honeymoon just for the two of them. Then they'll come back and the three of you will move into your new house like a real family. Just what you always wanted, isn't that right?"

"I guess so," she says glumly.

Poor Ananda. She's finding out a dream come true doesn't always turn out as you hoped.

Late that night, after Kit and Spence leave, I take a tearful Ananda home with me. The poor kid is exhausted and falls asleep right away in my bed.

I am awakened much earlier than I'd hoped by Lily on the telephone.

"Nell, I know this is lousy timing, but I need to go away for a while and I have nowhere else to leave Josh. Things are cooking on the story and Kilby wants me to follow up on a lead I have. It will take a few days. Is it terrible of me to ask you?"

"I guess not," I say. "Maybe Josh and Ananda will entertain each other."

Ananda looks depressed and mimes dramatic retching.

"What's the lead?" I ask.

"I think we better stick to what we agreed on. You're out of it for now," she says. "I'm going to keep things to myself a bit longer."

I sigh. "All right. Bring Josh over as soon as you're ready."

"I've got his stuff packed, but he hasn't had breakfast yet."

"That's OK," I say. "Neither have we. I'll take them out for breakfast."

"Thanks, honey. I'll be right there."

The three of us are making for the Last Chance when we see a crowd gathered on the sidewalk. We hurry forward to check it out.

At first I think it's just incredibly bad taste. In the infamous window of My Indiscretion one of the mannequins lies sprawled in black lace, one white stocking fastened to her garter belt, the other wrapped much too tightly around her neck. Then the ghastly grimace under the spill of shiny hair spells out the truth. This is no naughty window display. Claudia McKee lies dead, strangled, surrounded by her provocatively dressed mannequins.

Sirens wail and police cruisers screech to the curb. I'm dragging Ananda and Josh from the grisly scene when the police swarm about us and start to push through the crowd. Tom Waite and his mournful partner are among them. Ananda is full of questions.

"Who is it, Nell? Was she dead?"

"Yes, it's the owner of the store."

"Claudia! My mom knows her. She was at the wedding!"

Damn, I forgot she would know.

"What happened to her?" Ananda asks, as I steer us across the street. I don't know how to answer her. Then I see him. Benno, Will's big Nordic friend, is watching the scene from across the street. He is totally still, his beefy arms folded across his chest.

Ananda persists. "Why was she in her underwear? Did somebody kill her?"

"I think so," I say.

"Nell. I think it was *him*. You know, *Will*."

"Of course not," I say.

"We *know* he's a bad guy. I'll bet it is him. Nell! What if my mommy's in danger!"

"Honey, your mommy's in Mexico with Spence. She's perfectly safe."

"I want her."

"I know. This is very upsetting, and I'm very sorry you had to see it. I'm upset too. We'll call your mom tonight." I squeeze her hand.

"When we tell her people are getting killed around here, maybe she'll have to let me go down there with them. Do you think so?" she asks, tugging at my sleeve.

"Let's just wait and see what she wants to do."

I buy bread, eggs, juice, and milk at the store. Josh makes his hand into a gun, pointing his finger at Ananda and me, making shooting sounds.

"Stop that!" I snap, grabbing his hand. Both kids look shocked.

Back in my kitchen I make French toast and coffee.

"Do you think he met Claudia sometime when he was with my mother?" Ananda says, toying with her food.

"I don't want to talk about this anymore. I already said that it's ridiculous to pick on him and say he did it. Just try to eat and forget about it. You two go play something, or watch TV. I need some peace and quiet."

Ananda gives me the evil eye. It is a novel experience for me. I've seen her direct it at her mother, but this is the first time it's been aimed at me and I don't have Kit's immunity.

"And don't give me dirty looks," I say.

"C'mon, Josh," Ananda sulks and stomps out of the room. The TV clicks on in the bedroom.

I'm alone but not peaceful. I'm thinking about Will Trevane who probably just strangled his ex-wife or, more likely, had her strangled. I picture Benno's scowling face and big red hands.

My mail drops through the slot in the door. My passport is ready for me to pick up. As soon as Lily and Kit return, I can fly to New York and see my parents. I long for them. How good it will be to drink tea with them in their flower-and music-filled rooms. Then I will join Paul in Europe, far from this doomed place. Oh Merrivale, you used to be my sunlit haven. Now I can't wait to flee from you.

I decide to put the time to good use. I call Spence's mother about putting my house on the market.

"Don't worry about a thing," she says. "It will go like *that*. I'll be able to handle it all for you from here. I bet I can get you twice what you paid. The demand has been incredible these days. I wonder if there'll be a backlash from the murder. Did you hear about it?"

"Yes, it's terrible," I say.

"The second one this summer! It's incredible. It's got to be the drugs. Once they come into a community there's bound to be violence. Still, I've heard this was personal. I hear they're looking for the ex-husband. They think he did it. That would be so much better. Oh, that sounds terrible. But what I meant was, it wouldn't have to do with the town. I mean, a man can kill his wife anywhere." She sighs. "This used to be such a quiet little village, completely unspoiled. Victor is terribly upset. We sold her the house, you know."

I tsk. I wonder what she means by "looking for the ex-husband." Do they know he is here in Merrivale under an assumed name or not? And how did they find out so soon?

That afternoon I talk to Kit and Spence. Kit is distraught, but Spence decides she should stay in Mexico. He talks to Ananda, who is not too thrilled to be told to stay put.

"They don't care what happens to me," she says, after we hang up.

At six I turn on the news. Claudia's murder is the lead story.

"The sleepy seaside village of Merrivale was rocked today by the second murder of a young woman there in recent weeks. The body of Claudia McKee, a local entrepreneur, was found strangled in the display window of her high-priced lingerie establishment. Police refuse to say whether this murder is related to the still-unsolved death of police officer Marianne Banks two weeks ago. Officer Banks was killed while investigating drug smuggling incidents there. Her death was thought to be drug related. Now police are reevaluating. Police chief Arthur Hinckley says they have a suspect in the McKee death and are looking into possible connections to the murder of the policewoman."

Have they arrested him, I wonder. I see no one, not even the yellow dog Shiloh, from my window.

The phone rings. At last, I think, expecting Lily. But it is J.J., and she is crying.

"He's gone," she says. "We've been fighting all weekend.

He's been acting so queer lately. I want to have a baby so much and he won't even discuss getting married. Could I stay at your place? I feel so depressed. When he walked out he said he was sick and tired of tripping over me in this overstuffed Victorian chicken coop." She wails, "I just can't sleep in this bed alone."

I tell her to come. God knows where I'll put her. Ananda and I are sharing my bed. I was going to put Josh on the couch. Now I'll have to take Josh in with us and let her have the couch. And there's lunch. And dinner. I've forgotten I have to feed everyone. I call Pizza Hot Line. Tomorrow I'll have to go shopping. And surely Lily will be back to cover the murder.

Soon I hear brakes screeching. I look out the window and see J.J. pulling an inordinately large suitcase out of the trunk. Great. Looks like she's planning to stay for a week.

She struggles up the stairs, steps inside, and looks at me. Her chin starts to tremble. I have a box of tissues all ready for her. Then she spots the kids. They have all the sofa pillows and all the bed pillows propped up against the headboard of my bed, and are sprawled all over my down quilt watching a twenty-year-old rerun of "Family Affair."

"Ooh, Buffy and Jody, I love them!" J.J. says, and sits on the edge of the bed. "What's Mr. French doing?"

"Buffy lost Mrs. Beasley on a bus," Ananda fills her in. "Mr. French is tracking her down." J.J. settles cozily in with the children under the comforter. Our pizza arrives. Loud approbation from the gang. I'll put it on trays and let them eat it in bed. What the hell? As long as they're happy.

"I love you, Nell," J.J. calls from the bedroom, her mouth full.

sixteen

I SPEND A cramped and restless night. Josh squirms and tosses. Like all children and dogs taken into bed, he seems to grow in the night to immense size. I heave a grateful sigh when the kids get up, and move luxuriantly into the center of the bed.

"May I make breakfast?" Ananda whispers. I give permission, grateful she has recovered her good nature. They must be very quiet because I sleep undisturbed for two hours more.

When I get up I find a note from Ananda. She has left it for me stuck to the mirror, apparently with hair-styling gel. *We are going outside to play. XOXOX*, it says. I look out into the yard and Ananda waves up at me.

J.J. in a peach silk robe sits at my kitchen table and spares me not one painful detail of her troubles with Hal, while I drink my coffee and she sips tea white with milk and dense with sugar.

It is nearly an hour later when I realize it's been some time since I heard a peep from the kids. I go downstairs in my sleep shirt, but I don't see them anywhere on the front lawn or in the side garden. I walk around the house, calling, but they're nowhere to be found. A little worried, I go upstairs to dress so I can search the block.

"I can't find the kids," I tell J.J., pulling up my jeans, and I run back out. J.J. comes hustling after me to help. I think maybe they've gone down the block to their own house, or to Annie and Nicky's house, where they sometimes play. Their house is locked up and silent. Annie and Nicky haven't seen them. We walk briskly along the street, calling their names. Nothing.

I try to fight off the horrible pictures that start to form in my mind. A car stops and they get in *(but Ananda knows better)*. Maybe someone grabs them and they struggle but can't get away. Their bodies lie in the woods. I am sick with fear. "Please," I pray, "please."

"Let's call the police," J.J. says. We run back to my house. It is worse now that she is also so afraid. We run up the stairs. Josh is there, cowering on the floor in a corner of the kitchen. Towering above him like a mountain hulks Benno, his face contorted with rage.

"Where is it?" he shouts. "Tell me now, what haf you done wit it?" He looks up, startled, as we come in. For a moment, all four of us freeze.

Then there is a violent banging on the front door. "Open up! Open this minute, goddamn it. I know you're in there." It is a man's voice, desperate and terrifying.

Benno turns white and runs down the back stairs. I scoop the frightened little boy into my arms. The banging on the door becomes more frenzied. Shielding Josh with my body, I pull the door open. There stands Hal, wildly unkempt and hot. He pushes past me and confronts J.J.

"I've been waiting for you all night," he says. "Haven't you punished me enough? When you didn't show up this morning at the office, I went out of my mind. Don't you ever do that to me again."

J.J. throws herself at him. They cling to each other fiercely.

"Where's Ananda?" I ask Josh. He points down the back stairs. I run down the stairs with him on one hip. I put him down in the yard. Neither Ananda nor Benno are in sight.

"Where is she? Show me." He pulls me by the arm. I follow him to the potting shed; Ananda is inside.

"What's going on here?" I demand. She looks frightened.

"We found this," she says. It is a fishing tackle box.

"Where did you find it?" I ask. Josh whimpers. Ananda looks at her feet.

"In his toolshed," she says finally, in words so low I can barely hear.

"Will's?" I yell.

"Uh-huh. Maybe it's the one he showed those men the other night. We squeezed through the door of the toolshed. It was really hard work, but we pushed it open. You know what? Josh is really strong for a little kid. All there was in there was a refrigerator. This box was inside it. We took it for evidence. Am I in major trouble?"

I kneel down and hold her in my arms. She is plainly bewildered by my response—knowing nothing of the horrifying half hour I couldn't find her.

"I can't get it opened," she says. "I sent Josh to get a screwdriver or something."

Hal and J.J. come down the stairs. Hal looks flushed and sheepish, but triumphant. J.J. is holding his hand.

"Help me open this," I say. Hal pries at the lid. Inside are several plastic baggies. I pick up one. It contains several hypodermic syringes. Horrified, I let it drop.

There are also two clear plastic boxes wrapped with rubber bands. In one are what look like glass laboratory slides. The other contains five or six photographic slides. I open that box, and hold a slide up to the light. It is a picture of a large white boat surrounded by two small dinghies. The other slides show the same boats.

Josh reaches for the bag of syringes.

"No!" I shout. "Don't either of you touch a thing."

"You're touching it," Ananda says. I shoot her a warning glance.

"What is it?" she asks meekly.

"What *is* it?" Hal says. "What's this all about?"

"Nothing. I don't know. You kids should never have touched this."

What the hell am I to do with all this? Can I give it to Tom Waite? He'll never believe it isn't Paul's. Impulsively, I dash across to Will's toolshed and squeeze myself desperately through the door, scraping my skin. I shove the box into the refrigerator, my heart pumping. The back of my neck is tense and alert, as any minute I expect to be cornered by the menacing blond giant. But nothing and no one is stirring and I run home without interference.

I decide to give the kids a bath. They've gotten quite grimy and so have I this morning. While I scrub away at the three of us, Hal and J.J. are sitting in each other's laps in the living room, billing and cooing.

"This could be a fabulous house," Hal calls out. "You really haven't begun to bring out its potential."

"Thanks," I say. I'm at the bottom of my patience. I wish Lily would call. How could she leave her kid with me and not call to see if he's all right, not leave a number where she can be reached? Besides, I want to find out what she knows about Will, about Claudia's murder, about anything. Impulsively, I make a decision.

"I need to run out for a few things," I tell Hal and J.J. "Would you watch the kids for a little while?"

"Sure we will," J.J. says, wrapped in content as palpable as a quilt.

"Don't let them out of your sight," I warn.

I run across the street and almost right into Officer Dort, Tom Waite's thin, sad partner. He almost jumps out of his uniform.

"Sorry to startle you," I say.

"You just surprised me," he says. "What are you doing here?"

"I live across the street."

"Right, I know that, but I mean, do you know this guy or what?"

"He's my neighbor."

"Oh, right. Listen, I'd really like to thank you for being so understanding the other day with Tom, Officer Waite. We've all been so stressed out lately. I've been telling and telling the guys at the station that we should have someone come in and run some kind of grief sessions for us, you know what I mean. But they're too macho to think they need it and the chief says we can't afford it. But hey, everyone's got feelings, cops included, right?"

"Right."

"We need to be upfront with them, we can't afford *not* to be, for Pete's sake." He shakes his head sadly at the blindness of his peers.

"You're very insightful. It's too bad they won't take your advice."

"I'm going to tell you something. I probably shouldn't, but I can see you're very sensitive and I don't want you to be unprepared. Your friend, we're sure he's the guy that hired Fahey. He's the one who's been behind the smuggling all along."

"I see," I say.

"You're taking this awfully calm," he says.

"Well, I've suspected as much. What about the McKee murder?"

"Holy Toledo! You think he's involved in that too?"

"Don't you? He *is* her ex-husband."

"*Him too?* This case is getting weirder by the minute."

My heart stops.

"Wait a minute. Who are we talking about?"

"Varensky, Paul Varensky," Dort says. "We put out an

order this morning for him to be picked up and extradited back to the States."

"Oh my God," I say, and sit down on the curb. "This has to be some kind of terrible mistake."

seventeen

It is not easy to call off Officer Dort. He is relentlessly supportive and nurturing, but I finally escape. I walk aimlessly, trying to think. How can this awful thing be true? Paul, a criminal! The whole thing would be laughable were it not so frightening. I'll call Paul right away. What can the police be thinking of?

But of course they don't know Paul. If they knew him as I do, they'd realize this whole thing was a sham, a setup. But who . . . ? Then it hits me.

The banana peel on Marianne's foot. The store window. Weren't these evidence of a macabre sense of humor, of a twisted mind? Trevane or Pengryth, or whatever his name is, has been playing a game all along with the police, a sick game.

This was just another aspect of that game. He'd set it all up and arranged things to make Paul look guilty.

But why? He is a man full of rage, that I know. A dangerous rage that seethes beneath his smooth exterior. I've seen him rage, I've heard him lusting for vengeance. I remember the night of the dinner at Kit's. Paul and Will arguing. The air tense with competition out of all proportion. Will studying Paul through narrowed eyes, his expression mocking, mocking and *speculative*. A chill goes through me. He must have decided to go after Paul that night.

First though, he went after me. I writhe as I remember how I lapped it up—flirting back as Will humiliated both Paul and Kit. Even worse, I had run straight from Paul's proposal into Will's arms. How he must have enjoyed that! The ultimate screw-you. I burn with shame and rage as I remember how earnestly, how *nobly* he kissed me off.

"It's over because I'm living a life I can't ask you to share . . . I'd give you my heart if it was mine to give." God! I had wanted to believe it, so I'd swallowed that corny bull.

And then, more sinisterly, he'd set Paul up as his fall guy. Well, I'm not going to let him succeed. I know more than enough about him right now to interest the police in his activities. I'll sic the police on him and I'll find out what they think they have on Paul. Like any illusion, it will dissolve under close scrutiny.

I make straight for the Merrivale police station. I'll tell them everything—what we saw and heard through the window, the fight with Claudia. How could I have been so stupid, shielding this guy? It was only Paul's ethics about informing on people that had put him in this dangerous spot. I should have told what I knew from the first. I'll clear Paul and get Will's ass behind bars if it's the last thing I do.

The station house is beautifully situated on the Harbor Road, next to the town hall and the fire station, overlooking the harbor with its flock of pretty boats. Rosebushes climb its stucco walls and fat bees hum about the blooms. The sense of drowsy peace reassures me as I step decisively inside. Nothing could be less forbidding than these sunlit creamy walls and slowly turning ceiling fans. A white-haired policeman sits writing at the front desk, half-moon reading glasses on his nose.

"Can I help you?" he asks pleasantly.

I tell him I'd like to see the chief.

"What about?" he asks, looking at me over the half moons.

"I have information about the drug smuggling case," I tell him.

He purses his lips and considers, then asks me to follow him. We go into a small office with a bay window overlooking the harbor.

"I'm Chief Hinckley," he tells me. "Who are you?"

"I'm Eleanora Styles."

"I see. Paul Varensky's fiancée. Please have a seat." He smiles encouragingly at me. "What's on your mind?"

I sit down opposite a picture of three tanned white-blond children.

"My grandchildren," he says proudly.

"You're after the wrong man," I say. How melodramatic.

"How's that, Miss Styles?"

I tell him about Will Trevane, everything, from the beginning. He frowns as he listens.

"Officer Dort had no business discussing police matters with you," he says, shaking his head. "Now, how do I know you're not making any of this up to shield Varensky? You don't want to face an obstruction charge, do you? If you know where your fiancé is . . ."

"You can ask Kit Anglund when she returns from Mexico about what we heard through the window. She was with me. You can check with Donald Dugan. You can look in his shed."

"Did you know it is a crime to look into people's windows and break into their private property?"

"OK, arrest me, but what are you going to do about Trevane?"

"Miss Styles, I don't want to be unsympathetic. I can understand your feelings. Naturally, you're upset about your fiancé. But we have looked into this very carefully. We don't just arbitrarily fix on someone and make an arrest. We take our duties very seriously. We wouldn't be looking for Mr. Varensky's return if we were uncertain of our facts."

I start to sputter. "So you're just going to ignore all this stuff about Will Trevane?"

"Hold on now, we're aware of Mr. Trevane. We are not quite so sleepy here as we may appear. It was through him that we learned your fiancé was at the scene of the crime on the night of Officer Banks's murder—"

"There you are! Don't you see—"

"—which may or may not fit in with your theory. We are currently seeking out Mr. Trevane to discuss his ex-wife, and I'm sure we'll be talking with him quite soon. We will follow up on what you've told us. But in the meantime we have plenty to discuss with your Mr. Varensky as well.

"Why don't you go home now and let us do our job? I'll have one of my men drive you. Do you have anyone who could stay with you? Your mother, or a friend?"

"I don't need anyone to take care of me and I don't need a ride home. I'm telling you Will Trevane is the smuggler *and* probably the murderer of Marianne Banks or the one who had her murdered. *And* Claudia McKee. He's somehow managed to frame Paul."

"Even supposing he could, why would he want to?"

"He needs someone to pin it on. He and Paul quarreled. He must have decided it would be amusing to put it on him. But Paul Varensky is a respected research scientist—he's never done anything criminal. This charge is absurd. Just what do you have on him? I'll prove to you it's impossible."

"I'm sorry, Miss Styles. I can't discuss that with you. The district attorney's office will be glad to talk to Mr. Varensky and his representatives. I assure you, your fiancé will have every chance to prove his innocence. And as I say, we will be keeping a close eye on Mr. Trevane and his affairs. Thank you for the information. I'm sorry I couldn't be more satisfactory. If you talk to your fiancé, please impress on him how much better it would be for him if he returned voluntarily."

It is obvious there is nothing more to say. I stomp out of the station. They're idiots. How can I get in touch with Donald Dugan? He's the one I obviously need now. Is he still in town? I don't know where he lives, or even where he's staying if he is in town. Was he staying with Claudia? I never really grasped the nature of their relationship. I might as well try the hotels; there are only two places he might be, the Cutty Sark Inn or Mrs. Bunbury's bed and breakfast. I'll have to walk. If I go back for my car Hal will grab me. He's probably desperate to get back to the agency, and right now I need him and J.J. to deal with the kids.

Just as I reach the top of High Street, my search ends abruptly. Dugan is coming down the hill in his grey sports car. I wave both arms. He stops for me. He has the top down.

"Want a ride?" he calls.

"Yes, I do," I say, and trot across the street.

"Will wonders never cease? I thought I'd never get you inside this machine."

I climb inside. The dashboard is polished wood. The leather seat conforms exactly to my body, like an expensive oral surgeon's chair. Sinatra sings "Wee Small Hours of the Night" from the stereo speakers.

"Where to?" he asks.

"Actually, I was looking for you."

"At last!" He turns the car about so we can climb the cliffs. Soon we are hugging the hairpin turns with the spectacular view spreading out below. The wind whips my hair into my face. Dugan rummages in the glove compartment and hands me a white silk handkerchief. I tie my hair back into a ponytail.

"You look about sixteen," he says, and leans over to kiss my forehead. It is the ultimate drive—the winding road, the ocean below, and the car fast as hell but smooth as butter.

He pulls the car up beside a wall bordering a sheep meadow. We climb out of the car and sit on the crumbling stone. Overhead, gulls circle and cry, and in the grass the sheep baa comically.

"I'm sorry about Claudia," I say.

He nods.

"Who do you think killed her?"

His silent look is eloquent. "I told you about him, Nell. You didn't want to believe me."

"I want to help you get him," I say. "Will you let me?"

"I've wanted that all along," he says, "for us to work together. I got the feeling you didn't trust me, though."

"I'll work with you now," I say. "I guess you just seemed too good to be true."

He laughs.

"Tell me about Claudia," I say.

"Claudia was a fool. One of those beautiful doomed women who winds up jumping in front of trains, wrecking her life over men. Men always went off the deep end for her and she thought she could get whatever she wanted. But she never did. She always made disastrous choices, bungled things, wound up the victim. She was always in trouble. I felt sorry for her and responsible somehow for bailing her out. She and I were lovers once upon a time, years ago."

"Is that how you know Will? I thought you were investigating him professionally."

"I was protecting Claudia. Or trying to," he says bitterly. "Trevane's brother was killed. Claudia gave evidence that helped indict him. Charges were dropped because of a technicality, but we knew Trevane carried a grudge. I tried to keep an eye on him afterwards, but he dropped out of sight. When I saw your wine label I knew the vineyard was too close for comfort to where Claudia lived. But even knowing Trevane was in town didn't help." He stares silently into the horizon.

"Do you mind terribly?"

"I wasn't in love with her, if that's what you mean, but I promised her I'd protect her. I did a rotten job. Now all I can do is try to nail him."

"I want to help you."

"What made you change your mind?" he asks. "Do you

have your own beef with him or was it just Claudia's murder?''

I tell him about Paul and about my conviction that Will has framed him.

"Of course, drug smuggling!" He whistles. "That's just the kind of thing that would attract him. Danger, secrecy. He's an uncanny seaman, gutsy, smart, and elusive. He could definitely pull off an operation like that. The Finn he has for a baby-sitter, Benno Jikki, was with him in Alaska. I don't know who the other man is, a big-time drug dealer, sounds like.''

He thinks. "Any idea why he would fix on Paul? From what you've said, he seems an unlikely choice.''

"They quarreled. I got the idea he thought it would be funny.''

"Maybe. I guess he might be so egotistical that anyone disagreeing with him could get him enraged. Still, it hardly seems sufficient motivation. Are you sure there's nothing else? No other reason why Trevane might want to get at Paul? Something he wants from him?''

I hate myself, but I can feel the blood rising from my chest and suffusing my face.

"I see," he says. "I wondered if anything like that was going on. I know the guy has a weakness for beautiful women and by some crazy appeal I could never fathom he's incredibly successful. Don't feel too bad, Nell, we all make mistakes." Mercifully, he lets it drop. But something is nagging at me. Am I crazy or could it be possible?

"There might be something else," I say. "What you said about Will before reminds me of something. It was what he and Paul argued about. And the love of danger, the seamanship, the ruthlessness. He must have been afraid Paul knew something!''

"Nell, what are you talking about?''

"Dugan, do you think it possible—could Will be Henryk Rolfsen?''

He looks completely bewildered. "Who? The smuggler? He's dead. He died years ago."

"Did he? Didn't you ever hear that he escaped or bought his way out?"

"Yes, come to think of it, I guess I have. All right, Nell, you work on that end. Find out all the information you can on Rolfsen. Try to track down whatever news you can about his death and rumors to the contrary. I'll concentrate on the drug smuggling. From what you overheard, it sounds like they were planning some big deal very soon. Trevane's dropped out of sight because of the murder, but they might still try to pull it off. If we can catch them in the act, we can clear Paul. My organization is still keeping an eye on Trevane. I think they'd be willing to commit some staff to patrolling the shore hereabouts. Even if the locals are satisfied, maybe we can interest the Coast Guard in your information."

"That's wonderful," I say. "Thank you for helping me."

"Beyond the fact that I want to get Trevane too, I have to say my motives aren't completely pure. If I help clear Varensky, I won't have to feel so guilty about trying to move in on his woman."

I smile.

"Let's go, then," he says, jumping from the wall. "I've got things to arrange."

"I'll go to the library and start my research on Rolfsen."

"Good. But keep clear of my end of it and stay away from Trevane. I won't have you ending up like Claudia. At the very least I want to be able to imagine you, some lonely night, sitting by your fire, surrounded by a clutch of pink-cheeked children—"

"Apple-cheeked," I correct.

"—apple-cheeked children, but with a small regret in your heart for old faithful Dugan."

"Poor Dugan," I say.

"Yup. Always the bridesmaid, never the bride."

eighteen

I'M FEELING MORE optimistic when Dugan drops me off on Beau Cherry Lane. The first thing is to call Paul. I decide to call him from Lily's before I go back home to Hal, J.J., and the kids—more privacy and less noise. I have her keys.

I'm walking along the side path that winds to the back of the house and Lily's door when I hear something, a sound I shouldn't. Someone is washing dishes in Kit's kitchen. They must have decided to return early after all. I glance up at the kitchen window.

I am shocked to see Benno standing at the sink placidly washing up like it's the most natural thing in the world. He hasn't seen me. I creep over to the living room window and look in. Will is sitting right there with his back to me, his chair tilted back, his legs up on the coffee table. My heart is racing. What cool customers! They need a place to hide out and so they just casually break into Kit's and set up housekeeping. I am just about to go for the police when I am stopped short.

Will calls to someone who is out of sight. I peer further

into the room to see who it is. There, talking on the phone, stands Lily. She hangs up and runs to Will. I've never seen her look so happy or so carefree; she looks like a young girl. She says something to Will, who jumps up from his chair, swings her into the air, and kisses her.

I feel sick. Sick with shock, sick with some emotion I can't name. What has Lily gotten herself into? Has she fallen in love with him? Is he using her for a patsy the same way he's used me and Paul and Kit? Or is she working undercover, playing along while she tries to get her story? I don't know what to do.

How deeply is she involved? If I call the police, will I be saving her from danger or getting her in deeper? Would she be arrested? That could mean she would lose custody of Josh.

I hate him so much! Never before have I felt such a pure, strong, enticing hatred. I can't stop watching them. How naturally they sit and talk together. They are excited. What plans are they making? With a kind of sick fascination I wait for them to stop talking. I want him to take her in his arms and kiss her again. It twists my heart in some weird way that hurts deliciously. And I can hate and hate him and the most exquisite part of my hatred is this sick jealousy.

Oh, I must be insane. Despite everything he's done, to me, to Paul, I'm still drawn to him. But instead of having him, I will destroy him. I just need to figure out how to go about it so I don't bring Lily down too.

Lily. What are you doing, Lily? What was it you said? *"Oh, I would just retreat, waiting to see how things turned out. Then after he was tired of her, there I would be, laid-back and mysterious."* Does she know, has he told her about that day we spent before the fire? I am hot with shame at the thought. Has she been waiting all this time for Kit and me to throw down our hands?

Surely she knows what he is. What's in her mind? Do I pity her, or envy her? I know one thing. I can't let my feelings about him hurt my love for her. I have to save her. But how? She looks so very, very happy. All the hard edges rubbed off. Will she thank me for ruining their plans?

I've got to confront her. At least that way I'll be able to talk to her, figure out what she is doing there. All along everyone's been telling me to stay out of it—Lily herself, Paul, Dugan, even Will. I am not out of it any longer. It's time I became an actor in this little comedy. I remember another of Lily's speeches. *"You've never taken a risk in your life. The trouble with playing it safe is, you won't know when the right risk comes along."*

I had been angry then, but she was right. I've been a coward, playing it safe, and making a hash of things.

I march back to Kit's door and lean on the bell. A long silence follows. I ring again and again. Finally Lily opens the door. Behind her the living room is empty. She seems shocked to see me.

"Nell, what are you doing?"

"I saw you through the window. Needless to say, I was surprised. I thought you were supposed to be out of town."

"I just got in. I checked in at my place and thought I'd come down here and make sure everything was all right here too. Let's go back to your place and get Josh."

"Skip it, Lily. I saw Will and Benno too."

She sighs and opens the door wider. "Come on in."

"Lily, what are you doing with them? Don't lie to me now."

"OK, Nell. I'm working with Will and Benno and I can't explain to you what about. It's not that I don't want to." She seems uncomfortable. "I can't. I promised. But you have to trust me, I know what I'm doing."

I am beginning to give up hope that Lily is playing an undercover role. Her eyes shine with the fervor of the true believer. Or is it just post-orgasmic glow?

"Lily, listen to me. There's a lot you don't know. There's a man, a friend of mine, he can tell you about these two. The reason they have to hide out is because they are hiding from the police. They killed Claudia, and the police know it. They're pulling the wool over your eyes. I don't know what lies they've been feeding you, but . . ."

Will and Benno come into the living room. Will stands right behind Lily.

"A friend. She means Dugan. I tolt you she was workin' wit him," Benno says. "What haf you tolt him?"

"Hello, Nell," Will says. His eyes look away from mine, avoiding contact. No searching intimate glances this time, old buddy? I stare boldly but don't answer him.

"All right," he says. "What have you been discussing with Dugan?"

Defiantly I say, "Everything."

"Oh Nell, no," Lily moans.

"You stupid fool," Benno spits and starts towards me.

"Cool off!" Will yells harshly, grabbing his arm.

"Lily," I plead, "come with me now. It's not too late. I won't let you out of my sight for a minute."

"Stop being an idiot, Nell. I'm in no danger. You are. Just stay a minute and listen to reason. Will, you have to tell her. Make her understand."

He reaches for my arm. I pull violently away.

"Don't touch me!" I snarl. "I'm leaving here now."

Will lets my arm fall. Benno blocks the doorway.

"We let her go, she goes right to the police or to Dugan," he says.

I try to push past him. He picks me up off the floor and holds me in the air, as easily as if I were Josh. I kick and scratch. To my disgust, Will laughs.

"Put her down, Benno," he says.

"Nice friends you have, Lily," I say, once back on my feet. Benno still blocks the door. I see with satisfaction that his cheek is bleeding.

"Call Teague, Lily. Tell him Dugan knows we're making a move and to pick up immediately."

"But what about Nell?" she asks.

"I'll take care of Nell," he says. "Go."

To my disgust she trots off obediently. He's got her trained.

"Benno, get ready to move. This is it. Wash off your face first. That's one nasty scratch she gave you."

Benno looks recalcitrant.

"What's the matter, Benno? Don't think I can handle her? Go on."

We are alone.

"So you think you've got this all figured out, do you?" he says.

"You know it, and I know it," I say.

"I don't know exactly what Dugan's told you, but I can guess closely enough. He's lying. Don't let your personal feelings about me get you into trouble. You have every right to be angry at me, but don't get yourself mixed up with him to get even with me. He's big trouble."

This really makes my blood boil. "What nerve," I say. "Don't overestimate yourself. What happened between us was just temporary insanity, a mistake. It's your other activities that make me sick. And I'm going to stop you."

"I don't have time to explain. If I still have any chance to outfox Dugan and his friends, I have to move now, thanks to you. If it isn't to get even with me, I don't know why the hell you're cooperating with that creep. But nothing's going to stop me from settling his hash, not even you, you hellcat."

"I suppose you expected me to just let Paul be destroyed. But someone like you can't understand loyalty, I'm afraid."

"Well, I'll be damned. So that's it! I had no idea you knew about that. I seem to have misjudged you. Well, he's a lucky man. I wish I had you in my corner."

"You seem to have Lily."

"So I do. Well, good-bye and good luck."

"You mean you're letting me go?"

He laughs. "Did you expect me to bind and gag you and leave you in the attic? You've already done your damage. Go save your boyfriend if you can."

Lily hurries into the room. She is flushed and her eyes are bright.

"Teague says, 'Go!' "

"Right. Let's clear out. Benno's got the truck running."

"You understand now, Nell?" Lily says, rushing by me.

"I understand," I say, and watch them drive off.

I go to the phone and dial the police. My heart is heavy, but what can I do? Unless they catch Will in the act, how can I prove Paul is innocent?

"Police." I recognize Chief Hinckley's voice. I hesitate and then put down the receiver. I can't just send them after Lily. Even if she believes she is on some kind of mission, would the police believe her? She would go to jail and probably lose Josh forever. I have to think of some other way.

If only I knew what supposed evidence they had on Paul, there would have to be a way to bring it back to Will. Otherwise, I have to come up with something the police don't have. Like Daq Fahey! No one knows what he saw in the harbor. He told Marianne Banks and whatever it was must have fatally implicated Will; she was murdered to keep it quiet. If he's still alive, I have to find him right away.

I need to find Jean Fahey's mother. How I will convince Jean to help me, I'm not sure. But my first step is to go to the TipTop. Someone there will know.

The coffee shop is as smoky and bustling as ever, everyone companionably engaged in conversation. I don't know who to approach. I walk over to the cashier. She's very young, with spiky hair and long melon-colored nails.

"Order over there," she says, bored.

"Do you know Jean Fahey?" I ask. I can see her guard go up. The conversation in the immediate area stops dead.

"Umm," she grunts noncommittally.

"What was her name before she got married?" I ask.

"How do I know?" she says. "I wasn't born then, was I?" Someone laughs. I look around, but all eyes are on the tables. I start to walk uncertainly towards the tables.

"Over here," a man calls. I approach where two men in work clothes sit drinking coffee and smoking. Their arms are muscled but they have the beginnings of paunches. The man who spoke has longish dark hair and a mustache, both sprinkled with grey. He squints up at me.

"We know her?" he asks his friend.

"Yeah. You live in the old Cooper place? You a friend of Lily Brown?" the friend asks.

"Yes, I'm Nell Styles."

"A friend of Lily's, that's close enough," the first man says. "Sit. Why do you want to know about Jean?"

"I want to find her mother. I have a message for Jean."

"Margaret Labourne," he says. "Winter Harbor."

I thank him.

"Sure. Tell her Denny says hi."

"OK, Denny." I smile.

I head for the door feeling happy.

"Nice buns," someone calls out.

I turn around. Denny's friend is smiling innocently at me.

"Thanks," I say. "But you should lay off the pastry." Everyone laughs, including Denny and his friend.

A little later I'm on the green road to Winter Harbor. So far, so good, I think, babying the Duchess over the ruts. I realize that I'm enjoying myself. Well, why not? With considerably more confidence than I had entering the TipTop, I ask for directions to the Labourne house.

On a tree-lined road I find it, a tall white farmhouse, well set back from the road and maintaining a timeless grace amongst its stand of trees. I pull into the pebbled drive. Two girls, bare-legged and none too tidy, are chasing a small donkey through a grove of fruit trees. A thin, dark boy of about fifteen stands at the top of a rise looking through binoculars at the sea. Two smaller boys are recklessly riding double on an old bicycle. I walk towards the door and the dark young man comes down off his rocks to greet me.

"I'm looking for Margaret Labourne," I say, smiling at him. His thin face remains solemn.

"She's my grandmother," he says. "What do you want her for?"

"I just need some information. I will only take a minute of her time."

"I don't know," he says. "She's awful busy. What kind of information?"

"Jamie, is someone out there?" a woman calls from the house.

"Hang on a minute," he says sullenly, and steps up into the high, wide doorway into the house. He is back soon.

"She says to come in." He never takes his eyes off me as I walk by him and into the house.

"I'm in the kitchen," someone calls. I enter a long, cool, and tidy kitchen. The air smells of peppermint. The windows are so covered with curling vines and geranium leaves that the light has a calm green underwater cast. A white-haired woman sits with a colander of green beans in her lap. She stares straight ahead as she snaps the ends off the beans.

"Jamie says he doesn't know you," she says. I realize she is blind. "Are you with the police? I'm tired of talking to you people. I can't tell you anything 'cause I don't know anything."

"My name is Nell Styles," I tell her. "I know Jean."

"Oh yes? Styles? I don't recall her mentioning you."

"We don't know each other well. But I'm a friend of Lily Brown's." It has worked its magic before.

"Lily Brown, Lily Brown, oh yes, Terry's daughter. I heard she came back. Has a little boy that's not quite right, isn't it?"

"Josh is fine," I say. "He's just a little slow in learning to talk."

"Sure he is. I meant no harm."

"I'd like to talk to Jean. Is she around?"

"Not at present."

"Mrs. Labourne, I'd appreciate it if you could tell me how to reach her."

"Is that right? Well, I can't tell you, I don't know myself."
She does not seem agitated.

"Have you heard from her?"

She takes time to consider. "Yes. She called to check on
how we were making out. It was a shame too. She was so
upset she couldn't even talk to them kids. Jamie took it real
hard. He and his mother are awful close."

I am relieved. At least Jean and Daq are still alive.

"They sent me a bunch of money just this morning. And a
note saying they would start paying back the mortgage I
took out on this place when the trouble started. It makes me
uneasy. Where'd *he* get so much money, I'd like to know."

I'd like to know too.

"Did you keep the envelope the money and letter came
in?" I ask.

"Want a return address, do you?" she says sharply. "Why
are you here? You say you're not the police. Are you a reporter?"

"I'm not. I don't want to hurt Daq or Jean. My fiancé is in
trouble too, over this drug business, and I'm trying to help
him."

She sighs. "I can't understand why you girls mix your-
selves up with such men. They love trouble and it's their
women have to pay. Isn't life hard enough? I begged Jean to
stay away from Daq Fahey. Twenty years ago I could see
this day coming. Here I am with those five kids asking for
their mother and father and no idea what to tell them.

"Well, the envelope is on the counter, about three feet to
the right of the window. There's nothing on it, though, I
asked Jamie. It didn't come through the mail. Someone
must've stuck it in the mailbox last night."

It is as she said. The blank envelope is empty, the note
missing.

"Thank you, anyway," I say. "If you hear from Jean,
please ask her to call me. Eleanora Styles. I'm in the phone
book. Oh, and Denny says to say hi."

"That would be Denny Rourke. A good boy. Jean could

have married him, you know. She was such a bright little thing. Do me a favor before you go—look at those children and tell me if they're decent."

"I saw them when I came in. They all look fine."

"Thank goodness for that. They're good kids. Well, tell Lily to drop by some time and see me. I remember her mother very well. Good luck to you and your young man. Though if you'll take my advice, which you won't, you cut this one loose and find someone steady."

"Thanks," I tell her.

I walk down to the orchard and over to the biggest girl. She's bubbling over with health and high spirits, but her face is dirty and her dress torn.

"You kids do your grandma a favor and clean up before dinner," I say.

"Oh, we will," she says earnestly. "We're all going to take baths and I washed our good clothes."

"That's a good girl," I say. She laughs, looking almost fey.

"Most of the time, I can't see the point of it, can you? When we're just messing around out here? But *sometimes* even Jamie will take a bath."

"Oh, shut up, Nicole," Jamie says, looking miserable. "Why can't some people mind their own damn business?" he mumbles angrily as I get into my car.

Sometimes we just can't, Jamie, I say to myself as I drive away, pitying the thin angry young body perched on its rock.

I drive into the center of Winter Harbor. It's really just a crossroads with a few houses, a church, a gas station, and a combination grocery, liquor, and video market. I buy a Coke and sit on the bench in front of the market while trying to plan my next move.

I should try again to reach Paul. There is a phone outside the gas station where I can use my calling card. I try the number for the laboratory first. A woman answers, speaking what sounds like German, but when I ask for Paul she answers in English.

"No. No. Mr. Varensky is not here."

"This is his fiancée, Miss Styles. Can you tell me where I can reach him?"

"Wait please, Miss," she says. She discusses something with someone else in German. After a while a man gets on the line.

"This is Dr. Weber, Miss Styles. Your Dr. Varensky has nefer showed up. The police haf been here two days. We are very unhappy. Please do not call anymore." He hangs up.

I call the hotel. They inform me Paul has checked out. I ask if he's left a message for me. To my relief the clerk says yes, they have a message for me. He reads it. It is not a long message.

"Microbial Metabolites," he says.

nineteen

MICROBIAL METABOLITES. No matter how I look at it, the words signify nothing to me. Why would Paul leave me such a message? He must know the police are looking for him, but why is he running? Or is it the police he's running from? And what do microbial metabolites have to do with it?

Is there something I should know about them? I don't even know what they are. I guess I could look them up. Or maybe—yes, it could be the title of a book. I have cartons and cartons of books I am to ship to Luxembourg when Paul finds us a house. Is there something he wants in a particular book? Something that would be of some help to him now? Perhaps there is a name or address written in the book that will help me find him.

I'll have to go back to the house and unpack cartons. I hate to give up on Daq Fahey, but so far I have no lead to follow.

The envelope with the money was put into the mailbox by hand. Either Daq had someone nearby who was helping him or he was near enough to put it in himself. And if they *were* nearby . . . Jamie had been looking out to sea. Nicole had joked coyly about cleaning up for something special. I bet they are going to meet their parents this very night! I am sure of it. Jean wrote to Jamie, knowing he would reveal only what was necessary to his grandmother. That's why he was so strung up and Nicole so excited. I have to go back to the white house and wait.

I call J.J.

"Oh, thank God, Nell. We've been crazy wondering what happened to you. No, everything is fine. The kids are being great—we took them into the office while we worked, and they had a ball playing with your markers and the copier. Hal is grilling out in the yard now. He is going to try to educate their palates by giving them swordfish, but I got hamburgers just in case. He's got a big drink, and he and Josh are shooting at the flames with water pistols. So. When are you coming back?"

I ask her if it's OK for me to stay away a little longer, and she agrees. J.J. is so easygoing.

"I guess so. We'll just put them to bed and cuddle," she says cozily. "But what are you doing? Are you having an affair?"

I just laugh and say good-bye.

I provision myself with an Italian sandwich, an oversized peach, and another Coke. Then I drive slowly around looking for a back way leading to the house. I settle for parking in the lot of a public golf course and a thorny, brambly walk to an empty barn in back of the house. I sit just inside the huge open doorway on a box and eat my dinner. It's so peaceful here in the vast empty space with the sun slanting through the windows.

I awake with a start. I am cold and stiff and angry with myself. How could I have fallen asleep? What if I missed them? The last light over the trees has faded to a dusky lavender. A pale three-quarter moon hovers on a smoky wisp of cloud. The lights in the big old house are lit, illuminating the windows with that golden glow that fills a stranger with homesick and yearning.

I must have been kidding myself. There's nothing going on here tonight but a family of well-scrubbed children chatting with their grandmother over the last of their dessert. I've done it again—let my own desire reshape reality and called it intuition. Well, there's no harm in waiting a little longer.

When the sky and trees merge in shadow and the air is full of busy insect song, I see them—as hushed and ghostly as five solid children can be, they file from the back door and down the hill past me. Jamie goes ahead, his clothes dark, only his intense white face bright in the moonlight. Then the two smaller boys, heedless and springing, ignoring their brother's hissed commands to "be quiet, for godsakes." Then the two girls in fussy white dresses. The little one's legs are so thin. I hope she won't be cold.

They disappear down a gravel path. I follow, moving as quietly as I can. I wish I had sneakers. My sandaled feet scuttle on rocks and pebbles, and slow, fumbling moths bump blindly against me. I follow the children onto an empty moonlit stretch of highway and hug the shoulder as they do, about thirty feet ahead. Abruptly they disappear.

I walk past where they seem to have turned off but I see nothing, no path, no break in the scrubby bushes that line the road. I push through the bushes and into a weird empty expanse of big, smooth round stones. I hear and smell the sea. Taking off my shoes, I feel my way over the rocks. There is no sand, just the round, polished rocks like loose cobblestones. Coming over a small rise, I see them, huddled in a small clump by the shore. I can just make out the water in the moonlight.

I double back and come up behind them in a small stand of wind-twisted pine. There I stand behind a tree and watch with them, my arms wrapped around myself.

The children begin hurrying back and forth on the beach.

I can't imagine what their project is. Then the small girl comes quite close to me in the brush and starts snapping off dead twigs from the trees. Her little white face looks transported.

Jamie kneels over the pile they've collected, striking matches which are blown out instantly by the wind. Finally he throws his shirt over his head like a tent, and after a little while sits back. A flickering little fire wavers and then flares. The children crouch over it hungrily. I inch closer.

"There they are!" Jamie says, and points out to sea. I can make out nothing but the shifting moonlit path on the rolling water in the bay. After some minutes the other children all shout at once, "I see them, I see them too!" and then finally I also see. A small boat quickly approaches. A man jumps off into the shallow water and catches a woman in his arms, carrying her to shore. The children are all over them, hugging fiercely.

Daq unpeels himself and walks over to the fire, kicking sand onto it.

"This your bright idea?" he asks his son. Jamie shrugs. "We could see it from a mile out. Why not just send out an invite, 'Here's my old man—come and get him'?"

"Jeannie was cold," Jamie mumbles, kicking sand.

"Daq," Jean pleads, putting her arms around her son's shoulders.

"Well, the kid's gotta learn to use his brains. Still, it ain't a bad little fire in all this wind. We'll leave it goin' then, just smaller."

Jamie is inordinately pleased.

"Mom, see?" one of the little boys urges. "I lost another tooth."

Now that I'm here, I'm not sure what to do. Just jump out of the trees and say, "Hi, won't you tell the police who really hired you?" I wait and listen.

The little girl is nestled in her father's lap. He nuzzles her neck. "Is this my sweet little sugarpie?" he asks.

"Yes!" she giggles.

"Then I'm gonna eat it up," he says. She giggles wildly as he nibbles her. Nicole pushes into his lap too.

"God, you're getting to be a big horse," he says. "You're breaking my leg, stand up." She stands awkwardly. "I swear, you're taller than Jamie." She makes a face at her brother.

"Aw, she is not," the boy says angrily.

"When can we come live with you, Ma?" Nicole asks.

Jean pulls her big daughter into her lap and rocks her. "I don't know, baby. Soon," she says.

"Wait till you see the big, fancy house I'm gonna buy us," her father says. "Every one of you will have your own room. I'm gonna have my own bathroom too, just for me. That's all the luxury I ask outa life."

The kids laugh.

"That's neat, Dad," one of the small boys says. "And will it be up on the Cliff Road, where all the rich people live?"

"No, not in Merrivale, Teddy. Someplace much nicer. As soon as I see it, I'll know. 'This is a place for Faheys,' I'll say, and I'll come and round you up."

"No place is nicer than Merrivale," Nicole says.

"Shut up, Nicole. Have some sense. We can't go back there," Jamie says.

"The world is full of places," Jean says, "some so nice we can't even begin to imagine them."

"All right, Ma," Nicole says quietly.

"How's your Nana?" Jean asks. "She standing the extra work OK? You're helping her out, I know."

"She's fine, Ma. We're being good, except Teddy and Andy fight too much."

"No, we don't."

"Some people came," Jamie says.

"Who?" Daq is suddenly alert and wary.

"A lady today and some guy yesterday."

"You get their names?"

"Not the lady," Jamie says, nervously. "She was kinda young. Black hair, pretty."

Thanks, Jamie, I think. I knew I liked you.

Daq shakes his head.

"I got the man's name, though. Donald Dugan."

"Wha'd he want?" Daq says grimly.

"Wanted to know where you were. If we seen you."

"Checking up on me. Making sure I'm staying away," he tells Jean. "See now why we can't go back? He paid me to clear out, and if I don't keep out, just remember what happened to Marianne."

"I remember," Jean says hopelessly.

"You remember, you kids. You ain't seen me. Got that?" The children nod their heads.

My heart racing, I listen for more, but the rest is family talk, loving, hurting, joking, and quarrelsome.

When Daq says it's time to go, I can't bear to watch or listen anymore. Jean and the four younger children are crying as I quietly climb out of the brush and try to retrace my way to the Duchess.

Who is Dugan? That is what I keep asking myself as I drive back to Merrivale. Why did he pay Daq to stay away?

Everyone is asleep when I get back home. Hal and J.J. in my bed, Ananda on the couch, and Josh on a nest of cushions on the floor. I go into my studio and close the door. I start unpacking cartons, looking for *Microbial Metabolites*. In the third carton, I find it, a big book with a bright blue cover. There is no name or anything else written in it, but then I see an envelope tucked into the jacket flap. It is addressed to me.

I sit on the floor, next to the drying canvas of the streambed, painted for Paul, and open it.

Little Nell, it says. *If you are reading this now, it means that the police, slow as they are, have finally figured out that I am the mysterious drug smuggler of Good Harbor. Wait, let me clarify that—I've never done any actual smuggling, per se, myself—as a matter of fact, I get much too seasick to have anything to do with boats. I am, however, what the press so originally calls* The Brains Behind The Operation! *With any luck, as you read this I am still a free, though hunted, man. I've made excellent provisions for this eventuality. Money, a new identity, a place to go, all wait for me. Planning has always been rather a talent of mine. I don't know how many times I've stressed to you, Nell, the importance of organization.*

I don't know how closely you've been following the reports in the newspapers, but I've managed to carry out my little enterprise quite efficiently for some years now. Oh yes, I was already quite well-established in this business before I met you. It was really the most fortuitous situation that we met. It seemed like destiny—in addition to your considerable other charms, you gave me the perfect excuse to come and go often between the Good Harbor area and the city.

At first, I went almost three years without any confiscations. Then, though the heat was turned up, and runners will do the stupidest things, business was still remarkably profitable.

I am, in fact, a much wealthier man than you ever dreamed, my Nell. And happily for me, most of it is safe and sound where I can reach it easily. I will be a very comfortable though, it goes without saying, lonely man.

I've thought and thought, of course, about having you join me. I was so desperately hoping we'd be married and together before you had to find out about all this. I do love you, little Nell, but I'm afraid that you won't be as proud of my cleverness as you really ought to be. It is so amusing as I write this, to imagine your piquant little face. Do I see shock there? Certainly. Indignation? No doubt. Horror? Not too much, I hope. Admiration? Perhaps a bit. Knowing your quaint, rigid beliefs about right and wrong, I fear you may not be able to fully appreciate my exploits. I hate to say it, dear, but sometimes you can be a tad bourgeois. Now, don't get your feathers all ruffled. How I loved to see you bristle.

At any rate, I am unsure what your reaction will be. And I can't afford to be unsure. Do you love me enough to come to me, regardless of my little secret? I just don't know.

It shouldn't be like this, of course. If only you would say, "I love you completely, Paul, and want to be with you." If that were true, what a remarkable life we could live—a life of total luxury and beauty, free of the tedious cares of ordinary people.

But somehow, pretty though that picture is, I can't quite convince myself to believe in it. And hovering nearby is a less pleasant possibility. What if you should indignantly turn to the authorities and instead of being met by my blushing bride at our rendezvous, I should find a regiment of noisome officials? I can't allow all my most meticulous care to go in vain. I just can't risk my pleasant, secure future on the uncertain sands of love.

Perhaps, when I am more settled, I can come up with a foolproof plan to have you join me. What a happy reunion that will be. But as we must both be uncertain as to when and if that day will come, I will satisfy your curiosity and, I must admit, my own vanity in this letter. I will tell you "all about it," as Ananda would say.

How to explain the why of it all, I'm not certain. The profits certainly have been lucrative, but to tell the truth the money is really only the icing on this cake. The truth is, it's been the most tremendous fun, Nell—the ultimate game. You don't know this, but I've always enjoyed some kind of crooked enterprise. All those years following my mother's career from hotel to hotel, putting up with the dreary tutors and the awful parties. My only amusement came from getting into other people's rooms and lifting whatever interesting treasures came my way. (I could write a book about the peculiar things people keep.)

The basics have actually remained pretty much the same— the joys of planning every little detail, the excitement of carrying it out, the tremendous ruckus when the crime is discovered (and the suspense when it is not!), and then the rewards of cashing in.

This operation was of course more complicated than stealing fat ladies' brooches. Unfortunately I had to work with others —the suppliers, the runners, the distributors. I tried to be careful, never used the same runner twice. I'd investigate likely prospects until I found the perfect one, then put my proposition to him. Or her. I made all contact by phone, and left the payoff at a drop. One-third beforehand and the rest after. I must say I've been agreeably surprised by human nature. Only once did someone collect the prepayment and never show. Perhaps humanity deserves more credit than I've given it.

And then came the ill-fortuned Mr. Fahey. I fear it was my generosity over his bail (goaded as I was by a certain pair of soulful brown eyes) "what done me in." Otherwise, the police need never have glanced my way. Alas, Nell, you contributed to my downfall. Had you not pricked my conscience I never would have thought to connect myself to that loser.

Which brings us to the strangest part of this whole business. What happened to Fahey, that ungrateful rat who jumped bail with fifteen thousand of my dollars? Who killed the policewoman? I assure you I had no part in it. What's worse, I have no idea who did, nor why. Perhaps Fahey himself. But why? I just don't know, and it bothers me.

As you can imagine, it upset me rather badly. Especially as I had had the extreme misfortune to have wandered onto the scene of the crime and found the corpse! A most suspicious circumstance, I agree, but you simply must believe me. She was dead when I got there. That night, when Lily came to Kit's and said Daq had spilled his all to Officer Banks, I became uneasy. Did he know something dangerous to me? I had to find out. I went to see Banks after I left you at Lily's. I had some plan to pose as a federal agent and at least try to determine whether the information concerned my identity. Her door was open. I went inside and had a very nasty shock. I left immediately and ran right into your friend, the vulgar Mr. Pengryth, in the street nearby. Perhaps he is the one who did the dreadful deed, and was returning, pro forma, to the scene of the crime? I quickly seized upon him as an alibi. He wasn't likely to want his whereabouts known either.

Be careful, little Nell. No doubt when he finds me absent he will leap at the chance to fill the role of comforter. Don't accept. The man may be dangerous.

Good-bye, little one. I will think of you warmly and often.

Keep up with your painting, and try to be kind to my mother. She's in for unpleasant news and I can't really write to her. Love from your wicked and unrepentant

Paul

twenty

WEAKLY, I PUT the letter down. I shiver. Paul's letter, for all its matter-of-factness, reveals a madness that shocks and revolts me. It's almost funny. I'd clung to Paul hoping for security and for the comfort of the familiar. I hadn't known him at all.

And if *he* is the drug smuggler, who is *Will?* Who is Dugan? I try to work it out. Dugan wanted what Daq knows kept quiet. Marianne had known about whatever that was too, and she was murdered. Claudia had something Will wanted. She was murdered too.

It's too complicated. Don't you get it yet, stupid? There is no "good guy" here. Will and Dugan are engaged in some desperate private struggle and neither one of them is counting the cost. There is no white horse in this race. I've been like a child, wanting a hero and a villain. Good versus Evil. But I should have known—life isn't like that. There are no heroes, just two selfish animals ruthlessly seeking their own dominance. And sacrificing whoever gets in the way. The

Faheys, Claudia, Marianne, they were all just victims who'd been swallowed up and spat out.

I am filled with a sense of loss and indignation. Does it make any difference to them now, who won and who lost? Did they even know what the battle was about, a battle that had made their lives of no account, that had said they didn't matter? But they matter to me. I will not let them disappear silently, meaninglessly, like leaves in the wind. I am filled with a potent rush of certainty and purpose.

I make my plans. Marianne wouldn't speak. Daq, with young ones to protect, can't. But maybe, if I am lucky, Claudia can and will. I must find out what she was murdered for.

I write a note to J.J. and leave the house again with all still sleeping. I climb into the Duchess and force her up the Cliff Road, to where Claudia lived. It is not easy to find. All the house lights along the road are off and the street numbers indecipherable. By trial and error, I finally locate Claudia's stucco and glass villa. The doors have been sealed by the police, but I am sped along by an unwavering determination and I easily break in through a window.

I draw all the curtains and turn on the lights. The house is both dramatic and feminine. It doesn't feel like a house without a mistress. Her presence seems vital and immediate, as if she will step through the door any minute. I try to get to work but it is difficult. I don't know what it is I'm looking for. While I try to work out a plan I water the plants that are beginning to languish and die.

Others have searched here (I am sure Will has), searched and failed. I can't even be sure that whatever it is, it is still here at all. It could have been found. It may never have been here. It could be in the shop or, more likely, in a safety deposit box, or at a friend's house or a hundred other daunting possibilities. But I will not be daunted.

I might have one possible advantage. A woman hid whatever it was, and as a woman I might have a better chance of getting inside her head than those who went before me.

I start in the kitchen. I've hidden cash in my freezer. Claudia's freezer holds only a box of frozen blueberry muffins (one missing). It makes me sad, the box of muffins. I imagine her microwaving one muffin and I feel a stirring of compassion. She was lonely, I think. I look through cabinets and drawers. I probe packages and cookbooks. I search under and behind everything. I will be as thorough and patient as a spider.

It is getting light out when I finish the downstairs. Four hours and I've found every bobby pin Claudia ever lost and $3.61 in change, but nothing else. I wearily go up the carpeted stairs, sliding my hand under the bannister and behind the botanical prints hanging on the wall.

Claudia's bedroom is exactly like the bedroom I dreamed of when I was fourteen, a veritable boudoir. It's impossible to believe a flesh and blood creature ever slept here amongst the white lawn and lace. I move hopefully to the dresser. All along at the back of my mind I've been harboring great hopes for the panties drawer. Freezer be damned—this is the instinctive, the primal hiding place for a woman. The underwear lies in tissue paper, well-laden with fragrant sachets. I enviously flip through the tiny silk, lace, and embroidered items, but there's nothing here but a queen's ransom in lingerie. I am unreasonably disappointed.

Then I get a brainwave. I search through the trellised gardenlike bath. In a cabinet I find what I'm after. There are two boxes of tampons here, one partially empty. I open the full box and pull apart a pink plastic applicator. Eureka! Coiled inside, in place of the tampon, is a roll of narrow pages, like register tape. I uncoil one.

FROM: COMMAND CENTRAL OPERATIONS
4/17/85 18:24:31

TO: INTERNATIONAL COMPLIANCE AND SECURITY
Chief Officer

Central acknowledges receipt re: interloper presence. Believe our security seriously compromised. Evasive action approved at this time but continued presence enemy vessel unacceptable beyond 5/6. Can vessel and/or operations be rendered harmless? Advise.

-30-

FROM: INTERNATIONAL COMPLIANCE AND SECURITY
Chief Officer
4/17/85 18:40:00

TO: COMMAND CENTRAL OPERATIONS

Field 3 acknowledges receipt re: mechanical intervention. Interloper crew security-conscious and resourceful on mechanical failure but will attempt severe malfunction to structure of vessel. Crew usually aboard and may be severely inconvenienced. Advise.

-30-

FROM: COMMAND CENTRAL OPERATIONS
4/17/85 18:58:01

TO: INTERNATIONAL COMPLIANCE AND SECURITY
Chief Officer

Any and all actions including termination of enemy personnel necessary

to maintain security and facilitate
progress approved. Advise.

-30-

Sitting tailor-fashion on the carpet I search for the next
coil of paper.

"Clever lady." The voice comes from behind me. I jump.
Donald Dugan leans casually against the doorframe. He is
uncharacteristically disheveled and he needs a shave.

"Are you all right? You look rather green," he says.

"You startled me. I thought I was alone."

"Poor little buttercup. Let's see what you've found."

I hand over the open applicator with its cache of tightly
wound paper. He uncoils it. I try to calm my wildly beating
heart while he reads. Be careful, I remind myself.

"Yes. You got the goods all right," he says cheerfully. "I
can't imagine how you managed it."

"I'm clever. You just said so."

"So I did. But how did you happen to come looking for
something you didn't even know existed?"

"I heard Claudia and Will talking at the wedding. I figured she had something he wanted. And you said we were
partners. I couldn't just sit still while you had all the fun,
could I?"

"No, I suppose you couldn't. Well, I think this should settle Trevane's hash permanently. Where's the rest of it?"

I'm so sorry, Claudia, I think. I meant to avenge your
death and instead I'm handing over what you died hiding. I
give Dugan the open box of tampons.

"Great," he says, stuffing the first set of papers into the
box. "Let's go."

"Where to now?" I ask brightly.

"To hand these over to the authorities. You follow me in
your car."

"Why don't we just call the police and ask them to meet
us here?" I say.

"And get us both in trouble for breaking into an officially sealed house? No, angel. This is a murder investigation we've been messing with. This way is better. They don't need to know how we came upon this. The important thing is to nail Trevane and clear your fiancé, even though it means a broken heart for me."

How could I ever have found this sleaze charming? But then I seem to have made a specialty of terrible judgment.

Outside, he fixes the window to look as chaste as possible and climbs into his car.

"I'll meet you at the police station," he calls and roars off.

Like hell you will, I think. He's going to drop that package into the sea, or burn it. I remember the card he gave Hal. Dugan's the International Compliance and Security Chief Officer. I don't know what exactly these records prove, but it looks like Dugan, not Will, "terminated" someone.

I push open the broken window again and squeeze through. I have to move fast. I want to get out of here before he discovers I gave him the wrong box of tampons. I run back out with the full box and jump into the Duchess. I'm going to have to put the pedal to the floor, poor old thing. Get me out of here.

I speed down the Cliff Road, looking out for the grey car. I round a bend and see the road stretching before me mercifully clear all the way down to the harbor.

I'm going to make it, I exult, light-headed with relief and lack of sleep.

Then I hear the roar of an engine behind me. I look in the mirror. It's Dugan all right, coming down like a grey bat out of hell. He's honking his horn and motioning for me to pull over. I speed up as fast as I dare, but he's gaining on me. I can't go faster, so I slow down, my tires skidding sickeningly. I back onto the shoulder and turn my wheel desperately, trying to turn back. He reverses expertly and cuts me off. His car is in front of me, the cliff is to my back.

I look around wildly, but there's no one in sight. There is just Dugan and me in the silvery fog of dawn. Dugan gets out. He walks over to me and bends down to my open window. He hefts the tampon box I gave him in his hand, as if judging its weight. "Very cute," he says and throws the box at me. I roll up the window and jam his arm in it, and jump for the passenger door. He has me in an instant, writhing on the ground. He sits on me. The rough pebbles cut into me cruelly. He jerks my arm behind my back and holds it there.

"Get up," he says, and half pulls me to my feet. "Where are they?"

"What?" I say.

He hitches my arm higher. My shoulder feels like it's going to give. It only takes about two seconds for me to tell him, "In the car."

He pushes me over to the Duchess. The pale pink box sits foolishly on the floor. He picks it up and tosses it into his car, never loosening his grip on my arm.

"Look at this terrible mess you've gotten us into, Nell. Why'd you have to go and play a lone hand? I suppose you thought Trevane would pay a pretty penny for these? He would have cut your throat. Now what am I going to do with you?"

"Forgive and forget?" I laugh. "After all, you haven't been exactly straightforward with me either."

"No, I guess I haven't. Still it's no good, angel. I'm disappointed in you. I thought you were such a sweet, straight little thing. How I've dreamed about those soft trusting brown eyes." He sighs.

"No. I'm afraid you're going to have to have a little accident." He pushes me over to the Duchess. We stand there together, him behind me. He talks softly, dreamily, his breath tickling my ear.

"Now let's see. You are driving along alone, enjoying the early morning air. You pull onto the shoulder, and watching the sun come up, you start to feel romantic. You leave the car running to listen to the radio. One of your old favorites comes on. You get turned on, thinking about old times, perhaps. You pull down your panties and start to, um, reminisce. In your excitement, you flail out, releasing the brake and your car tragically rolls off the cliff. Brilliant, I think, don't you? Artistic, ironic, tragicomic."

In a panic, I wrench myself away, stomping with my heel into his instep. He shouts with pain and releases his grip on my arm. His face is contorted, dark with rage as he grabs for me again. Suddenly I hear Lily in my mind, instructing Josh:

"Make a fist, tight! Go for the nose, one, two!"

I bring up my right fist. It catches him in the jaw. My left hits him right on the nose. Torrents of bright red blood pump over the hand he raises to his face. He swings at me. Something explodes in my face as he connects. I am stunned.

"Duck! Weave! Keep moving!" I hear Lily exhorting. I bob to the right and swing at him again and miss widely, but I'm off balance and my head smashes into his by accident. He howls and holds his nose. I run for my car. Blessedly the motor is still running. I gun it into the sports car, and with the grey car wedged against the front of the Duchess, I push the pedal to the floor. My wheels spin in the dirt.

"You bitch," Dugan yells, and leaps for the passenger door. I throw the bug into reverse, then into second. I hear a scream of metal as my bumper rips loose and then I pull free with Dugan hanging on to the open door. I speed up and he brings his feet up off the ground, swinging his legs to jump into the seat. His weight is too much for the rusty old Duchess and the door snaps and hangs, dragging him on the asphalt. He drops and rolls to the side of the road. I race away to the sound of his curses.

"It works, Lily!" I shout into the morning. "It really works!"

My hands are throbbing with pain. I can wiggle the fingers, so I don't think anything is broken. My left eye is closing. Dugan has the papers. He may even have a chance to destroy them. But I am alive, in fact I am exultant. From

somewhere deep inside me comes a strange, primitive shout
—a shout of victory and the fierce joy of life.

The few people about as I pull into the lot at the police
station stare at me in a kind of fascinated horror. I'm bleeding, my clothes are torn, my poor little car looks as though
it's been attacked with a sledge hammer, but I am smiling
broadly as I go up the steps.

The station is bustling; very different from the torpor I
found it in the day before.

"I want to see Chief Hinckley," I tell the man at the desk.
He takes one look at me and says, "Sit down. The chief is
pretty busy but I'll check. Do you need an accident report?"

"No, I want to report an attempted murder."

"Sit right down here," he says, looking at me like I'm a
gun about to go off. "I'll be right back." He makes me hold
a wet towel to my eye and soon ushers me into Chief Hinckley's sanctum.

"Who did what to you, Miss Styles?" the chief asks.

"A man named Donald Dugan tried to throw me off a
cliff," I say. "I hit him and got away from him."

He whistles long and low.

"Where and when was this?"

"About fifteen minutes ago on the Cliff Road."

"Move it," he tells his subordinate, who rushes from the
room. The chief picks up the telephone. "We've been looking
for Mr. Dugan all over hell and gone," he tells me. "One
minute and someone will take your statement."

I hear police cars leaving the station, sirens wailing.
"What about Will Trevane?" I ask.

"You don't know?" he says, then speaks into the receiver.
"Hi, Demaris. Hinckley. We have a report that Dugan was
on the Cliff Road here about a quarter of an hour ago. . . ."
He is still enmeshed in his conversation when my buddy
Officer Dort comes to take my statement. I answer about a
thousand questions, but Dort will answer none of mine. He
is pale, distant, and speaks to me in formal monosyllables.

I think he must have gotten a lecture on releasing police information to civilians. I refuse to go to the hospital. I will tend to my own wounds, I insist. Finally, I am free to go but not before receiving a stern warning that I may face charges for breaking into the McKee home and removing evidence.

The Duchess, bless her stalwart heart, starts up at once, but she looks terrible and groans ominously all the way to Beau Cherry Lane. What *was* the chief surprised I didn't know about Will? Have they been arrested? Are they all right? Where is Lily?

twenty-one

THE FIRST THING I find at home is a note from J.J. left on my kitchen table.

> *Nell, where were you and what on earth are you up to? The kids are with Kit and Spence. They were quite surprised to find Hal and me here instead of you. I didn't know what to tell them! Lily Brown called and said for you to meet her at Will Trevane's at noon. What is going on??? Call me!*
>
>

Love,

J.J.
>
>
> *P.S. Hal just loves this house. He was wandering around murmuring, "Pastels, pastels," and wanting to knock down walls. Tee hee. Call me.*

It is ten-thirty. I feel just terrible. I look in the mirror. The sight is fairly lurid. I have a black eye. Or I should say a purple and yellow eye. I feel like "The Winner," the Norman Rockwell girl grinning outside the principal's office.

I put some ice in a kitchen towel and gingerly hold it to my eye, sitting on my bed. All my bones and muscles are stiff and painful. I ease myself back against the pillows. I'll just rest for a little while, I tell myself. I sleep like a stone until five-thirty.

When I awake I'm still sore, but at least I've slept. I've missed meeting Lily at noon. Maybe she's still there. I grab some leftovers from Hal's barbecue and turn on the TV as I wolf them down. I look for the news. I tune in a picture of men in business suits trying to avoid the camera as they're led away.

" . . . the arrest today of top officials of EcoTech, a private organization purportedly operating to promote environmental concerns. The arrests followed the discovery today of huge illegal caches of toxic wastes in hidden storage on the Baldur Islands, a chain of offshore islands newly designated as a federal wildlife refuge area. Several hundred barrels of these wastes have been discovered so far, some of them in stages of severe deterioration. Search teams expect to find many more.

"Wildlife experts say they cannot yet estimate the extent of the damage done to the colonies of seals, schools of whales and food fish, and over twenty species of wild birds, including some endangered species who have found refuge on or near the islands.

"EcoTech was incorporated in 1979 as a research and lobbying organization. Since that time many environmental action groups such as Greenpeace, Earthwatch, and Earth Haven have challenged EcoTech as a wishy-washy or counterproductive agency. They claim EcoTech weakened efforts to pass and enforce meaningful legislation both internationally and at home. Government officials, however, such as the Department of the Interior and the Environmental Protection Agency, have often praised EcoTech's efforts, calling the organization responsible and reasonable.

"Today, however, a task force led by Congressman Teague Duprey gave evidence that EcoTech was in fact engaging in the illegal transport and disposal of toxic wastes and suggests that the organization may have been involved in illicit international sales of radioactive materials."

No wonder Teague looked familiar! I watch his long spiritual features as he speaks into the microphones. He is my congressman. Lily must have recognized him at once from my drawing. Standing in a row behind the congressman are a jubilant Will, a beatific Lily, and a solemn Benno. What a fool I've been.

"We are proud and pleased to have put a stop to this outlaw organization," Teague says. "Masquerading under the banner of environmental protection, they have stolen our contributions, poisoned our waters, wantonly destroyed endangered wildlife, and, under the guise of donating fertilizer to third-world nations, have dumped tons of toxic ash on their shores."

The announcer now continues, "EcoTech officers face charges of tax fraud, illegal toxic waste disposal, misuse of federal funds, and mail fraud. Illegal profits over the years are estimated to have run into hundreds of millions.

"Still at large is this man, Donald Lorenzo Dugan, EcoTech's chief field agent." Lorenzo? Dugan's elegant, smiling image broadcasts well.

"Officials believe he masterminded the Baldur Islands operation and he is being sought for questioning in what may be related murders in the nearby village of Merrivale. In other news, the Senate today—"

I click off the TV. No matter how humiliating, I must find Will, Lily, and Benno. I had warned Dugan and endangered their campaign. Thank heavens I hadn't scuttled it completely.

I run a brush through my hair and change into clean clothes. Should I put on lipstick? I can use purple to match my eye. I can't believe I'm fussing over how I look. I'm just going over there to offer congratulations, eat humble pie, and slink away, aren't I? I walk in dread to the yellow house. Laughing, happy people I don't know are milling on the front porch. Will's guitar lies in its case next to the red sofa. How long ago it seems since I listened to his music sweet in the summer nights. Soon it will be fall.

"Hi," the folks on the porch greet me. They think I am a friend. I walk into the house looking for Lily. A noisy crowd is in the living room gathered around the TV. All-news radio is on in the kitchen. I hadn't counted on a crowd.

"It's Nell!" Will shouts warmly, like he's just spotted his best friend. How nice he is, I think, how really nice. He looks a different man—happy, expansive, and exuberantly alive.

"Nell," Lily says joyfully, and falls on my neck. "We were so worried about you. I'm so sorry we couldn't tell you, but . . . Anyway, it's all worked out splendidly, hasn't it? Will is something else. And have you seen the *Examiner?* Front-page exclusive by Lily Brow . . . My God, what happened to you? Look at her, Will."

They fuss over me like parents. I tell them the story of Dugan and me. Will tenses, turning back into his grim self.

Benno says, "Don't worry. We get him too, soon, I tink." He towers over me and examines my eye critically, holding my chin in his huge hand and tilting my face.

"You say you punched him in his nose?" he asks seriously.

"Yes."

"Twice? It bled?"

"All over the place. I hit him once with my fist and once with my head."

He laughs heartily. It's the first time I've seen him smile.

"You look great. Dot is one beautiful eye." He shakes my hand, then changes his mind and kisses me. "Haf a beer," he says, handing me one. "Haf two."

"Thank goodness you're safe," Lily says. "Let me introduce you to Teague and the rest."

"No, Lily. I only came by to congratulate you and apologize for the trouble I caused."

I turn to Will. "I really am sorry. I guess I misunderstood, and I mixed myself up in your business and almost wrecked things."

"That's my fault too," he says. "If I had trusted you, had told you why I was here, you wouldn't have gotten things wrong. You wouldn't have almost gotten yourself killed."

"You had no reason to trust me," I say.

"I had some."

I look at Lily. She is watching the two of us anxiously. When she catches my glance, she walks off. I go after her.

"Lily, do you want me to pick Josh up from Kit's for you? He could stay with me tonight, if you're busy."

"Josh is here."

"Oh, he is? I didn't see him."

"He was outside playing with Shiloh a minute ago. Where's he got to now?"

She steps out onto the porch. "Josh. Joshua!" There is no answer.

"I haven't seen him for a while," a woman standing on the porch says.

"I have to go look for him," Lily says.

Will joins us. "You see them?"

"Uh-uh."

"That's strange. I told Shiloh to stay. He wouldn't take off."

"Even to follow Josh?" Lily asks.

"I don't know." A chill goes through me. I walk out into the street, calling Josh. Lily and Will join me, calling him, calling Shiloh.

Lily hurries down the block towards her house. Will goes inside.

"Josh! Shiloh!" I call. My voice sounds inadequately thin and high. The rest of the party pours out of the house. Lily comes running back.

"They're not there," she calls to us. Benno gets into his truck and cruises slowly down the street.

"I think we'd better call in the police," Teague says. "I hate to say it but . . ."

"It smells like Dugan," Will finishes.

twenty-two

THREE HOURS LATER there is still no sign of boy or dog. I sit
with Lily in the dark in her kitchen. She refuses to let me
turn on the light until the sky is completely black. Even then
she will only allow the light in the hall. In the kitchen we
sit in a tense dusk. Josh is so little to be out in that great
darkness. He cannot speak. So we sit in the dark too, and do
not speak.

The phone rings. It is not the first call. The phone has
been ringing and ringing and I must tell callers to keep the
line free. The tracing equipment and tape recorders click
on. Will and a state police officer come into the kitchen.

"Hello," I say, trying to keep everything out of my voice.
Hope is as dangerous as fear.

"Mommy?"

The voice is small but true.

"Who is this?" I ask, not daring to breathe.

"I want my mommy. I want Lily."

Each word is a miracle.

"Hold on, honey. Mommy's right here. Don't hang up."

Lily takes the phone, holding the receiver as she might hold a baby bird. I put my ear close to hers.

"It's Mommy, Josh. Where are you?"

"A man taked Shiloh. I'm saving him, but I'm losted."

"What man, baby?"

"I don't know. A bad guy. He's mad at me."

"Why? What's he done?"

"I sneaked into the car after he put in Shiloh."

"Did he hurt you?"

"Just yelled. I wouldn't talk. I didn't want to."

"Do you know where you are, honey?"

"In a house. It's dark out. I want to come home now. Won't you get me?"

"Yes, honey. I'll get there as soon as I can." Lily is crying. I take the phone.

"Joshie, this is Nell. Are there numbers on the telephone?"

"On the buttons?"

"No. On a little piece of paper under the buttons."

"Oh, yeah. Three."

"What else?"

"Seven. Oh."

"What else?"

"Goddammit!" I hear a man's voice yell, then the receiver crashing down.

"Josh? Josh?" The line is dead.

"NO!" Lily screams.

"Did you trace it?" Will asks.

The policeman shakes his head. "Not enough time," he says.

Lily looks to Will.

"Do something," she says. Her faith in him is absolute.

"Call the operator," I say. "Find out what exchange or area code starts 370."

There is a city exchange starting 379. The state troopers amend the All-Points Bulletin and contact the metropolitan police.

Will turns pages in a worn leather address book.

"Claudia's parents had a vacation house up at Feeding Lake," he says. "That's a few hours north of here. That exchange is 307."

"It's worth a shot," the trooper says. "I'll contact the police up there too."

Half an hour later, the Feeding Lake police call back. The McKee's house is empty, all locked up.

Two more hours slowly pass with no new word. Lily is grey and silent.

"I can't just sit here," Will tells us. "I'm driving up to the lake house. I know these folks think it's useless but I have a hunch about it. It can't hurt, and I need to do something. Do you mind?"

"No, go," Lily urges. "I'm going with you."

"I don't think you should, Ma'am," the trooper says. "The police there found no sign of them and you've got to stay by the phone." Lily nods her compliance. We watch the door close behind Will. The room seems very empty.

"Nell, you go with him," Lily urges.

"I'm staying right here with you."

"Go with him. Find my Josh. If he's there he'll need somebody he knows. I'll have Kit, if you'll get her."

I run after Will. "I'm going with you," I say.

Fifteen minutes later we climb into Benno's blue pickup truck.

I ask the question I've been afraid to ask in front of Lily. "Will, if Dugan has Josh, why hasn't he called? Wouldn't he want to make a deal?"

"He didn't mean to take Josh," Will says. "He just wanted Shiloh. That means there's something he wants from me. What, I don't know. You said he already has the EcoTech communiqués."

I nod, but something nags at me.

"Turn back to my house," I direct.

He pulls into the driveway behind the wreck of the Duchess. I lean down and look behind the seats and on the floor. I start to laugh.

Will looks at me.

"Twice in one day," I say, waving the pink box in my hand.

"What?"

"Dugan," I explain. "He took the wrong tampons."

twenty-three

"WAIT ONE MORE minute," I say. "I want to get something."
Will agrees without questioning me. I know he's anxious to
get going, but he has a deep well of patience along with the
fierce resolve. I change into a long-sleeved shirt, jeans, and
sneakers. This time I want to be adequately dressed. Then I
search among Paul's cartons. I soon find what I'm after.

We drive north. After we pass the exits for the city the
traffic dies off. We turn away from the coast and into the
deeper darkness of the trees. Beside me, his face revealed
occasionally by passing lights, is Will, his flame as constant
and purposeful as a torch.

"Tell me," I say.

"Tell you what?" he asks, his eyes intent on the road, his
fingers tight around the wheel. Then he turns and looks at
me as if realizing for the first time that I am here in the cab
with him. He seems to come back from somewhere far away
where he is alone in his desperate quest. And then he smiles
warmly at me. It is so good to be here, riding alongside him.

"Tell me all of it, about you and Claudia and Dugan," I say.

He looks off into the far darkness again and is silent. It is a while before he starts to speak.

"Lewis was my older brother," he says. "It all really starts with him. He was two years older than I. Good-looking, smart, a great outdoorsman, a great sailor. Everybody loved Lewis, knew he was something special. If there was anything going on, Lewis was at the center of it, laughing, yelling, making it special.

"We weren't just brothers, we were best friends. I knew people wondered if I was jealous of him, but I wasn't. You couldn't be jealous of Lewis, he was unique. He made you feel special too. Just being with him automatically brought out the best in you.

"The best times we had were when we went off by ourselves, hiking, camping in the mountains, or sailing in the boat we built. Then we'd talk about the things we were going to do. We had it all planned. We were going to study marine biology and travel the world like Cousteau.

"After he graduated, Lewis went to the university in Santa Barbara. I followed two years later, and it was like old times. Hanging out, working together, making our plans. Then I met Claudia."

He frowns. "She was the most beautiful woman I'd ever seen," he says flatly. My heart contracts in an ugly way. This is no time to be jealous, especially of a dead woman.

"She seemed different then, softer, not as screwed up, and just incredibly lovely. I was blown away. Lewis didn't like her. He thought she was empty, I guess. He tried his damnedest to talk me out of marrying her. When Claudia found out about that she started to hate him. She saw him as an enemy, was always on me about him, saying I couldn't be my own man until I got out of his shadow.

"Lewis graduated and got a job with Earth Haven. We both saw them as the most serious about fighting for the environment. He'd send home these incredibly exciting letters. He was going all over the world, just like we'd planned —fighting whalers, saving seals and dolphins, fighting major polluters. I was desperate to join him, but both he and Claudia insisted I stay in school. It was the only thing they ever agreed on.

"When he came back home for visits, it was bad. I'd be torn between them. There was Lewis sitting on Claudia's silk couch in his work clothes, smelling of salt and the wind, telling these great stories, drinking beer, showing slides of himself and his crewmates in action. And Claudia, all dressed up, was throwing coasters under his beer, and pouting that I was ignoring her.

"When I graduated, Lewis had a slot waiting for me on his team at Earth Haven. Claudia insisted on graduate school. She said when I got out, I could do more good in an executive position. We fought. Finally I agreed to go for the master's if she'd agree that when I finished I would work as an activist. She was like a lamb the whole time I was in graduate school. She supported us, she was getting to be pretty successful as an interior designer. I was convinced we'd worked it all out.

"She and Lewis still squared off when they met, but he toned down the stories and I guess she thought I'd been domesticated. I finally got through the whole ordeal. The last happy peaceful day we had was when I graduated and we went to the marine outfitters and bought my kit. Claudia pranced around, posing in her foul-weather gear. Then we went up to the base camp in Alaska, and she started to make my life miserable.

"The camp was in this isolated outpost, very stark and primitive, but surrounded by mountains and glacial lakes. God, it was beautiful. The air was so clean, Nell, it was like wine. But Claudia didn't know what to do with herself. It was no good. She couldn't stand the life, and I couldn't leave it. She didn't get along with the few other women stationed there and she flirted with the men. There wasn't much there, but there was a bar. She started to drink. Then EcoTech established a station there, and Claudia got an organizational job with them. She seemed happier."

He falls silent. I look into his face, which is dark and troubled.

"Dugan was the field officer," he spits out, and then turns to me. "God help him if he's hurt Josh or Shiloh, Nell. They've just got to be at that lake house." He pushes the truck even faster along the dark road. The trees whip by.

"Anyway, Lewis and I began to have our doubts about EcoTech," he continues. "They already had a bad reputation among the environmentalist groups, for bullshit policies and extravagant administrative budgets. There's always some competition between different groups for funding, or differences of philosophy or tactics. But EcoTech was really different from any of us. These guys were unbelievably slick. They talked a good line but they never seemed to do much. And their equipment! We were always going begging for a new engine and patching holes in the hull with spit and scrap iron. These guys were totally computerized, navigational equipment out of NASA, amazing stuff.

"We'd go out on a mission and a few days later there would be Dugan and his dream machine right smack in the middle of our operations. We'd ask him to back off—it's impossible to do the kind of work we did in the limelight they brought to the whole arena. But he always insisted they were conducting necessary research.

"Research, balls. They were purposely fouling us up and, we later found out, locating dumping locations for private industry. They were going to foul the bay so badly it would make the North Sea look like a kiddie pool.

"I confronted Claudia, told her what her boss was up to, and she laughed. She said Lewis and I were paranoid, crazy. When I insisted she quit, she said I was just jealous of her and Dugan. That's when I found out they were doing a thing. It was the last straw. I kicked her out.

"Then she wanted money. She came to me with this long

bill, everything from the last three years itemized, from my textbooks to my underwear. She insisted I repay her for her "investment" in my career. It was totally impossible. I was making forty dollars a week on top of my living expenses from Earth Haven. I didn't have anything.

"It was like a nightmare. Wherever I went she hounded me. She took my diving and photographic equipment. And then she went after Lewis.

"After he was dead, she acted as if they'd been lovers. That's how she convinced the authorities I was responsible for his death. But it wasn't like that. She had pursued him, insisting she was in love with him. She made it her mission in life to seduce him. Wherever he was, she showed up. He'd be having a beer in the bar, and she'd stand behind him brushing up against him with her breasts. She'd sit across from him sucking her thumb and parting her legs. It was so fucked up. At first Lewis tried to laugh it off, but he finally stopped going out.

"We were on an over-winter watch. There was nothing much to do that winter but a little ice fishing, a little repair work, and hanging out. We were starting to get on each other's nerves. I decided to clear out for a while. I went with a Greenpeace crew on an overland trek for a few weeks. When I got back, Lewis told me what had happened.

"He said he woke up one night and Claudia was in his bed. She'd just walked in and climbed under the covers while he was asleep. He woke up and found her there naked. He kicked her out. After that she just tried to seduce as many men as she could."

His voice is unemotional, but I can see the pain in his face. I take his hand, but he gently removes it to shift.

"That's OK. Anyway, Lewis was waiting for me when the truck pulled up. I guess he knew Claudia wouldn't wait to throw something in my face and he wanted to tell me the truth first himself. I went crazy. I wanted to strangle her. Lewis and Benno propped me up through the next couple of weeks. Lewis talked to her, tried to get her to go back to

California. She refused. I guess she was getting some weird pleasure out of torturing me. I think Dugan had broken it off, but there were plenty of guys around to take up the slack. She was throwing whatever she could in my face and all I could do was drink myself into indifference or give up and clear out. I was just hanging on, and I don't know what would have happened if Lewis hadn't died. But he went down with the *Reckless Abandon*, and as Claudia loved to remind me, it should have been me."

He falls silent. I can see his pain.

"You don't have to tell me," I say.

"I know," he says. "It's OK. Lewis and I started working like maniacs. Usually early spring is still a quiet time on the wintering-over stations. You can't really take the boats out yet. The harbor is full of floating ice blocks. But we needed to keep busy, so we put the *Reckless Abandon* into the water early, and set to work completely refurbishing her.

"She was a beauty. Built expressly for our fleet, not a castoff like our other boats. We were raring to go. That spring we were going after whalers with so-called research exemptions. There's nothing like facing down a thousand tons of steel, weaving between the harpoons and a beautiful pod of whales, for driving the personal misery out of your head. And we also had a few nasty surprises planned for EcoTech and Dugan.

"Ever since the *Rainbow Warrior* was bombed by the French secret service, we'd all been nuts on security. It was my turn to stay aboard overnight. Lewis, Benno, and I were alternating until the rest of the full crew joined us. It was my night, but I was hungover and I couldn't face a long night alone in my berth with my demons. I would try to concentrate on a book, but before long I would be making pictures in my head of Claudia and Dugan, Claudia and anyone. I'd imagine grabbing her, choking her—it was pretty rotten.

"I asked Lewis to take my turn. He was feeling so bad for me he'd have jumped overboard if I'd asked him to. He was eager to do anything for me and I guess if I'm being honest, I liked him taking care of me.

"That night the *Reckless Abandon* was bombed. A diver attached explosives to her hull underneath the waterline and set them to go off in the middle of the night. I'll never forget the blast. I was playing chess with Benno. Nothing is more silent than a long cold night in the north when there's no wind. There was an enormous crack, then three tremendous booms as the tanks exploded. We ran out of the house. It looked like the sea was on fire. We did what we could, but it was too late. Lewis drowned. He must have been asleep and couldn't get out."

He's staring at the road ahead, his head rigid, but tears are running down his cheek.

"Benno and I were certain it was Dugan. I don't know how much Claudia knew about our plans to dog his boat or what she'd told Dugan, but it made sense that EcoTech needed the *Reckless Abandon* out of action, and it seems they didn't much care who went down with her.

"I went out of my mind, Nell. Imagine what it's like knowing you sent your own brother to his death in your place. The better man went down that night and I can't forget it."

I explode. "Will, you mustn't say that. It isn't true. Your brother was a wonderful man, someone to be proud of, but so are you."

"Yeah, thanks," he says. "Anyway, I was insane with grief and rage. I wanted to kill Dugan—that's all I wanted. Benno and the other Earth Haven warriors who flew up there after the blast almost sat on me to keep me away. There was an investigation, but nothing to connect Dugan or EcoTech to the bombing. I'd lost Lewis, I couldn't get Dugan—I thought nothing more could happen to me. I was wrong.

"Earth Haven insists on insuring its field workers for their lives. Dodging harpoons, getting bludgeoned by angry crews, diving into toxic wastes—it's not the safest life. Claudia was still my beneficiary and it turned out I was Lewis's.

As soon as Claudia discovered I was collecting two hundred grand, she was at the door looking for spoils.

"Seeing her acting like the bereaved on the one hand and grasping for his blood money with the other was too much for me. I literally kicked her out the door. Then she went to the authorities. She painted them a sordid picture—her supposed affair with Lewis, my switching shifts with him, the insurance money, the fact that I'd been diving near the boat. They went for it. I spent almost a month in the crappiest jail you ever saw. They finally dismissed the whole case because there was nothing to show I had access to explosives. In a way it was worse than going to trial. There I would have been found not guilty. This way it was just insufficient evidence.

"Earth Haven relieved me of my duties at the station. They said it was nothing to do with the arrest, just that they didn't believe I could function efficiently in that environment. So I quit.

"I'd lost everything, my brother, my boat, my work. Three things kept me going. One was Shiloh, who was just a pup then. Then there was Benno, who kept me from going over the edge. And there was revenge. I was determined to nail Dugan for Lewis's death and to bring EcoTech down.

"Dugan knew that I knew. I don't think he considered me a danger, which was a big advantage, but it galled me. The arrogance of the bastard is incredible—the smarmy way he acted at Lewis's funeral. He even made a donation to the memorial fund.

"I swore I'd get him. When Benno wasn't on active duty with Earth Haven, he helped me. I disappeared for a while, Benno kept track of Dugan's whereabouts, but EcoTech was slippery and very highly connected. Once you realized what they were, it was obvious, but it was damn difficult to prove. Benno persuaded me that uncovering EcoTech's illegal activities would get the authorities to look into Dugan's role in Lewis's death.

"When we discovered that Claudia was in Merrivale, not far from EcoTech's headquarters, and suddenly very prosperous, we became suspicious. It turned out she was in touch with Dugan, but we didn't know if it was professionally or just privately. We hired an agency to check her out. It turned out EcoTech had been paying her over fifty grand a year. She was on their books as a consultant. We figured it had to mean a payoff.

"Whatever she had was buying her more than a hefty paycheck. I had no doubt Dugan would have soon got rid of her if there wasn't something he was afraid of. It couldn't have just been something she knew or she would have been dead sooner. You know how dangerous he can be." He lifts his hand and very tenderly touches my eye. I'd forgotten about my shiner.

"It was the transmission records from the *North Star*, of course. But I didn't know that then. I just knew it was probably something concrete that tied Dugan to the explosion, and that I wanted to get my hands on it. So I came down here using a false name."

"Weren't you afraid she'd recognize you?"

He laughs. "Yeah. I knew there wasn't a chance if she ever got a good look at me but I did what I could to keep out of her sight, and I shaved my head and grew a beard."

I am shocked. "You're not really bald?" I blurt tactlessly.

He laughs. "I don't know. It seems like I don't have to shave quite as often as I did at first."

I try to remember the picture Dugan showed me in Hal's office. I conjure up an image of his chin clean shaven and with a head full of red-gold curls. Foolishly, I comfort myself that the noble bone structure, the fine humorous lines of his face, and the intelligent gold-green eyes remain. No matter what, he'd still be a beautiful man—his beauty relies on his inner fire. Not that it concerns me, I remind myself. It was Lily who'd been at his side when he needed her, Lily whom he'd kissed in the joy of victory, Lily who was relying on him now to recover Josh, and Lily who might still require his comfort in a way I couldn't dream of diminishing.

"What's the matter," he asks slyly. "Can't feature me with hair on my head and none on my chin?"

"It's hard," I force myself to banter back. "But go on. What happened next?"

"You pretty much know the rest. I broke into her house and her store, but I don't have your brains. I didn't find anything. Then your wine bottle blew my cover. Claudia knew where I was and Dugan did too. He came to town, but so did Benno, and Dugan couldn't get near me.

"When he saw that I hadn't made a move on EcoTech I guess he figured I was just after Claudia. He realized she was a weak link and tried to get her to hand over the communiqués. She panicked and tried to sell out to me. I guess she was going to run for it and needed the cash. I didn't know whether they were working together, laying a trap, so I didn't bite.

"By then we had Teague Duprey's ear and I knew we were going to get EcoTech, if they didn't get us first. You know, you almost blew that too. Until you talked to Dugan, he didn't know we were onto the Baldur Islands dump or that a congressman was involved. It was pretty close. If we hadn't moved when we did, EcoTech would have had that whole mess cleaned up."

"Sorry," I say. "I know it's hard to believe, but I thought you were smuggling drugs."

"I know. Lily told me. It must have been a shock, learning about Paul."

I nod. He squeezes my hand.

"I thought you were setting him up," I say.

"And I thought you were trying to pin his mess on me in order to clear him. I didn't really blame you. But at least you know now it was Dugan who killed the policewoman. At the time I thought it was Paul. I ran into him outside her house soon after she was killed."

"Why did Dugan kill her and not Daq Fahey?"

"I guess he knew he couldn't buy her off. And it was enough to scare Fahey off. But he's not going to get away with anything. EcoTech's through. My name is finally cleared." He pats the tampon box. "For now he's got Josh and Shiloh, but we're gonna get them back, you and I. Do you know that?"

"Yes," I say, but I don't know any such thing.

Suddenly he pulls the truck onto the shoulder and stops. "Nell," he says, "look at me."

I look over at him. He's turned towards me in the seat. "In Earth Haven, when we go out on missions, you know what we call ourselves? Peace warriors. That means we go out to do battle, but we don't endanger anyone but ourselves, right? You go out against people armed with guns, bludgeons, harpoons. They're in much bigger boats that can ram and sink you, and all they'll have to say is that you got in the way. Now I'm not telling you this to pat myself on the back. Here's what I'm saying. The only thing standing between you and death is your brains, your instinct, your skill. You have to be in an almost mystical connection with the righteousness of your task. You have to have the heart of a warrior, and your weapon is love. Love of the earth, love of your fellow creatures, love of your fellow warriors. Do you understand?"

Something fills my heart as he is speaking, some inexplicable substance starts to pump through my veins. I am in a state of heightened awareness. Somehow, I am plugged in. I nod.

"Good," he says. "Place your hand on my heart." I reach out my right hand and place my palm against his chest. He covers it with his. I feel something like an electrical charge coursing back and forth between us.

"We have to trust each other, rely on each other, put our lives in each other's keeping. Doubt is like a hole in our armor. If you feel doubt, cast it out now.

"Now concentrate on Josh and Shiloh," he says. "Send them your energy and your love."

I concentrate. I see little Josh with his big wet eyes and his dark curls. I see him watching Shiloh being hustled into the back of an open car and jumping in, intent on helping the dog.

"Josh has the heart of a warrior," I say, filled with understanding.

"That's right," Will says. "It has nothing to do with age or size. That's why when he needed to contact us, he could speak."

I see Shiloh licking Josh's face and giving the boy comfort and courage. I am filled with certainty and love. Fear is not in me.

"Let's go," Will says. "This is why you came with me, we are going to do battle well together. Do you know it in your heart now? Are we going to get them?"

"Yes," I say. I know it in my heart.

twenty-four

IT IS THAT grey hour before dawn when we reach the winding road that leads to Feeding Lake. Although it isn't raining, the trees that line the narrow track of road and the windows of the truck are drenched with the cool heavy dew. I can smell the deep doggy smell of the nearby lake, so different from the clean salty ocean scent I am used to. Bumping and turning, we twist up one heavily forested side road after another as Will searches his memory for the right house. Finally he says, "This is it."

We drive past the house and pull into an empty driveway several houses down the road. The mist is cold and thick and noisy with the chirruping of insects. I shiver and Will rummages in the space behind the seats. He hands me a huge woolen sweater.

"We'll cut around on the lake side and approach the house from the back," he says, his voice low. "Try to step carefully and quietly. I don't want to use the flashlight unless I have to. If we can avoid Dugan altogether and just recover Josh and Shiloh, that would be best. We'll leave it to the authorities to deal with Dugan. As far as we know, he hasn't contacted anyone. We'll assume, if they are here, he thinks no one knows where he is. If we do have to confront Dugan, leave him to me and try to get away with Josh, and Shiloh too, if you can. Then go for the police. Got it?"

"Yes. Uh, Will," I say, "I have this." I draw Paul's small revolver from the pocket of my shirt.

"Umm," he grunts. He takes it from me and hefts it gently in his palm.

"Is it loaded?" he asks.

"I don't know. I didn't find any bullets for it."

He examines it. "There are two bullets in it. Put it back in the truck, Nell. I don't use one."

"It might come in handy," I say. "I think we should have it, but I don't know how to use it. Do you?"

"Yeah, I do, but I won't take it."

"Dugan will probably have one."

"I like to think there's a difference between Dugan and me. You take it if you want. I can't tell you what to do."

I hesitate. He is so compelling, part of me longs to just follow him and his certainty. But I can't. I remember Dugan pushing me against the cliff wall and my feeling of helplessness. I'll take whatever odds in my favor I can get.

"I'm taking it," I say.

"All right. You flip this to remove the safety only if you really want to fire it. Squeeze your finger back on the trigger. Don't jerk. Don't shoot near anyone you don't want to hit. Got it?"

The sky is lightening, but the mist is terrific, it's like walking through a cloud. I follow behind Will, trying to concentrate on walking as quietly as he. We pass over one lawn and across someone's wooden deck. Will halts.

"That's it," he whispers.

I look over his shoulder through evergreens into the next lot. An imposing redwood and glass chalet floats silently in the mist. Will takes my hand and we push through the wet, scratchy trees. In a minute we are on the raised deck. Will cautiously tries the sliding glass door. The screen is locked, but he quietly pulls at it until it lifts off its track. He pushes up on the catch with a pocketknife and it comes loose. He lifts the whole screen and passes it to me. We silently prop it against the house. He jiggles the glass door. It doesn't budge. He points down towards the floor on the inside. There's a broom handle wedged into place, keeping it shut tight. He shakes his head.

We descend from the deck and he leads me around to the side, where he points to a basement window. The screen here doesn't open. He works at it with his knife, cutting a small opening. I fit my smaller hand through and undo the catch. The screen grates horribly as we slide it open. We wait silently, my hand on the gun in my pocket. No one comes. Will easily slides the window open and peers inside. He slips through, feet first, and drops to the floor, making not a sound. Heart pounding, I follow him.

We are in a good-sized room fitted out with an oversized fieldstone hearth, a wet bar, a media wall, and a plethora of electronic games and equipment. Will slowly opens a wooden door under the stairs. Inside, it is dark. Will turns on his flashlight—we are in a utility room containing a washer, dryer, and furnace. Then Will points.

On the floor is a bowl of water. The water looks fresh. Could it have been a water bowl for Shiloh? There is no other sign.

We climb the stairs to the main floor of the house. It has one big room with a high vaulted ceiling. We look into a closet, nothing doing. All that remains is the loft above. We start up the stairs.

Then the lights flash on. "Hold it right there," a voice orders. I freeze.

"Put your hands in the air and turn around. Slowly."

I am somewhat relieved to see two policemen standing in the doorway below, one with a rifle raised, its barrel trained right on us.

"Come down slowly now," one of them bids. We walk down carefully, hands raised.

"What are you doing here?"

"Same thing you are," Will says. "We're looking for Joshua Brown, the boy who was kidnapped in Merrivale. Along with my dog. We're friends of the boy's mother. My name is William Trevane. This is Nell Styles. We thought Dugan might have brought them here. The Merrivale police know who we are."

"Take them out to the car and check their IDs," the policeman tells his partner.

They stand us up against the car. One of them starts to pat Will down. Oh God, I think, the weight of Paul's revolver heavy in my pocket.

"Chief says bring them in," his partner says. "I'll stay here and watch the house."

Temporarily reprieved, I climb into the back of the cruiser. On the way, Will tells him about the water bowl.

"Well, we're keeping an eye on the place. We haven't seen anyone *until now*," the policeman says grimly.

We sit on a bench in the small one-room station while they check us out. A number of men dressed in fishing gear drift in from the mist, stopping by to sip coffee and chat with the men on duty in the station. They look us over thoughtfully, silently convicting us of something.

Finally the chief gets off the phone with the Merrivale police and reluctantly tells us we can go, but not before administering a thorough tongue-lashing. *And* my second warning that I might face a charge of breaking and entering. I wonder how many counts before you're put away? Fortunately, they never get around to checking me for concealed weapons. The guy who brought us in gives us a lift back to our truck.

"Go home and quit playing cops and robbers," he says. "You probably scared your man off for good, *if* he was ever here to begin with, which I doubt."

"What now?" I ask Will as he drives off.

"They've definitely been there," Will says. "Don't you think so?"

I agree.

"Maybe he saw the police show up earlier and moved on. But he must know the net's closing in, Nell. He may be feeling desperate, and that's not good for Josh and Shiloh. We've got to find them soon."

"Is there anyplace around here he could hide with a kid and a dog?" I ask.

"There's miles of woods around, but they seem to be getting pretty closely built up. Must be ten times as many houses as when I was here last. Of course, there's the boat house. We should try there."

"What's that?"

"Down by the lake. It's a private yacht club with a boat house and a sort of recreation center where they hold dances. The McKees keep a boat down there too. Let's try it."

We drive towards the lake. Any minute the sun will rise and burn off the mist. We pull into a gravel lot alongside the boat house. There seems to be no one about. The heavy front doors are locked. We look through one of the high windows. It appears to be empty inside. We walk around the dock overhanging the lake. Many good-sized boats are docked there, cruising yachts and smaller, more delicate sailboats.

"The McKees used to have a cruiser called the *Marisol*. Let's see if we can find it."

We walk out onto a wooden pier.

"Hello, hello! If it isn't Trevane and his lady fair." Sitting high on the deck of a small yacht is Dugan. He's smiling, the two hundred kilowatt special.

"Don't make a move, don't make a sound," he says pleasantly. "I've got a hefty .38 pressed right against your little friend's head." We look at where his right arm rests on a pile of canvas. He lifts his wrist slightly so we can see the gleam of metal.

"This is most fortunate for me. I don't know how you manage it, Trevane. You're always where you shouldn't be. I was at a loss for what to do next. This place is crawling with police. I figure the population is about 200, and 199 of them are on the force. Now you're going to get me out of here."

"Am I?" Will asks.

"Oh, I think so. *How?* You're going to sail me across this lake and down the river to Brewster Bay. I figure it's about thirty or forty miles. *Why,* I think, speaks for itself."

I stare in horror at the canvas which lies unmoving at his feet.

"Josh, are you all right?" I ask.

"Buster Brown and Tyge are fast asleep," he says. "You have no idea what a terrific pain in the ass a kid and a dog can be. It was like the "Ransom of Red Chief." I had to give them both a nice dose of medication. But don't worry, they'll be fine if you get me safely out to sea. And by the way, where are my communiqués? You do have them with you?"

"Turned them over to the authorities right away," Will says impassively.

"How prompt. Righteous indignation was always your least attractive quality, Trevane. But at least you can make yourself useful by sailing me out of here."

"There's only one problem with your neat little plan, Dugan," Will says. "The Grapevine River does feed out of this lake into the bay, but you have to pass through a series of shallow streams and estuaries—much too shallow for this cruiser."

"I know that, you ass. Why do I need you if I can motor out myself? You're going to sail us out in that." He points to a small sloop which bobs in the water, near the end of the pier.

"You're the hotshot sailor, not me. Here I was, wondering

how I'd get myself down those nasty little creeks, maybe sailing right into the arms of the harbor police. 'If only Trevane were here,' I was just lamenting, and voilà, here you are, ugly red beard and all. It's really like an answer to a prayer.

"What a nightmare it's been up to now. I never meant to take the kid. I have no idea how he climbed into the car. Now I just want to get out of here. Come aboard and help me transfer our precious cargo."

Will helps me climb aboard the yacht and swings up behind me. I wonder if I can get my gun out, but Dugan is watching too carefully.

"Good," he says. "Come here, Nell. Pity about that eye. But then again, my nose is not the thing of classic beauty it once was either."

He transfers the gun to the small of my back.

"I hate to be melodramatic, but one false move and you never walk again," he says. "Uncover them, Trevane."

Will lifts the canvas. I gasp. Josh and Shiloh lie limply on the deck.

"You bastard," Will says, feeling first Josh's wrist and then the pocket between the dog's leg and trunk.

"Just sleeping, as I told you," Dugan says. "You carry the dog. Nell, you take the boy."

I bend slowly, the gun clinging to my flesh like a leech. Awkwardly and slowly we move our ghastly procession down the pier. I sweep the deck with my peripheral vision, but no one is about anywhere. At the end of the pier lies the little boat.

"The *True Love*, isn't that sweet? Can she make it to the bay?" Dugan asks.

"We'll be low in the water with all this weight," Will says, "but she can make it."

"Go aboard then, Mr. Christian," Dugan says.

Will carefully lays Shiloh on a blanket inside the little cabin, stroking his head, and I, with Dugan right behind me, lay Josh down on a small berth.

"Mama," he mumbles in his sleep. I stroke his brow, which is white, cold, and moist, and cover him with a blanket.

"Wait, put this on him," Will says, handing me a life jacket. He straps one around Shiloh too.

"Now to raise the sails," says Dugan happily, and we climb out into the cockpit. Dugan pulls me down next to him on the padded seats, and we sit there together, his arm around me, the gun nestled into my kidney. We both watch Will expertly fitting up a sail. He finishes tying his line and says, "Is someone helping me, or do I do this alone?"

"Alone, I think. I want to concentrate," Dugan says.

"It'll be slower," Will tells him. "We won't be able to use the jib."

"Do your best, Trevane," Dugan says. "Just make sure we get out to sea."

"We're ready, then."

"Then cast off and no funny stuff. I want a nice, uneventful trip. Understand?"

Will nods. He loosens the painter from the pier and pushes us off. He takes the tiller in one hand and pulls on the line. The sail catches the wind. It fills instantly, and we take off with a lively leap into the lake. The sky is rosy in the east and from far off a loon's weird call welcomes the rising sun.

Dugan settles himself and me more comfortably in the cockpit. His free hand rubs my shoulder and upper arm, and brushes my breast. I try to wriggle my body away to keep him from feeling the revolver in my pocket.

"Stop brooding," Dugan tells Will, who frowns out at the water. Then Dugan sniffs inquiringly.

"I hate to say it, dear, but this sweater is not all it should be," he tells me.

"It's Benno's," Will laughs.

"Ugh!" Dugan grunts and pulls away a bit.

Will looks considerably cheered.

twenty-five

FOR A WHILE we tack uneventfully out into the middle of the lake. The promise of the sun never really materializes. The morning settles into a chilly grey day, and we are alone on the water. Once we are well out from shore and a fairly stiff wind is blowing steadily we no longer have to shift about, but can sit fairly comfortably, raising ourselves occasionally if the little sloop heels too sharply. Dugan and I watch Will's back. I admire his broad shoulders and his muscular arm, relaxed and competent on the tiller. What Dugan is thinking, I don't know. He is uncharacteristically quiet as he, too, watches Will work.

"I can't figure why you took the dog, Dugan. You could have been well away by now," Will says quietly, not turning around.

"It was a stupid move," Dugan laughs ruefully. "I couldn't stand you having everything your own way. I thought I'd make you jump through hoops to hand over those effen communiqués. I got myself into a sticky situation that you are going to get me out of."

"Out how?" I ask.

"He's got a yacht, a stinkpot with high-tech navigational equipment, in a small harbor outside Brewster Bay," Will says.

"How the hell do you know?" Dugan asks, surprised.

"Just a good guess," Will says. "Going to try to make Mexico or the Caribbean?"

"That's all. Be quiet and sail. Go into the cabin, Nell, and see if there's any way to make some soup or some coffee."

"One more question. At least satisfy my curiosity," Will says.

"What?" Dugan sighs.

"Where the hell did you put your car? I didn't see it anywhere."

Dugan laughs. "It's lying under about ten feet of water in this lake. It was wrecked anyway, thanks to Nell. I pushed it off the dock. No loose ends, you know?"

What about us, I think ominously.

Dugan transfers the gun to the back of Will's neck. I gratefully climb away from him and through the shallow hatch. First I check on Josh. He is still sleeping heavily, but his color looks a little better. Shiloh's legs are bicycling, the way a dog's do when he's dreaming of running. I wonder if that means he's coming around.

There is a tiny galley with a minute sink and a two-burner cooktop, even a miniature oven you could roast a small chicken in. There are plate racks and cunningly designed cupboards that hold an amazingly complete set of necessities. I boil some bottled water for instant coffee and open a can of potato-leek soup. Plenty of daylight comes into the cabin from the portholes. This could be very nice under different circumstances.

All the while I wait for the water to boil I am thinking furiously. This is the perfect opportunity. I can watch from the hatch for the right moment and surprise him with my gun, taking his from him. I go up one step and look out. I have a clear sight of Dugan, who sits there rumpling his hair. He looks tense. Then he catches my eye. "Find any-thing?"

"Yes, it will be ready in a minute. Can I bring some for Will and me, too?"

"Of course!" he snaps. "What do you take me for?" He seems really offended.

I go back into the cabin. That's the real crux of the whole matter. What do I take him for? Will he really let us go once we get out to sea? We know about his yacht; Will probably has an idea of where he's headed. He knows we'll be in touch with the authorities. He's killed for security before. He's going to kill us, I think.

But then again, he could have gotten rid of Shiloh and Josh—dumped them by the side of the road at the least. And he didn't murder Daq Fahey either—just paid him off. He paid Claudia off for a long time, too, until he decided she was unreliable. He's not a maniac, just ruthless, I think. It's some small comfort.

He may decide we're a risk he can't take. I have to decide if he's a risk I can take. I know one thing, after watching him from the hatch. I can't bring myself to shoot him. I'll have to try to surprise him, threaten him, make him drop his gun. I put my hand into my pocket and grasp Paul's revolver.

I'll bring the soup out first. Then I'll come back in for the coffee, I plan. He'll be holding the soup. I'll crawl behind him and put down the tray. The gun will be on the tray under a napkin. I'll put the gun to his head. I rehearse it in my mind as I put the soup in mugs and carry it out. Dugan lifts his gun and keeps it trained on me as I put the tray down.

"I'll get the coffee," I say.

"We'll drink this first," Dugan says. Both Will's hands are busy. I can't hand him the mug.

"You can hold the sail for him," Dugan says graciously. He seems eager to oblige. Holding a gun to our heads, he still worries what we'll think of his manners.

"Take hold of the main sheet," Will tells me. "Pull it in until the sail is not fluttering—see how the wind fills it fully?"

I sit down beside him. I hold the line. The feeling delights me, it's like holding a live thing.

I adjust slightly to a change in the wind.

"That's good!" Will says, smiling at me. I search his eyes for a message. Can't he sense what's in my mind? Does he give me a slight nod? The message is so subtle, I'm not certain it's real.

"Well, you two look very cozy," Dugan says. "But I think I prefer the other arrangement. Go get the coffee, if you would, Nell, and we'll resume our former positions."

I collect the mugs and the tray. OK, I steel myself, this is it.

"There's the mouth of the Grapevine," Will points out.

"Good, how long until we reach it?"

"About twenty minutes."

"And then to the bay?"

"It's hard to say. The banks are enclosed by the trees, the wind won't be as stiff, I don't know what the current is like. Four hours maybe."

"OK," Dugan says. "Is there anything to have with that coffee, Nell?"

"I'll see." The condemned man ate a hearty meal. I reheat the coffee and rinse out the mugs. It will have to be after I hand him his coffee, I think, while I'm resettling to take the sail. In my head, in the safety of the cabin, all goes smoothly. The heart of a warrior, I repeat to myself, but I can't make myself believe it. I'm afraid I'll fluff it. Do it, do it, I urge myself. You coward. We'll all die because you sat and waited for Will to do something. I'm terrified, but I'll do it anyway. Anything not to ride passively down the river, serving refreshments and pretending there's no danger, hoping something will happen to make it turn out all right. *I* have to make it turn out all right.

Then Josh begins to moan. I bend over him. He is tossing

and turning. I sit down and gather him up into my arms. He is still out of it, but he opens his eyes for a minute and looks at me. Then he begins to vomit.

"What's going on in there?" Dugan calls.

"It's Josh, he's sick."

"Shit!" Dugan curses. "Bring him out on deck."

"I can't."

"All right. Hold on, I'm coming in. Don't screw up," he tells Will. "I've got this trained right on them."

He appears with gun in hand in the hatchway. Then I hear a ferocious growl, and a streak of gold flashes past me. Shiloh leaps for Dugan's throat. Dugan jumps back. The dog crashes to the deck.

Shiloh must still be groggy; he's confused by the bulky life jacket tied about him. He shakes his head and tries to fix his eye on Dugan. Dugan aims the gun at the dog. Will throws the tiller to one side. The sail whips around and the heavy wooden boom crashes into Dugan's ribs. He goes down. Josh and I fall from the berth amid a crashing of crockery. The boat heels sharply. We're going over. The cabin is turning upside down in slow motion. I clasp Josh to me.

But Will must still have control over the boat, which joltingly, sickeningly rights itself. Holding Josh, I crawl up onto the deck.

"Dugan and Shiloh are overboard," Will shouts. "Get the ring." I look stupidly about for the life ring.

"There, there," Will points. "I'm going to bring her about. Keep your eye on them." He sails away from the two heads bobbing in the water. I clutch the ring attached to the boat by a loosely coiled line and turn myself as the boat curves in a figure eight back to where Dugan's sleek black head bobs like a seal's. Josh is crying softly to himself. "It's OK now, honey," I tell him.

"How's Shiloh?" Will yells.

"He's swimming towards shore," I say. The dog, incongruously buoyant in the life jacket, is steadily pumping towards the shore.

"It's too far," Will says. "And I don't know how I'll get him back aboard."

Will brings the boat around into the wind, and the sail hangs loose. We come to a sudden stop. I throw the ring to Dugan, who swims to it, awkwardly, and one-handed. He maneuvers himself into it. Will tows him closer.

"Should I cover him with the gun?" I ask. Will doesn't answer. I take the gun out and point it at Dugan's head, but I leave the safety on. Will struggles with Dugan, dragging him aboard. Josh lets out a cry when he sees Dugan coming over the side.

Dugan is sodden, dazed, and pathetic, shivering on the padded seat of the cockpit. He brings up some lake water, and stares at my gun in disbelief. He raises his own hand, looking at his gun as if he doesn't recognize it.

"Drop it," I say. He lets it fall heavily into the cockpit. Will quickly kicks it into the lake.

"Get out of those wet things," Will says coldly, slipping off his own jacket and tossing it to him.

"The complete gentleman," Dugan says, trying gamely for his old zip. Will picks up the tiller and the main sheet, and sails towards Shiloh, who is slowly paddling towards the still-distant shore. Soon we sail alongside the dog. I briefly take my eyes off Dugan to look at Shiloh. He doesn't look up, just tries desperately to keep paddling forward. I can see he's frantic and exhausted.

"I'm going in after him," Will says, bringing us to a stop. He rolls himself off the boat, which rocks violently.

"Shiloh! Shiloh!" Josh calls.

Dugan watches me intently. I force myself to stare him down, keeping the gun on him. Will is crooning to Shiloh. "OK, Shiloh, OK, boy. It's OK."

"Does he have him?" I ask Josh.

"Yes," Josh says.

"Grab him, Dugan, bring him up," Will calls from the water. He is struggling with the dog, who is paddling his paws, trying to get away.

"No way!" Dugan says. "He'll rip my throat out."

"Do it!" I say, pushing the gun into his face.

Dugan reluctantly leans over and grapples with Shiloh, who by now is flailing wildly. Will curses and pushes; Dugan curses and heaves, and finally, Shiloh is aboard. He shakes himself violently, and falls in a heap on the deck, too exhausted to do more than bare his teeth and growl at Dugan.

Dugan looks from Shiloh's teeth to my gun.

"I guess I'm not the most popular member of this crew," he says.

"Help Will aboard," I tell him, gesturing with my gun. I'm really getting to like this.

He leans over and extends his hand to Will, who is clambering up. As Will starts to come onto the deck, Dugan stands, kicks at Will, who manages to hang on, and dives into the water.

"Hey!" I shout, enraged. I aim the gun at Dugan, who is swimming for shore. "Stop or I'll shoot!"

"Nell!" Will shouts. "No!"

Startled, I drop the gun, which falls into the water. I look at Will and then at Josh. They are both staring at me, horrified. I collapse into the cockpit. Will swings himself up and holds me, rocking me as I cry tears of frustration, and rage, and shame.

"He's getting away! I didn't do anything!" I wail.

"I know you didn't," Will says consolingly.

I am furious. He doesn't understand.

"No!" I yell. "I mean I didn't do anything to help. You and Shiloh did it all."

"Oh yeah? What about my main man here? He puked at the strategic moment."

I laugh, but I insist, "I did nothing—I was just . . . frozen."

"That's not true," Will says. "Nell, you were brave, you were perfect. Josh and Shiloh are safe here with us. We're all alive and unhurt. We did what we came out here to do. Be glad! We're gonna sail back to the dock and take Josh home, and let the police take care of Dugan. He won't get far."

We look out to where Dugan makes a small dark dimple in the grey surface of the lake.

"I want Mommy," Josh says.

"Oh, baby," I say, scooping him up. "You're talking so good!"

twenty-six

WE CAN SEE the crowd gathered on the boat dock from the lake. There is quite a commotion as we dock. The owner of the *True Love*, having found his pretty little boat missing, is going out of his mind. He's an older guy who looks quite a bit like Groucho and he has to be physically restrained from attacking Will. Will has to do some mighty fancy tap-dancing to appease the guy and the police, who are pretty reluctant to swallow Will's story twice in one day.

Finally, I call Lily from the yacht club and she persuades Josh to tell the police about Dugan. Very reluctantly the two cops who'd surprised us in the house go off to hunt for Dugan, but they turn their heads in their patrol car to stare after us longingly as they drive away.

The state police arrange to fly Lily up from Merrivale in a helicopter. Fortunately for Josh we don't have long to wait. About an hour later Lily steps out of the helicopter.

"Mama," Josh sighs softly to himself, then Lily rushes forward and enfolds him in her arms. Lily and I are crying and Will is grinning like mad. Then Lily puts Josh down and runs at Will and throws her arms around him. I wander off into the yacht club, where a kind of party has developed, and get a nice hot mug of coffee. I let a blond young man in a windbreaker pour a shot of whisky into it from his hip flask. We eye each other half-heartedly.

Lily and Will come in search of me.

Lily hugs me tight. She looks into my face and we just stare into each other's eyes. Our feelings are beyond words. It doesn't matter. Words aren't necessary. We are all just so glad to have our Josh safe.

"It's time for us to be headed back, Ma'am," the helicopter pilot says.

"Am I going to ride in that?" Josh asks, his eyes shining.

"Uh-huh," I answer. "Me too."

"I thought you'd ride back with me," Will says.

"I'm afraid you'll have to," the pilot tells me. "We don't have room for you."

We watch Lily and Josh lift off and bid good-bye to the boat crowd. Even the owners of the *True Love* have become friendly since they've determined that there's been no damage to their craft. They've even rustled up some dry clothes for us to change into. Will is given a snazzy warm-up suit that forces me to bite my lower lip very hard. I get some jeans and a tee shirt that must have belonged to a teenaged son. I just make it into the jeans, but the white tee shirt is snug and embarrassingly sheer. Will starts to compliment me, but I quickly squelch him with a fatally nasty look. I make him hand over the warm-up jacket.

We climb into the truck and he smiles at me. I turn my head and stare out the window. He takes my hand, but I pull it away. What does he think he's going to pull here?

"What will happen to Dugan?" I ask.

"They'll find him," he says. "He'll go to prison. I'm not sure how much they'll be able to prove on top of the Eco-Tech stuff, but probably they'll indict him for Claudia and the policewoman. And the communiqués will get him at least a felony murder charge in my brother's death."

I reach for his hand on the gearshift. He pulls the truck onto the shoulder. He turns to face me.

"Stuff your pity," he says. "Dammit, Nell, I don't know how you feel about me, how you feel about the love we made. If I hurt you then, I'm sorry. I didn't know what else I could do. I had no idea how this whole mess was going to turn out, if I'd even make it out alive. I was prepared to bring Dugan and EcoTech down with my life, if necessary. I couldn't be in love, I couldn't—"

"It's OK," I interrupt. "These things happen. I didn't know what I was doing either. We got carried away and it was very nice. You don't owe me anything. Not even an explanation."

"It's not OK with me," he says, his voice exasperated. "I love you. I want you. I want us. I *have* to tell you and I need you to tell me."

I am speechless, consumed with anger.

"Tell me," he says again.

"What is wrong with you?" I shout. "Do you think you can just hop from Kit's arms to mine, to Lily's and back again? How can you even think of hurting Lily like this? Or believe that I would? You have no idea what kind of pain she's been through. I'd like to kill you for doing this to her!"

"This is insane!" he shouts back. "What are you talking about? There's nothing going on between me and Lily. Nothing! She's great, she was great in the EcoTech thing, but there was nothing between us. Nothing romantic or sexual. And I didn't make love to Kit. She was playing and so was I."

"I saw you," I hiss. "When you and Lily and Benno were hiding out in Kit's house. I saw you kissing each other."

He falls silent and looks at the floor of the cab, shaking his head sadly. A little flame of hope that had flared in my heart flickers and dies.

"Nell, I don't know what you saw. Maybe we were hugging each other because our plans were working out, I don't know, but it wasn't what you thought. Since the first time I saw you, it's never been anyone but you."

"Oh," I say. I watch myself lace and unlace my fingers in my lap.

"So?" he says.

"So?" I say.

"So, is it OK that I love you?" he asks softly, desperately.

"Yes," I say. I look up at him. His green eyes are tender and fierce. "It's very OK."

He takes me in his arms and kisses me as well as he can with the gearshift in the way.

"And you love me?" he asks, his face in my hair.

"I love you," I whisper. "I love you."

We are sleeping in an airy room in a beautiful old inn, high in the trees, overlooking the cliffs and the sea, somewhere between Feeding Lake and Merrivale.

Driving up to the inn wrapped in dizzy anticipation, walking into the office with our arms around each other's waists, being shown up to this big, sun-filled room, all the while knowing that soon we would be making love, was the second most wonderful experience of my life. Only actually loving Will was better. We had infinite time and no more secrets except the best kind. I am sleeping a deep, deep, dreamless golden sleep, every pore of my body sated with sweetness. If I start to surface, I feel his warm arms draw closer about me, and I dive back down, to this deep, voluptuous peace.

At last I start to wake again and find it might be more interesting to be awake together. I turn my breasts towards him and rock sinuously. His hot flesh answers mine, I feel him awaken and rise, and we are lovers, my sweet lover, my sweet Will.

We laugh at our sweet mischief, conspirators of the flesh and the spirit. Whatever we can imagine we can do, and we can imagine all manner of delightful things until, for the moment, enough is enough. It is five o'clock. We can dress and go downstairs and have food and drink and try to listen to the news. We both want to know what's become of Dugan. How locked together we all are.

We shower and dress in our borrowed clothes, and try to find faces to face the public with. I feel sure the afterglow of our afternoon shimmers around us like neon auras.

The lounge is nice, neither too crowded nor too empty. The other guests are caught up in their own lives and don't pay us much attention. We ask the bartender to turn on the news. When we hear that so far Dugan has eluded capture, I am oddly relieved. I ask Will if he minds. He smiles at me.

"It would be incredibly ungrateful of me to mind anything right now," he says.

In the morning we return to Merrivale. We have made our plans. I hope to simply begin to live them out without a lot of fuss. But Benno, Lily and Josh, and Kit, Spence, and Ananda have been watching for our return. The newness of our love has to bear the scrutiny of our friends, who gather round us on my front porch. I gaze at its flower-filled, shady comfort and console myself that Hal and J.J. will make loving new owners.

Lily watches with a shining joy as Josh romps in the grass with Shiloh and then lifts his head to say happily to Will, "He likes me!"

"Tell Nell about your new job," Kit urges her.

"The *Examiner* has hired me," Lily says casually. "City desk."

"Oh, Lily, that's wonderful!" I say.

"The salary ain't too shabby either," she laughs happily.

"But what about Kilby and the *Meridian?*" I ask.

"I worked it out so that I'll commute four days to the city and still have one day on the paper here."

"Kilby is just happy she'll still be around at all," Kit says.

"And what about *your* promotion, Kit?" Spence says, rubbing her shoulders. I look at Kit, who smiles.

"Mother of two," she says serenely. "Won't my mother

have a fit when she finds out I was a pregnant bride again?"
I hug her and Spence. I look around for Ananda. Hers is the
only unhappy face. I feel a tug—I haven't talked to her in so
long, and I wasn't really there for her during her mother's
honeymoon.

"Hi, big sister," I say.

"Hi," she says, trying to smile, but casting sideways
glances at Will, who's got his arm around me.

"You know what, Ananda?" I say. "I haven't even seen
your new room yet. Will you show it to me?"

"OK. Can I, Mom? I have my own key." Ananda holds up
the key, tied around her neck on a ribbon. Kit agrees, and I
walk along with Ananda under the sun-dappled leafy canopy the short distance to her new house.

"You're upset about me and Will, aren't you honey?" I
say.

"Nope. I've given up being upset by the things grown-ups
do," Ananda says unemotionally.

"Oh, Ananda," I say, dismayed. "I'm me, Nell, not 'grown-
ups'."

"How could he do it, Nell?" Ananda cries. "How could
he?"

"Who?" I ask.

"Who? Paul! My friend, the guy you were supposed to
marry, remember him?" she screams, hitting me with her
fists. She is hurting me. "The drug dealer!"

I hug her as tightly as I can without hurting her. She
struggles to get free, and then collapses against me, crying.

"I don't know, Ananda. It hurt me too and it scared me.
It's scary to think you know somebody, trust him, and find
out there was something else, something wrong. But Paul
must have been sick in a way we couldn't see. Everybody
isn't like that."

"How do you know?" she says. "What if Spence turns out
to be bad, or you, or Mommy?"

"Ananda, just because Paul was doing something wrong,
that doesn't make him all bad or wipe out the things that

were good, like his friendship with you, or his feelings for me. They were real," I say, uncovering this truth for myself as well as for Ananda. "And the things we loved about him were real too. It just wasn't the whole truth. I can't promise you that no one you love will ever hurt you or disappoint you again. It's just a risk you have to take when you care about people. I love you and I care about you and I will try my hardest to never hurt or disappoint you. Do you believe me?"

Ananda nods and hugs me. "I love you too, Nell. I'll even try to love Will, if you do," she says earnestly.

I laugh.

"Thank you, sweetheart. Do you think it will be really hard?"

"I guess he's OK. Mommy says he sails like Spence does, only on bigger boats, and that he saves whales and dolphins and stuff. That's pretty neat."

"He is pretty neat," I say.

"Are you going to go off on a boat to save whales and stuff with him?" she asks, still suspicious.

"Sometime I will. I think next spring we'll go for a while. But for now we're going to live in his house, right on Beau Cherry Lane, and you and I can fix up a room for you to stay in sometimes overnight there, if you want to. How will that be?"

"That will be excellent," she says comfortably.

I am feeling happily certain that from now on everything will be extremely excellent, as I sit in front of the fire a few nights later. We have had dinner, Shiloh lies snoring at our feet, and Will plays his guitar. The music is sad and beautiful. I watch his handsome face as he stares into the flickering orange hearth.

"What are you thinking about?" I ask.

"Hmm? I don't know, nothing." He smiles at me and reaches for my hand.

"I suppose things will seem rather dull, now that the

whole EcoTech thing is over," I say, waiting to be contradicted.

"I suppose," he says.

"What's wrong?" I ask, dismayed.

"I was waiting to find the right time to tell you, Nell. I got a letter today. From an old friend. An old friend who's in bad trouble."

"Yes?" I prompt.

"She needs me."

She?

"She's asked me to come to help her out. It's far. The Caribbean, and I don't know how long she'll need me. I don't know what to do." He looks miserable.

I think quickly. "You must go, of course," I say.

"Really?" he asks. He's starting to look excited. "Nell, you're so wonderful."

"I know," I say modestly. If he's impressed now, just wait until he sees how quickly I can pack. I'm going with him, of course. No way is he going off alone to an old girlfriend in distress on a tropical island. I'll have to break the news gently. Let him think it's all his own idea.

"Will you be leaving right away?" I ask.

He grins and reaches for me. "Oh, I think it can wait a couple of hours," he says.

About the Author

Sharon Singer Salinger, a poet and lay psychotherapist, was born into a distinguished literary family on the Palisades above the Hudson River. She lives near Boston with her husband Seth, an attorney, and her children, Natasha and Gabrielle. She is currently at work on her second novel.